Instru

the Devil

by

Debbie Burke

Instrument of the Devil

© Copyright 2017 by

Debbie Burke

Media Management LLC

PO Box 8502

Kalispell, MT 59904

debbieburkewriter@gmail.com

Acknowledgments:

Many friends and colleagues offered invaluable assistance with this story. Sincere thanks to editor Ray Rhamey (*Flogging the Quill*); tech guru Tom Kuffel; ever-patient critiquers and beta readers: Betty, Bev E., Val, Katie, Bev Z., Marie, Ann, Karen C., Karen L., Debbie E., Sami, Dawn, Constance, Leslie, Sarah, Sue, Holly, Jenn, and Phyllis. Their help and encouragement can't be measured, except by the depth of my gratitude.

Most of all, love and gratitude to Tom. Because of you, I'm living the dream.

Table of Contents

Chapter 1: Happy Birthday

Kahlil Shahrivar strode down the dim, quiet street, parka hood over his head, swinging the leash that would support his cover story of a runaway dog. Even at one in the morning, he didn't expect to be challenged. Residents of this small Montana town lacked the knife-edge of suspicion prevalent in most places he worked. He stopped in front of an old single-story Craftsman bungalow. A porch light glimmered, but its illumination didn't reach the mailbox at the curb.

He checked the block: No approaching headlights. Houses dark, safe, and sleeping. From his pocket, he took a postcard and a book-size package and inserted them into the mailbox.

On the side of the house, light from a small bathroom window spilled into the yard.

She was awake. He smiled.

For two patient years he'd waited to see Tawny Lindholm in person. Finally, here was the chance. Dense lilac bushes gave cover as he crept close and crouched in shadows a mere ten feet from the house.

Framed by the bathroom window, she brushed long coppery hair that was lightly streaked with gray. An oversize threadbare T-shirt hung loose on her slender frame. Probably had belonged to her dead husband. High cheekbones and delicate features bespoke the modeling career of her youth. And the lovely wide-set brown eyes he remembered from online photos.

Her shoulders tensed, and she turned to look out into the darkness.

His heart quickened, even though he knew she couldn't see him. She lowered the shade, and the light went out.

He left the cover of the lilacs and returned to the sidewalk, thrusting his hands into his pockets against the chill, smiling as he turned the corner.

The final stage of his attack on America's electrical grid had begun.

* * *

Tawny Lindholm made her way to the mailbox in April-morning fog. As she hurried back to her warm house, she thumbed through the envelopes. AARP had sent birthday greetings and yet another invitation to join, which she tossed into the kitchen trash along with a postcard advertising a smartphone class. A couple of bills and a bubble-wrapped package from an online retailer. Strange— she hadn't ordered anything.

At the chipped Formica breakfast bar, she tore open the package. Inside was a new smartphone. The message on the label read: *Happy 50th Birthday, Mom. Love, Neal.*

Crap. Her son meant well, but he knew how much technology intimidated her. With him in the army seven thousand miles away in Afghanistan, he couldn't even show her how to work it.

When she picked up the device, a bell started to ding. She tried pressing buttons on the side. The sound changed to a whistle, a woodpecker tapping, a chainsaw buzzing. She swiped the screen as she'd watched other people do, but the display remained a shiny black mirror, reflecting her scowl. It was laughing at her.

"Dammit, if you're ringing, I can't even answer you." The gadget had her talking to herself.

Despite Tawny's frustrated prodding, the screen remained blank, indifferent. Since Neal must have ordered it online, she couldn't even take it back to a local store. She didn't want a phone smarter than she was. But Neal apparently thought differently. She could almost hear him scolding: *Come on, Mom, it's 2011. Time you joined* this *century.* If it weren't a gift from her son, she'd gladly smash it against the wall. Still might.

A different tone warbled five times. Was this an incoming call? Or had she accidentally told the thing to launch a missile?

She twisted the tail of her french braid. "I ought to call you Lucifer."

It chirped.

"You like that name, huh? Well, it fits you."

Tawny had used a basic cell, no problem, when her husband, Dwight, was sick. All she'd had to do was flip it open, punch in numbers, and connect with doctors, the oxygen company, the pharmacy, and finally, on a July night nine months ago, make one last call—the funeral home. Her throat constricted at the memory.

But with Dwight gone, she'd canceled the cell to save money and only used her home phone. How could she afford the service for this fancy new smartphone? She'd have to ask Neal the cost . . . if she could ever figure out how to make a call.

Then she remembered the postcard and fished it out of the trash: *Baffled by your smartphone? Free class. Easy, fun, impress your children and grandchildren. 7:00 p.m. at the library in downtown Kalispell.*

The class was tonight. *What lucky timing,* Tawny thought. Although if she went, she was afraid she might be the dumbest person there. But dammit, she wouldn't let an electronic device outsmart her.

Besides, she didn't have anything better to do than sit home in the silent old house, listening to the phone's mysterious beeps and whistles.

* * *

As Tawny walked through the entrance of the hundred-year-old library building, her palms began to sweat. The same wood table still sat in the corner where she'd spent endless hours of her childhood with a tutor, struggling to read. Her dad had always said, "Good thing you're pretty, hon, cuz you sure are dumb."

Years later, when her daughter, Emma, couldn't read, either, Tawny had learned about dyslexia, but knowing what to call her problem didn't cure the weakness she still felt deep in her core. What a rotten joke to name a reading disorder so its victims could never hope to spell it.

This night, kids sat cross-legged on the carpeted floor, hunched almost double, their little noses buried in books. Adults wearing reading glasses tiptoed fingers along the shelves. How she envied people who read easily, even doing it for pleasure, something she couldn't imagine.

At the front desk, she found a kind-faced young librarian. Showing her the postcard, Tawny said, "There's, uh, a class, I think . . ."

The librarian nodded and pointed to stairs at the far end of the room. "Second floor. In the meeting room. Lots of seniors."

Seniors? How old did she think Tawny was? Well, according to AARP, she was now technically a senior, an uncomfortable milestone better forgotten. Thank goodness no one besides Neal had remembered her birthday. Tawny turned toward the stairs.

"Good luck," the woman called after her.

Was she being sarcastic?

Tawny skipped up the steps two at a time. *I'll show her who's a senior . . .*

On the second floor, walls of books hemmed her in, making her claustrophobic. She followed a pathway to a glassed-in cubicle. About a dozen gray-haired people milled inside the room, chatting and comparing smartphones. Did she really look as old as these folks? Probably, in the eyes of the young librarian. At least Tawny had company in her ignorance.

A dark, attractive man at the entrance made her draw in a breath. Strong, wiry build, six feet, or maybe a little taller. Crisp white shirt, ironed chinos, tweed sport coat. About forty, she guessed, with shaggy black hair and a thick mustache.

And startling, soulful green eyes.

He held a clipboard. Must be the teacher. Tawny approached. "Smartphone class?"

He grinned, showing perfect white teeth below the mustache. "Welcome," he said.

Would that tickle if he kissed her? *What are you thinking? Stop that!* Guilt welled over feelings she thought had died with Dwight.

The man's eyes crinkled with warmth and humor, almost as if he'd read her mind. "I am asking people to sign in with their name and cell number." A hint of an accent she couldn't place touched his speech. He handed her the clipboard and a pen.

"I can give you my name, but I haven't a clue what the number is. The phone was a gift. It goes ring-a-ding-ding, but the screen just stays blank."

"May I?" He held his hand out for her phone.

While she wrote her name on the sign-in sheet, he tapped and flicked the screen with a feathery touch. Suddenly the phone lit up: a bright, glowing mountain scene. His index finger flew, changing the screen to strange icons she didn't understand. Might as well have been hieroglyphics scratched on a pyramid wall.

After a few more flicks, he handed it back to her, the heat of his palm lingering on the device. "This is your number."

Tawny felt embarrassed that she needed to put on her glasses to see the display. "How'd you do that?" Her voice sounded breathy. Must be amazement, or a surprise rush of hormones. Yet when she looked into his green eyes, she felt a connection that stirred deep inside.

How she'd missed her man's closeness during the eight long years of Dwight's illness. She hoped she'd never let on to him the hunger she felt when he'd pulled away, no longer able to make love.

She shook the memories from her mind.

The dark man studied her, black brows drawn together, searching deeper into her thoughts. "Are you all right?" He glanced at the sign-in sheet. "Tawny? May I call you Tawny? I'm Kahlil Shahrivar."

"Nice to meet you." Beyond his good looks, she sensed concern, empathy, and maybe sadness in those eyes. "Thanks for making it work."

His smile warmed her. "The brightness display was turned all the way down to save battery life. That is why you could not see anything. No magic."

"Might as well be magic," she murmured. "To me it is."

His hand brushed her upper arm, directing her through the door. "Let me give you a peek behind the curtain. When you're finished with this class, that phone will do everything for you except fold the laundry."

She moved into the room, wishing his touch had lasted longer. "In that case, I need a different model. I specifically asked for one that does housework."

* * *

Kahlil was a patient teacher as he explained how to take photos, record appointments on the calendar, and track heart rate. "If you think your phones are amazing now," he said, "wait a couple of years." Enthusiasm raised his soft voice. "Now we must remember a PIN or pattern code to unlock the phone. New devices are coming that will use your thumbprint, so no one except you can access your information. You will be able to lock and unlock the doors in your home and see inside, even if you are half a world away. Your phone will track your grandchildren so you can keep them safe."

An older gentleman with a pinched expression said, "Sounds like Big Brother," which made everyone laugh.

Students practiced calling and texting each other. Tawny discovered a text from her son already on her phone: *Hv fun w/ ur new toy. Watch 4 email w/ updated contact #. Love, Neal.*

I ought to spank your butt, you little brat, she thought, even though the *little brat* was now a six-three, no-nonsense army sergeant.

As people tried various tasks, she felt relieved not to be the dumbest student, even though Kahlil seemed to spend more time with her than the others. Hopefully nobody picked up on how she inhaled his masculine scent when he leaned close—close enough that she spotted a small hearing aid inside his ear. Seemed young to be going deaf. Probably too much loud music as a teenager.

When the class broke up, a white-haired lady winked at Tawny. With a sly smile, she said, "Teacher's pet." Tawny's cheeks burned. So she *wasn't* the only one who'd noticed.

This is ridiculous, she thought. *I can't be interested in a younger guy, or any guy.* She hurried from the room ahead of the other students and skipped down the stairs, out to Dwight's old Jeep Wrangler.

She now knew the basics of using Lucifer. Mission accomplished.

* * *

The next morning, wrapped in her blue fleece robe, Tawny sipped coffee and nibbled rye toast while she labored to compose a reply text to her son, although she didn't know when or if he might receive it.

Neal's deployment to Afghanistan three months ago made her heart ache with worry, since he was often out of touch for weeks. She was proud when he made sergeant early, even though he never talked about his work except for vague mentions of "intelligence." She guessed he'd confided in Dwight, a Vietnam vet. Father and son used to talk for hours, huddled in the downstairs den, turning up the TV to cover their conversation.

Now silence hung heavy in their old house, so empty and hollow. How she missed them both. At least, one day, she'd be able to hug her boy again, admire the square jaw and steady gaze he'd inherited from his father. *Please, son, come home safe . . .*

She tapped the phone's virtual keyboard, which kept correcting her spelling, changing *Neal* to *neat*. "Dammit!" she muttered. "What were you thinking, sending me this instrument of the devil?" She wanted to write, *Dear Neal, thank you for the phone. I hate it.* But that would be ungracious.

Fed up, Tawny padded barefoot down the hall on the hardwood floor to check her email in Neal's old bedroom, now her office. On her laptop, she found the promised message from him with a new phone number to the Rear Detachment. Dwight used to poke fun at the "rear echelon motherfuckers" in Vietnam who stayed safely behind the action at a base. He scoffed that they were only useful for emptying trash cans.

But Tawny appreciated Rear Detachment for the emergency lifeline between deployed soldiers and family back home. They had treated her kindly and helped her get a message to Neal during the last gasping week of Dwight's life. On the smartphone, she carefully created a new contact for "Rear D" and saved the number.

She finished off the thank-you text to Neal and sent it. At least she hoped it had been sent. Every time she touched the smartphone, a new unexpected screen popped up, full of choices she didn't understand, like *Tethering, NFC, Air View.*

Kahlil had helped her through basic tasks at the library. She might've learned more if she hadn't been so distracted by his sensual way of stroking the screen, his softly accented speech. He reminded her of Omar Sharif from the old movie, *Dr. Zhivago.*

Kahlil. What kind of name was that? It sounded exotic, romantic . . . yet vaguely familiar. Then it hit her. In her daughter's purple bedroom, Tawny pulled down a box of books from the top shelf of the closet and set them on the furry zebra-striped bedspread. She'd wanted to donate them to the Salvation Army, but Emma protested. Somehow, unlike Tawny, Emma had overcome her reading difficulty and loved books. Whenever she came home, she promised to get her own place and take the books with her. Hadn't happened yet. She lived like a nomad in a van with her tattoo artist boyfriend.

Tawny dug among the books. *Phew, mildew.* The slim volume she was looking for turned up near the bottom.

The Prophet by Kahlil Gibran. Emma had all but memorized the book during high school. At the dinner table, she was forever quoting passages of romantic, mystical poetry that didn't rhyme. Tawny understood the appeal. Dwight would never speak such words to her, but that didn't mean she wouldn't have loved to hear them.

Tawny carried the box to the patio and spread the books on the picnic table to air out in the warm sun. Then she got dressed, pulling on black leggings and a sleeveless coral spandex top for Zumba class. Working out had been her salvation while Dwight was sick. Now, though, she had to force herself to leave the house. Exercise temporarily lifted her out of the pit of loneliness, but it didn't take away the ache in her heart or the pressure in the back of her throat.

In the mudroom, she donned a denim jacket and went out the back door. In the detached garage off the alley, she climbed up into Dwight's Wrangler. The rig bounced like a balky mule, but her brawny husband had loved it. She'd sold her comfortable Explorer because driving the Jeep made her feel closer to him—and besides, she couldn't afford the expense of two cars.

On the way to the gym, Tawny stopped at the bank's drive-up ATM and withdrew $200. The balance on the receipt caught her eye . . . it couldn't be right. She dug in her bag for her readers, put them on, and verified the amount.

$47,281.06.

Impossible.

The checking account normally hovered around $5,000. This was $42,000 too much. Must be a computer error.

She parked the car and went inside the bank lobby, irritated. Once she'd badgered herself into leaving the house, she hated to miss Zumba class, especially for a mistake.

Her favorite teller, Margaret, was on duty. The plump silver-haired woman listened to Tawny's explanation and tapped the keyboard to access the account. She rotated the screen to show

Tawny. "Here's the deposit yesterday. Forty-one thousand five hundred dollars in cash."

Tawny stared at the screen. "But I didn't make that deposit. It's wrong. Can you tell where it came from?"

Margaret shrugged. "If it was a check, we could backtrack the account number. Cash is harder to trace."

Tawny's checkbook always balanced to the penny—a source of pride. She might struggle with reading, but she knew her numbers. "I did not make that deposit," she repeated, as if her protest would alter the figure on the screen.

Margaret tapped again. "It wasn't made at this branch," she agreed. "Let's see . . . it was done in Helena."

"That's a hundred and fifty miles away," Tawny answered. "I haven't been to Helena in more than a year." An unwelcome memory flooded back of that last agonizing trip to the Fort Harrison VA, when doctors finally admitted defeat and pronounced Dwight's death sentence. She shoved the bitter memory aside. "I couldn't have made the deposit."

"I don't know what to tell you." Margaret glanced over Tawny's shoulder at customers lining up, then glared at a couple of young tellers chatting as they ignored the growing queue. She raised her eyebrows and shook her head.

Ridiculous. In the age of computer tracking, IRS monitoring, and surveillance cameras, a bank *had* to be able to figure out where the cash came from and where it should rightfully go. "Is the manager in?" Tawny asked.

"Sorry, he's out of the office." Margaret pursed her lips and gave her a you-know-how-things-are shrug.

The bank had been going downhill ever since a multinational conglomerate bought it a year before and renamed it United Bankcorp. The former manager had taken early retirement, replaced by a man from San Francisco who'd made the front page of the newspaper when he flew into town in a Learjet emblazoned with a gaudy United Bankcorp logo. Tawny hadn't met him yet and didn't particularly want to. Once she'd caught a glimpse of him glaring down from the mezzanine like an emperor. He'd averted his eyes, as if she were a peasant.

Margaret had confided that her new boss didn't like being exiled to the backwater town of Kalispell. One by one, familiar employees left, replaced by twentysomethings with inflated titles like *Account Management Specialist*. They worried less about customer service than kissing the manager's behind. Only Margaret remained, trying to hold out till she could collect social security. How much longer till she, too, was swept aside?

Tawny leaned forward. "I better see the operations supervisor."

Margaret spoke into the phone, then gestured at a desk on the opposite side of the lobby. "He'll be with you in a moment." She mouthed *good luck*, as if she expected Tawny would need it, and then made a face that warned *you won't like him*.

Tawny sat at the desk and scanned the employees—all strangers now—behind sterile glass cubicles along the wall. Back when she'd kept the books for Dwight's diesel repair business, an error like this would never happen. Or if it did, the problem would be solved immediately, with apologies and a hearty handshake.

The once-neighborly atmosphere had been wiped clean. Gone were the days when a banker's three-piece suit meant jeans, a plaid shirt, and down vest.

A young man of about twenty-five emerged from behind a wood partition—newly built since the takeover. He approached, looking as bored as if he were flipping burgers and scooping fries. A black shirt, black tie, and black horn-rims emphasized his vampire-pale complexion.

Tawny pushed the ATM receipt across the desk. "I have a problem. Someone deposited forty-one thousand five hundred dollars into my account yesterday."

"Wish somebody'd do that for me," the kid scoffed.

Tawny forced herself to keep smiling. "It's not my money. Obviously someone must have keyed in the wrong number, and it got put into my account by mistake."

He stared at her through his horn-rims, blank with apparent indifference.

This nitwit was the operations supervisor? Trying to hide the irritation in her voice, Tawny said, "I'm sure whoever this money belongs to is expecting it to be in their account. Maybe they're writing checks that are going to bounce. Don't you think they might be a little upset?"

"The manager's out," he answered blandly.

"So I hear. Meanwhile, how do we straighten this out?"

With a put-upon sigh, he asked, "Are you *sure* it's a mistake?"

She wanted to reach across the desk and swat him. "Look, a forty-one-dollar error, maybe I could've screwed up. But I guarantee you I didn't screw up forty-one thousand dollars' worth." She sucked in a deep, nerve-settling breath. "Why don't you call the Helena branch and talk to them?"

He peered over the top of his glasses, plucked a bank business card from a holder, circled a phone number, and handed it to her. "Here's the eight-hundred number. You can explain directly to them."

She took it. "Is this the branch number?"

He heaved another sigh. "It's the central number for the whole bank. They'll help you."

It was useless talking to this clown. Tawny grabbed a pen and scrawled her name and phone number on a slip of paper. "When the manager gets back, please have him call me right away." She rose and stalked toward the door.

"Have a wonderful day," he called. How politely and professionally he had told her to go screw herself.

* * *

Tawny couldn't wait to get home. When Dwight heard about this ridiculous mess, he'd blow a gasket, and they'd be out looking for a new bank tomorrow . . .

Realization hit her like an ice cube down the back.

Dwight was gone. Forever.

Tears burning, she pulled over and parked. "Dammit, Dwight!" She pounded the steering wheel. "Why aren't you here to help me?"

Most of the time, she held grief at bay . . . until the smallest trigger set off the horrible replay of his death. She felt as if she'd been hanging on a sheer cliff with one hand, desperately clinging to her husband with the other, until her strength ran out and she could no longer hold him. When he fell into the abyss, she'd been torn apart, and half of her had fallen with him.

She knew it wasn't the bank and its corporate indifference that troubled her—it was the silent emptiness she faced at home, where there was no one to talk to or share her frustration with. Guilt filled the hollowness inside her, multiplying and swelling like Dwight's cancer, seeping into the ragged edges of her soul.

It was her fault—she had wished for an end to the relentless pain, the vomiting, the sleepless nights. Now she regretted the wish with all her heart. Their bed was silent and empty, with only his childhood teddy bear to hold. A pitiful substitute.

Still sniffling, she pulled herself together and blew her nose.

No matter how much she screamed and pounded, Dwight would still be dead, and she still had $41,500 of someone else's money. She needed to fix that.

* * *

At home, she steeled herself and called United Bankcorp's 800 number. The automated response runaround offered to help her make a loan, open a credit card, or consolidate her debts and then rattled off locations of branches in fourteen states. She heard a prompt for every possibility except what to do when someone else's money winds up in your account.

After twenty minutes of merry-go-round trips back to the main menu, she repeatedly pressed zero, hoping to connect with a human being. The recorded voice apologized sincerely but did not recognize that command. When she heard for the eighteenth time how important her call was to them and how valued she was as a customer, she disconnected. She wished she'd used the landline phone so she could at least feel the satisfaction of slamming the receiver down. Damn smartphone deprived her of even that.

"'Valued,' my ass," she muttered. "If I'm so important, why can't I talk to anyone but a machine?"

Then she thought of the Slocums, her neighbors who had retired from banking—Sheryl as a loan collector, Phil as a vice president. Maybe they could give her advice.

Tawny walked down the avenue under red maple and linden trees past well-kept old bungalows like hers. On double corner lots sat the landmark mansions built by Kalispell's movers and shakers in the early 1900s. The Slocums' house was a two-story pillared Colonial with a carriage house converted to a double garage.

She rang the bell and heard Sheryl lumber across the hardwood floor with heavy dinosaur steps.

"Hi, Tawny, what's up?" Sheryl always looked vaguely annoyed, as if her bunions hurt or her bra chafed.

"Hi, I wondered if I could talk to you and Phil about a banking problem I'm having."

Sheryl looked her up and down, eyes gone flinty. Heaven help anyone who might fall behind on their payments to Sheryl. "You know we're retired. We really don't care to talk business anymore."

Phil approached behind Sheryl with a leering smile, the kind Tawny dreaded from husbands because it made wives hate her. "Howdy, neighbor!"

Tawny took a step back. "I don't want to bother you."

"So what's the problem?" Phil all but pushed Sheryl aside. "I heard something about banking?" He motioned Tawny into the house. "Come on in, sit down. Want some coffee?"

"No, thank you. I won't take up much of your time." She grimaced an apology to Sheryl, who narrowed her eyes and closed the door.

In their lavish great room, Tawny sat on an uncomfortable—but no doubt expensive—antique chair. Sheryl took the matching chair while her husband filled a tapestry love seat.

"Now, what's this about?" Phil asked.

Tawny released a breath. "This is going to sound weird, but United Bankcorp put money in my account—a lot of money—and I don't know where it came from. I think it must be a computer mistake, and it should have gone into someone else's account. But I can't get the bank to look into it. They insist I made the deposit yesterday in Helena. I haven't been to Helena lately, so it can't have been me."

Phil hunched forward, elbows on knees, belly hanging. "How much are you talking about?"

"Forty-one thousand five hundred dollars."

He whistled softly. "You sure it couldn't have been a direct deposit, like from a life insurance payoff, or a tax refund you forgot about, or a settlement in Dwight's estate?"

Tawny shook her head. "None of those. I think I've got the finances pretty well squared away. No, this is completely out of the blue. And it was cash. The trouble is, I can't get anyone at the bank to pay attention. I've told them it's an error, but they blew me off."

Phil rubbed his chin. "This could be more of a problem than you think. Even before 9/11, regulators tightened restrictions and increased reporting requirements to track money laundering that finances terrorism. Anytime someone makes a cash deposit of more than ten thousand dollars to an account outside the normal ordinary course of business, banks have to file a CTR within fifteen days of the transaction."

"What's a CTR?" Tawny asked.

"Currency Transaction Report. That goes to the feds so they can monitor unexplained movements of large amounts of cash— you know, like from drugs or weapons smuggling. If something alerts the teller to unusual behavior, he or she fills out an SAR—a Suspicious Activity Report."

Tawny's stomach clenched. "What the hell? I'm no drug smuggler or terrorist. I just want the mistake fixed."

"That's all well and good, but the bank has probably already filed the CTR, so you may still come under scrutiny unless you can explain the source of funds."

"What's to explain? I don't know where it came from. It isn't my money."

"You need to talk to the manager and ask about putting the money in a suspense account until they find out the source."

"What's a suspense account?"

Phil lifted his double chin and smiled while looking down his nose. "To put it in basic terms that you could understand, it's an internal account where banks stick money they're not sure what to do with until they figure it out."

Tawny tightened at his condescending tone but said nothing. She needed the ex-banker's information.

Sheryl cleared her throat. Tawny recognized the wifely signal—*wrap this up, and get her out of our house.*

Phil leaned forward. "You're absolutely sure you don't know about this cash? You've had a lot to keep track of with Dwight's illness and passing. Maybe something slipped your mind."

Tawny read doubt in his eyes and pulled herself straight. "More than forty thousand dollars didn't slip my mind." She rose. "Thanks for your time. I'll see the manager tomorrow." As she went toward the front door, she felt Sheryl's glare on her back and heard Phil mutter something to his wife.

They think I'm crazy. If my own neighbors don't believe me, how can I convince the feds I haven't done anything wrong?

Chapter 2: Windfall

The next morning, Tawny dressed in cocoa-brown slacks, a cream silk blouse, and a copper-colored scarf that matched her hair, determined to talk to the bank manager. She stood at the entrance when the bank opened, watching the operations supervisor unlock the door. He held it wide for her but otherwise gave no sign he recognized her from the previous day.

"Is the manager in?" she asked.

"No, he's at a meeting."

"Who's in charge while he's gone?"

He jerked a thumb at a glassed-in cubicle across the lobby. "She'll help you." He made his escape, disappearing behind the wood partition.

Margaret stood at her window. She caught Tawny's eye and offered another helpless shrug.

Tawny crossed the lobby to a door with a nameplate that read Guadalupe Garza, Consumer Lending Facilitator. Dwight always said big corporations gave inflated titles to employees instead of decent pay. Tawny knocked. A round-shouldered woman in her midfifties looked up from her monitor and gestured to come in. Gray-brown hair fell in lank curtains on either side of her face, reminding Tawny of a lop-eared rabbit.

This time, Tawny felt more confident, having learned banker's jargon from her neighbor. "Good morning, Ms. Garza. I'm Tawny Lindholm. My husband and I have banked here for fifteen years. I have a big problem, and I need your help. Someone deposited forty-one thousand five hundred dollars in cash into my account a couple of days ago in Helena. It's not mine. The manager is out and hasn't answered my messages. Your automated phone system makes it impossible to talk to a human being."

Tawny paused to refresh the banking code words in her mind. "I need to get this straightened out because I don't want you filing a CTR or an SAR that will make the feds look at me suspiciously. You need to put that money in a suspense account. And you should look at the surveillance video from Helena to find out who the money really belongs to and get it in their account." She finished the rehearsed speech without a glitch. *Wow, I did it.*

Guadalupe Garza spread her hands in a helpless gesture. "Mrs. Lindholm, first of all, I'm very sorry you're having this problem. But I'm sure you can understand why federal auditors would frown on us allowing a customer to determine what reports we do or do not file, as well as what funds should be put in suspense. To act simply on a customer's say-so would violate more regulations than you can imagine."

Tawny's short-lived confidence disappeared. Garza had shot down ex-banker Phil Slocum's suggestions in seconds.

"Besides," she continued, "I'm a loan officer, not operations. That really is an operations matter."

"I will not be put off again." Tawny's jaw tightened. "I'm a customer, and there has been a serious error, and you need to take care of it. I don't care what your internal—" *What was that big word Dwight used to say?* "—hierarchy is. You need to correct this."

Garza reached for the ATM receipt. "I'll see what I can find out." She tapped her keyboard and then studied the screen. "OK, what you were told is correct: forty-one thousand five hundred dollars in cash was deposited at the Helena branch." She typed for a minute. "I've sent an email to branch operations and the manager, asking them to look into this. Now, is there anything else I can do for you?"

"Can you tell if one of those SARs or CTRs has been filed?"

Garza gave an apologetic shrug. "Again, that's an operations matter, not my department."

At least Garza had been more helpful than the guy in horn-rims, but Tawny still felt the brush-off. "Would you please write down the manager's name, email address, and a *direct* phone number so I can follow up?"

"Of course, I'd be happy to." Garza penned the information on a bank business card and handed it to Tawny. "Again, I'm very sorry you're having this problem, but I'm sure they'll get to the bottom of it." She rose and offered her hand.

Tawny shook it. "Thank you." But she sensed she'd been shuffled down the line.

Her suspicion was confirmed when, back at home, she sent an email to the address Guadalupe Garza had given her. An unsigned reply appeared instantly: *Thank you for contacting United*

Bankcorp. Your business is very important to us. Your message has been forwarded to the appropriate department. You'll receive an answer shortly. A stock acknowledgment intended to fend her off while her question dropped into the black hole of corporate indifference.

The so-called direct phone number snared her in the same automated phone tree as before.

Short of driving to Helena, what else could she do?

* * *

After Zumba at the gym the next day, Tawny ran into her friend Virgie Belmonte, a petite woman in her late thirties with mahogany-colored hair cut in an asymmetrical bob. Her long plaid skirt brushed the floor and a gray turtleneck molded her sprung-steel figure. When they hugged, Tawny apologized, "Sorry I'm sweaty, but am I glad to see a friendly face."

Virgie held Tawny at arm's length, looking up, studying her. "I've got about a half hour before I go to work. Let's have coffee."

Virgie had been Dwight's urologist at the Kalispell VA clinic when they still held hope the cancer could be contained in the prostate. She was one of Tawny's few friends who hadn't drifted away when Dwight's condition became hopeless. Tawny understood the desertion—people didn't like to associate with dying and death. But the abandonment still stung, making her value Virgie's loyalty even more.

At the coffee shop adjacent to the gym, they ordered lattes and settled in a corner away from other customers. Virgie reached across the table. "Let me see your paw."

Tawny extended her left hand. "The ring finger still won't bend, but it doesn't bother me that much, except in the cold."

Virgie examined the hand, turning it over. "Arthritis. Joint's pretty swollen. If you ever want to take off your wedding ring, it'll have to be cut."

"Good thing I don't want to take it off." *Not ever,* Tawny thought, rubbing the gold band with her thumb.

"This is what I call *cancer's collateral damage.*" Virgie cocked her head. "The caregiver sometimes winds up in worse shape than the patient. You got off fairly light, just breaking your finger wrestling with Dwight's wheelchair. One of my couples, she was helping him from his walker into the tub, but *she* slipped and broke *her* hip. Got pneumonia and the poor dear died a month before her terminal husband."

"How sad." Tawny flexed her fingers. *I'm lucky . . . I guess.*

Virgie said, "So tell me what's going on, kid? How are you adjusting?"

A surge of gratitude welled in Tawny's throat. Virgie understood, really understood. Her questions went deeper than polite inquiry. She'd accompanied many patients on the long seesawing road of life and death.

"OK, sort of. I think most of the estate business is finished—notifications, life insurance, transferred the house deed into my name alone and all that."

"Good for you, but don't be surprised if things continue to pop up that you didn't expect." Virgie leaned forward and studied Tawny's face. "But cut the crap, sweetheart. How are *you* doing?"

Tawny grasped the paper cup between her palms, letting the warmth seep into her aching finger. "Lousy, if you want to know the truth. You know, when we were going through it, all I wanted was to get it over with. Have Dwight be done with the pain. Sleep through a whole night without a crisis." She grimaced. "Now, I feel guilty, like I wished him away, and he's gone and it's my fault."

Virgie gave her a crooked smile. "That's completely normal. You want the suffering to stop. When you poke an amoeba in the lab, it jerks away. It doesn't want to hurt. That's how living beings are programmed. Avoid problems, avoid pain. But we humans are cursed with guilt and remorse, like if we don't suffer, we're somehow immoral." Virgie flipped her bangs out of her eyes. "It will get better, but it takes time. You guys were married, what, over thirty years?"

Tawny nodded. "I was right out of high school. Of course, Dwight was so much older, and my parents didn't approve. He was only seven years younger than my dad."

Virgie snorted. "Thanksgiving dinners must have been a little tense. But you hung in there. That's what counts."

Tawny pulled on her braid. "The days are so pointless now. For so long, no matter how hard I worked, there wasn't enough time to get everything done. Now, I feel empty, useless."

"Also normal. You got laid off from your career as a wife."

Virgie's understanding opened the floodgate of concerns Tawny couldn't share with anyone else. Problems tumbled out of her mouth. "I can't concentrate. I forget. I do goofy things and don't remember doing them. Like, the other day, the TV remote somehow winds up in the freezer, and I find my leather boots in the washing machine. I'm the only one in the house, so I must have put them there, but I sure as hell don't remember doing it."

Her friend leaned closer, an encouraging smile under her frown.

Tawny gnawed on her lip, wondering how much to confess. Virgie might think she was crazy, but Tawny had to go on anyway. "A few weeks ago, I guess I came out of a trance and found I'd driven fifty miles west of town, no clue where I was or why. Sometimes I'm scared I'm losing it."

Virgie reached over to tuck a stray lock of hair behind Tawny's ear. "That's called depression. No fun, but also completely normal after what you've been through." Her voice dropped low. "Do you think about hurting yourself?"

Tawny shrugged, trying to appear casual. Virgie's question dug into the depths of too many sleepless nights in her empty bed. Sometimes the yearning to join Dwight almost felt like a physical pain.

Virgie patted her hand. "Listen, sweetheart, if these symptoms don't improve, you might think about trying an antidepressant for a little while to get you over the hump."

Just talking to her friend reassured Tawny. "OK. Thanks."

In her pocket, Lucifer trilled. Lousy timing. She pulled it out to send the call to voice mail. Caller ID read *Kahlil*. What the hell? She swiped the screen to dismiss it.

Virgie said, "New toy?"

Tawny grunted. "My son sent it to me, and it's been making me crazy. I call it *Lucifer*."

Virgie chuckled. "Isn't that the new model advertised on TV all the time? My office manager keeps pestering me to trade up to that from my old Blackberry, like I need more aggravation in my life." She peered closer at Tawny. "Hey, how come you're blushing?"

Tawny touched the back of her fingers to her cheek. "Blushing? Must be a hot flash."

Virgie's stare bored through Tawny's embarrassment. "All right, spill. Who's calling that's got you all pinked up?"

Tawny stuffed the phone deep into her gym bag, eager to change the subject. "Nobody. I'm not ready to even think about that."

"So it *is* a guy."

How did Virgie know? Was Tawny that transparent? She gave up trying to distract her friend. "He taught a class on how to use smartphones. He put his number in my contact list in case I had questions. I thought I'd erased him."

Virgie folded her arms and leaned back, casting a dubious smirk at Tawny. "OK. If you say so."

Tawny swished her hand back and forth. "He looks like Dr. Zhivago—remember that movie? When I was a kid, I had a terrible crush on him."

"Good taste."

Would Virgie never let it go? "But I've got a lot more serious issues than him to figure out, speaking of unexpected things that pop up."

Virgie lost the teasing smile. "What?"

Tawny related the story of the strange cash appearing in her account and her frustration over the bank's unwillingness to look into the error.

"Well," Virgie said, "if it were me, I'd withdraw the money. When they find the mistake, they'll have to come to you."

"But it's not mine. I'd feel wrong taking it."

"You're not taking it permanently. You'll give it back. You just want to get their attention."

"Might get someone else's attention. Like the FBI or Homeland Security." Tawny explained the banking laws she'd learned from her neighbor. "They're probably already aware of me with this"—she made air quotes—"'*unusual transaction.*'"

Virgie finished her latte and licked a thin line of foam from her lips. "Well, the choices are you can be under scrutiny *without* money, or you can be under scrutiny *with* money. Personally, I'll

take the latter. But you know me, I'm the brokest doctor you'll
ever meet." She glanced at her watch. "I better go. Let me know
what happens, OK?"

After Virgie left, Tawny pondered, twirling her empty paper
cup. Was her friend right? She was an educated, sophisticated
woman, more so than Tawny could ever hope to be. It felt wrong,
but maybe bold action would get the bank's attention.

Tawny rose and flicked her cup into the trash, plan in mind. If
she could see the manager today and get the mistake corrected,
OK. If not, she'd withdraw the money and stash it in Dwight's gun
safe.

* * *

"I'm sorry, the manager isn't in," said yet another new teller
Tawny didn't recognize.

"Where's Margaret?" Tawny asked.

"She's no longer an employee."

Uh-oh. "But I just saw her yesterday. She didn't say
anything."

The teller drummed pink-and-white nails on the counter. One
side of her maroon mouth turned down. "How can I help you?"

Tawny's hopes sank. The last friendly face of the old bank,
dumped out with the trash.

She took in a deep breath, opened her checkbook, and
carefully wrote *Forty-one thousand five hundred dollars and no
cents*. She signed it and pushed it across the counter.

"Driver's license."

Tawny presented it.

The teller wrote identifying information on the check. "You
want this in cash?" The last word ended on a high note.

"Yes." Tawny hoped the pulse in her neck didn't show. She
should have changed from her still-damp workout gear into the
outfit she'd worn yesterday, clothes that made her look more like a
self-assured woman accustomed to withdrawing large amounts of
money.

With a sigh and an eye roll, the teller said, "I'll have to get
approval."

"Fine."

She picked up the check and driver's license and disappeared behind the partition.

What went on behind the partition that hid the inner workings of the bank? Tawny had suspected employees lounged back there, playing video games and laughing about how long they made customers wait. Now, though, she wondered about one-way mirrors, squinty-eyed security guards, and direct phone lines to the FBI.

She glanced around the lobby. Other patrons lined up in the rope queue. Several minutes passed. She fidgeted with the cup of giveaway pens. Waiting people shot annoyed glances at her. Her skin prickled, like a rising fever. She stared straight ahead, trying to ignore the stink-eyes.

At last, the teller returned with a man of about thirty. He noticed the long line of impatient customers and gestured to employees to open more windows.

In the lobby, he scanned Tawny from head to toe while holding her check and driver's license like hostages. "Good morning, Mrs. Lindholm." His starched green shirt rustled when he moved. "This is quite a substantial request for cash."

"So?"

"Our policy is that we require a forty-eight-hour notice for large withdrawals."

What the hell? "This *is* a bank, isn't it? Where you keep *cash*?"

He stiffened. His eyes were bright blue, too bright not to be contact lenses. "Would you please step over here?" He escorted her across the lobby to the same desk where she'd faced off with the operations supervisor in horn-rims. He nodded to a chair. "Have a seat."

Tawny stood her ground. "How long is this going to take?"

"I need to ask you a few questions. What did you plan to use the cash for?"

Tawny's dry throat tensed. She didn't expect to be interrogated. "Why are you asking?"

"Just routine. We want to make sure our customers are not withdrawing cash for questionable reasons."

"Questionable? What's questionable?" Should she explain? Suddenly Virgie's idea of getting the bank's attention seemed idiotic, maybe even illegal. But she forged ahead. "Is there enough money in my account or not? Or do I need a note from my mother?"

He gave an oily smile. "Of course, it's your money, and you're free to use it as you choose. We simply want to be certain, for instance, that cash isn't being withdrawn under duress or false pretenses. There are many scams targeting seniors, and we feel an obligation to protect our older customers."

Older? Resentment smoldered inside her. "Thank you for your concern, but I'm not feebleminded enough yet that I need your protection."

"I'm sure you're correct. Now, what's the reason for this withdrawal?"

Tawny couldn't bring herself to lie. She should just snatch her license back and leave. This whole harebrained plan was leading her into quicksand. But Virgie was a lot smarter and more sophisticated than she was. She should trust her friend's advice. "I believe the bank has made an error in my account, but you won't check it out."

The supervisor drew himself back, apparently horrified by her accusation. "I assure you, United Bankcorp has a stellar reputation for accuracy."

Behind his blue contacts, a different expression emerged. Before, Tawny had sensed pompous nosiness. But now his face reflected doubt, suspicion, accusation. He must be thinking that she intended to use the money for illegal purposes.

Heart throbbing in her ears, she forced her voice to sound strong. "If the account has enough funds in it, what right do you have to deny my check? Are you going to honor it or not?"

The oily smile reappeared. "Naturally, we'll honor it." He rubbed her driver's license and check between his fingers. "Within the confines of the forty-eight-hour policy, that is."

Or maybe to give him time to report her to law enforcement. Tawny pressed her lips together. "Then how much can you give me today?"

"Mrs. Lindholm, this is an unusual transaction out of your normal banking pattern. We're simply looking out for the safety and security of our customers."

She squared her shoulders. "Sounds like the bank is trying to hold onto money that I have a right to take out." An idea flickered. "What if I need this cash to buy a car today? Is there a law requiring forty-eight hours, or is this just your internal policy?"

His chest thrust out. "It is the bank's official policy." As if bank policy obviously trumped the law.

She tightened her muscles to keep from twitching. Dwight's voice played in her mind: *Look him in the eye, don't blink.* "Then I'm asking you to make an exception. I need the money today."

His shoulders shifted. "Are you sure there isn't anything you want to tell me?"

"Positive." Actually, anything but positive. Maybe she was rationalizing. She hated to mislead him about buying a car, but she'd had it with the bank jerking her around. She'd tried to be straight with them, and they blew her off. Virgie was right—get their attention, then let them fix the mess they'd made.

Long seconds passed as they stared at each other, the only sound the beat of her heart in her ears.

Finally, the supervisor blinked first and returned to the teller window, where he initialed the check and handed it to the clerk with a curt nod. Tawny followed, hoping he didn't hear her sigh of relief. *It worked, Dwight, thank you!*

The feeling of triumph lasted only long enough to put on her reading glasses. When the teller returned from the vault with an armload of bills, regret bit Tawny. She shot quick glances over her shoulder, wondering how many people watched as the teller counted out hundreds in piles of a thousand dollars each. Once Tawny had the money, could she get home without being robbed?

After an eternity, the teller snapped the last bill down. "You want a bag?"

Tawny stared over the tops of her readers until the young woman seemed to recognize the stupidity of her question. She loaded the stacks in a paper sack. Tawny retrieved her driver's license and hurried away, gripping the bundle of cash. In the vestibule, she whipped her head side to side, peering through the glass doors, scanning the parking lot for threats.

What if a thief tried to jump her? She mentally ran through defensive moves—knee to the groin, karate chop to the windpipe, smash the nose with the heel of the hand. *You were right, Dwight, insisting I take that self-defense class even though I didn't want to.*

Tawny raced across the lot and climbed into the Jeep, immediately locking the doors. *Virgie, I hope your advice doesn't backfire,* she thought, driving home as fast as she dared.

With the money locked in the gun safe inside her closet, she breathed easier. In the kitchen, she made a salad and iced tea. While she ate, she set the smartphone on the counter and noticed a message. Playing it back, she heard Kahlil's softly accented voice: "Hello, Tawny. I hope you are doing well with your phone. If you have any questions, I'd be happy if you'd call me. As a matter of fact, I'd be happy if you called me without questions, too." A teasing lilt came through, turning the comment into an invitation.

"Honestly!" She deleted the message and started to remove Kahlil from the contact list but hesitated. She might have more questions.

In her head, she heard Virgie's mocking voice: *Damn right you'll have more questions for that hunk.*

* * *

Two days later, Tawny wasted forty-five minutes searching the house for her checkbook. She finally located it in the garage trash bin, under empty plastic bottles from the previous afternoon when she'd changed the oil and filter in the Jeep. "I am losing it," she muttered. Despite Virgie's assurances, her memory lapses and zoning out weren't improving with time.

She wiped oily grime off the checkbook and sat at the breakfast bar to review her finances. Ignoring the mysterious windfall, she knew the day fast approached when she'd need to find work. Expenses that the VA didn't cover had gobbled up most of their retirement savings. Dwight's life insurance dwindled fast despite her thriftiness. She wouldn't be eligible to draw on his social security or VA pension for ten more years.

She planned to go back to her old summer job leading tours at the Hungry Horse Dam, but four months of seasonal paychecks wouldn't stretch far enough to live on. She needed more.

But what business would hire an absent-minded fifty-year-old with no degree and rusty bookkeeping skills after eight years out of the workforce? Even tech-savvy young college grads struggled in this recession, forced to live at home with their parents.

Tawny had years of hands-on caregiving experience. But with her reading difficulty, she feared she'd never pass the bookwork required to earn official certification.

Maybe she could teach Zumba at the gym. She'd check with the instructor, but substituting was hit and miss, at best. Employees clung to their jobs with a death grip.

Cleaning houses didn't need a license. But in the troubled economy, the housekeepers she knew were losing clients, as even wealthy people had to cut back.

That left her with either the thrilling prospect of fast food or retrieving shopping carts.

Her hand rubbed worn spots on the counter. When she and Dwight sold their business, dreams of carefree retirement had filled their imaginations—an RV, travel, remodeling the kitchen—until cancer changed everything. A sharp flake of Formica splintered under her fingernail, leaving bare wood exposed. Those dreams would never come to pass now . . .

. . . unless she used the cash in the safe.

No!

That money wasn't hers, no matter what the bank claimed. Her conscience was grated by the fact that the idea even occurred to her.

The smartphone trilled beside her.

Kahlil's name showed on the screen. She hesitated, remembering his soulful green eyes. A tickle of excitement ignited during two more rings. *Dwight, forgive me.* She swiped the answer arrow. "Hello, Kahlil."

"Tawny, it is so good to hear your voice." His velvet tone caressed her ear.

Thank goodness he couldn't see her blush over the phone. "How are you?"

"I am well. Are you doing OK with your phone? Have you come across any new mysteries?"

"As a matter of fact, it trumpets at me sometimes, and I don't know what for. Also a screen keeps flashing with something called *world clock* that gives the time in Abu Dhabi, Kazakhstan, all these weird places. I really don't need that."

"Didn't you say your son was overseas? Might be helpful to know when it is a good time to call him."

Had she mentioned Neal? Who knows? She felt so flustered the night of the class, she could have blurted out anything. "Yeah," she said slowly, "if I knew where he was."

"Well, if you find out, I can help you set the time for that location."

"OK, thanks."

"Tawny, I must be honest. I am not really calling about your phone. I would very much like to see you again. May I invite you to dinner?"

A breath caught in her throat. How long since she'd been asked for a date? She had no idea what people did at her age. Or at Kahlil's age. He certainly looked too young for her. "I-I don't think so." Her voice wavered. Dammit, she needed to sound sure of herself, not wishy-washy.

"I should explain," he went on. "When I first saw you, I sensed we shared a common understanding—a connection, you might say—even though we'd never met before."

So he'd felt it, too, that intensity vibrating between them. She waited for him to continue.

His voice softened, even gentler than before. "My dear lady, I do not wish to intrude on you. I only wanted to . . . well, if I may, I would like to tell you a little about myself. The other evening, I sensed great sorrow within you because I know sorrow of my own. Sometimes it helps to share the burden with one who has gone through similar loss."

How did he know? She tried to cover her grief around people but didn't always succeed.

After several seconds, he said, "My beloved wife died almost two years ago. We had been together since we were children. I never knew another woman." He took a deep breath. "As much as I wanted to see you again, I did not want to overstep boundaries. I must confess that I looked you up online and was saddened to read your husband's obituary. I did not mean to pry."

Damn. Nothing was private anymore. Or sacred. She never mentioned being widowed to strangers, but with the all-pervasive Internet, her caution hardly mattered. She wondered if she should be flattered or creeped out by his interest. "Look, Kahlil, I appreciate your help with the phone, but I'm not ready to think about dating."

His response came quickly. "Inexperience makes me clumsy. I will not bother you again. But please, say you will forgive me for being forward."

Had Kahlil explained the reason for the vibration between them? Mutual sorrow. Empathy. Unspoken understanding. "There's nothing to forgive. Honestly. I'm sorry about your wife."

"And I for the loss of your husband. Now I will leave you in peace. However brief our friendship, you have brought light into my life."

He even talked like a poet.

What was wrong with seeing him again? He was easy to look at, certainly charming, making her feel a giddiness she thought was long gone. "Listen, why don't we meet for coffee?"

"Oh yes!" His tone sounded boyish with enthusiasm. "I would be so honored."

They made a date for the following day. As Tawny tapped the call off, she thought, *Wow, I never saw this coming.* A quiver of anticipation teased her. *Dwight would understand, wouldn't he?*

* * *

The next morning, Tawny pawed through her closet. What to wear? A skirt and blouse with a scarf? Capris and a sweater? Makeup? Or just mascara and lipstick? No blush, that's for sure. The mere thought of Kahlil heated her cheeks.

This is stupid. It's not a date, just coffee. He's a kid anyway.

When had she grown so conscious of age? Fifteen years' difference between her and Dwight hadn't mattered. At least, not most of the time. But he'd left her a widow much too young. She never wanted to go through that kind of loss again.

In the glaring lights around the bathroom mirror, she noticed new wrinkles. Without her readers, seeing up close grew more difficult every day. Tiny print on food labels and in the phone book reminded her constantly that fifty might be the new thirty, but her eyes were anything but new.

The last couple of years, she'd given up makeup as a pointless waste of time when she needed all her energy for urgent caregiving tasks. Now, as she tried to focus on her blurry reflection, she feared poking her eye out with the mascara wand. *Makeup by Braille.* Brown smudges appeared on her skin. With a wet swab, she cleaned off the unwanted smears. When had her eyelids started sagging? She remembered a catalog featuring makeup glasses that allowed one lens at a time to flip out of the way. Maybe she should order a pair.

She dressed in khaki capris, a long-sleeved forest-green T-shirt, and added a paisley scarf knotted loosely around her neck. Dressier than workout clothes, but nothing glamorous. Simple, casual, the right note to convey this was most definitely not a date.

He probably just wants a motherly shoulder to cry on about his late wife. Had he mentioned kids? She didn't think so.

Really, they had nothing in common, except the premature loss of their spouses.

Tawny checked herself in the full-length mirror on the bathroom door. Not bad, but, oh, where had that young girl gone?

Regret nibbled at her for committing to this date with Kahlil. She would always be Dwight's wife. But it was too late to cancel now. She drove to the coffee shop near Woodland Park.

Through the window, she saw that Kahlil already had a table with his paper cup and a plate of pastries. His shaggy dark hair was neatly combed, and he wore a black turtleneck under his tweed sport coat. She hesitated, wanting to study him for a few more seconds, but he must have felt her gaze because he jumped up and waved.

She took a deep breath and went in. *Here goes nothing.*

He greeted her. "Good morning! What can I order for you?"

"A mocha latte, please."

He pulled out a chair, seated her, then went to the counter. While he placed her order and paid, a new regret seized her. She should have bought her own coffee. Dammit, why hadn't she thought of that earlier? Such unfamiliar territory. So uncomfortable to be with a man other than Dwight.

What should she say to this stranger?

Kahlil returned with her latte and smiled. "May I see your phone? I'll look at the clock settings."

She gave him the cell, grateful he'd taken her off the hook of starting the conversation.

He swiped back and forth on the screen, dark brows drawn together. Then he scooted his chair around beside her. She caught a hint of aftershave—lime, maybe—and an underlying earthiness.

He held the phone up. "See, this is the world clock." A list of exotic-sounding cities filled the screen. He scrolled down page after page.

"I've never heard of most of these places," she said.

"OK, say, for instance, your son is on holiday in Hobart, Australia. It's nine thirty a.m. here, while it's three thirty a.m. there. If you call him now, he will wake up grumpy." Mischief touched his smile. "Or you could wait until this afternoon, and he would be most happy to receive your call. Do you have relatives in other countries?"

She shook her head. "No, fourth-generation Montanan." She broke off a morsel of glazed huckleberry scone and nibbled it. Not bad, but she baked better.

He flicked the screen. "My mother lives in Paris. It's five thirty in the evening there, so I could call her."

Curiosity gnawed at Tawny. She took the opening he'd offered. "Are you from France?"

"I was born in Iran, but my parents immigrated to France in 1979 when the Shah was deposed. We moved around a great deal during my childhood. Then I went to university in Glasgow, Scotland, and postdoc at Texas A & M." He picked up a scone and ate the corner.

No wonder she couldn't pin down his accent—such a blend of places he'd lived. Postdoc? Did that mean he had a PhD? "How on earth did you wind up in Montana?"

"I'm here on a contract job for several months."

"What do you do?"

"I'm a psychologist."

Tawny drew back, staring at him. "Really?"

He gave an apologetic shrug. "Not the kind who sits in a chair, listening and nodding." He mimicked an old-fashioned stereotypical analyst, stroking an imaginary goatee. *"Vhat vas your relationship vith your father, my dear? Vere you toilet-trained too early?"*

She had to laugh. "Sorry, you sound more like Groucho Marx than Freud."

He threw up his hands. "Alas, I am a failure as an impersonator." He smoothed his mustache. "My career is not very exciting, I'm afraid. An industrial–organizational psychologist for electrical generation companies. I try to improve work production and efficiency, and place the right person in the right job for their temperament. Quite dull, except for the travel."

"Should I call you *Doctor*?"

"Please, just Kahlil. I only use the title when I'm writing grants or authoring a case study."

Tawny blinked. "Over my head. I've never read a case study."

He pulled an amused grimace. "You have missed nothing unless you enjoy boring statistics."

She leaned forward, surprised at her hunger to learn more about this fascinating man. "Where do you travel?"

"Anywhere there's a position. Egypt, Dubai, Turkey, Germany, the Czech Republic." A flick of his hand indicated more countries, too many to count.

This man was sophisticated, educated, a world traveler. Why was he sitting here with her, a small-town nobody? "What brought you to Montana?"

His smile glowed. "I've read your eloquent authors, Ivan Doig, Rick DeMarinis, and James Welch. After their books, how could anyone resist? When I learned of the contract here, I jumped at the opportunity."

Tawny recognized the names but felt too embarrassed to admit she'd never read them. "How does it compare with the books?"

"Even more beautiful than their words expressed. People are very hospitable."

She shrugged. "We don't know how else to act."

"It's very charming. The people in the class the other night were so friendly."

"That's because we were all drowning, and you threw us a life preserver."

He laughed, a warm throaty sound that made her toes curl.

"I have to ask ... if you're a psychologist, why are you teaching about smartphones?"

He rested an elbow on the table. "Wherever a job takes me, I try to reach out to the community that is hosting me, offer a small token of appreciation for allowing me to join them." He hefted

Tawny's phone. "Since my hobby is playing with these new toys, I try to help people become more capable at using them. If they leave the class with confidence, it pleases me."

Tawny snorted. "It'll take more than one class to teach me the ins and outs of this monster." As soon as the words left her lips, she cursed silently. *Why did I say that? Sounds like a come-on. How stupid.*

He wiped his mouth with a napkin. When his eyes met hers, she looked away, pretending interest in her scone. The next bite tasted like a dry sponge. She left the rest.

He finished his scone without comment, only a faint smile. She felt an odd gratitude toward him. She'd stuck her foot in her mouth, and he didn't take advantage of her awkwardness.

"Do you like to walk?" he asked. "The park is nearby."

Relieved, she nodded and rose. "Too pretty a day to sit inside."

They left the shop, carrying their coffees, and approached the park. He matched her quick pace on the sun-dappled pathway. Light green leaves unfolded on towering cottonwoods. Blades of young grass poked through winter thatch. The smell of new growth floated on a light breeze.

"This is a nice town in spring," he said.

"How long have you been here?"

"Since February. I'm renting a furnished house. As beautiful as Montana is, I'm not a fan of your snow and ice."

"It's OK if you like winter sports. I snowshoe and cross-country ski. See that pond?" She pointed to the expanse of water, where swans drifted. "People ice skate there when it's frozen."

He hugged himself and pretended to shiver. *"Brrrr."*

Waddling ducks and snowy geese chortled as they parted to allow the couple through. "Should have brought the rest of my scone," she said. "It's fun to feed them."

Kahlil spotted a duck-food dispenser, immediately headed for it, and bought some. He grasped her hand and poured the food into her palm. How warm his touch felt.

She scattered pellets on the ground. The fowl clustered around her, gobbling and quacking for more.

One duck stayed off to the side of the flock, beady eyes focused on Tawny. It favored a deformed foot. "Poor guy." She shooed the other birds away and bent down with her palm open. The duck didn't hesitate to take the food, its bill lightly scraping her skin. She straightened, brushing her hands on her capris. When she faced Kahlil, the intensity of his green-eyed stare almost made her jump back. "What are you looking at?"

His dark brows softened. "Your kindness."

She resumed walking, quickly, to escape a blush trying to overtake her. He caught up in an instant, near enough that she felt his breath on her neck. She said, "My husband used to get mad because I always picked up some lame, injured critter and tried to nurse it back to health. Half the time, they died anyway. He called them my 'lost causes.'" Her throat tightened. "He was my final lost cause."

They walked in silence for several moments. Kahlil remained quiet, and Tawny felt grateful that he didn't push her. Finally she brought up the question she'd been longing to ask. "If you don't mind talking about it . . ." She glanced sideways at him. "How did you lose your wife?"

Head bowed, eyes hooded, he kept walking and didn't answer.

Uh-oh. She'd asked too much, too soon. How she hated it when nosy people she barely knew pressed her for personal details about Dwight's illness. Now, dammit, she'd overstepped those limits herself.

Another moment passed. She opened her mouth to apologize when he finally spoke: "She died in childbirth. It would have been our first. A little girl."

A wave of sympathy, empathy, surged over Tawny. "I'm sorry."

"She was thirty-nine, a year younger than I. She was an engineer. Our careers had been our lives before then. The doctors warned us about possible complications. Perhaps we shouldn't have waited so long. But we did." A tremor shook his voice. "My heart was torn from my chest."

How well Tawny knew that wrenching grief. She squeezed Kahlil's arm and held on.

He started to turn toward her but stopped and looked away, maybe to keep her from seeing the sheen of tears in his eyes. For a second, his fingertips barely brushed her hand, still gripping his arm. His shoulders shifted and relaxed, as if he could finally let down the mask hiding his grief.

She didn't let go of his arm as they continued over a footbridge that crossed the pond. They moved in silence, her hand tucked in the crook of his elbow, feeling the sinewy muscle through the texture of his tweed sleeve. Their steps fell easily in sync. It felt natural, as if they had strolled linked together for years. As if they shared a long, deep history of memories and heartaches. She hoped he felt the comfort she wanted to give him, and she soaked in the quiet consolation he offered.

Ten peaceful minutes later, they completed the circular path around the park, ending at their cars parked on the street.

He faced her and tilted his head. "I must go to work now. May I see you again?"

She nodded, unsure of her voice.

"I will call you." He reached to touch her cheek but stopped himself, as if worried he was being too forward. Instead he extended his hand to shake.

She took it, instantly aware of the electric heat of skin contact. They stood, gazing at each other for a long moment. She didn't want to give up the warmth of his grasp.

He finally spoke. "You have given me the first day of joy since my wife died. Thank you." He released her hand and slid into his car, a silver BMW convertible with the top down. After he started the engine, he looked over his shoulder and smiled. As he pulled away from the curb and drove down the avenue, his eyes watched her in the rearview mirror.

Tawny leaned against Dwight's Jeep, letting out a huge sigh. "Oh my God." She had to wait for her rubbery legs to regain strength before she climbed up on the pipe running board.

In her pocket, the smartphone trumpeted. Another new noise she didn't know the meaning of. She pulled it out and stared at the screen. "What are you saying to me?"

* * *

It had gone perfectly. Kahlil could not have rehearsed it better. Tawny appeared impressed with his education, profession, and travels, related in an offhand manner to sound modest and likeable.

Having been sheltered, she would likely build up glamorous illusions about the adventurous life he tossed out, like a casual jacket over a chair.

He also noted her look of admiration at the BMW he had rented. He downshifted through the curves on the highway to the Hungry Horse Dam and felt the Z4's power surge. A prior search of vehicle registrations revealed the Jeep Wrangler he'd seen her drive, aging and utilitarian, lacking glamour. He'd chosen the convertible, hoping its sportiness might appeal to her, in bright contrast to her sensible, dull vehicle. Soon, he hoped, she would be riding beside him, the top down and her titian hair blowing in the wind. The image caused a stir in his belly.

He felt especially pleased with the inspired tale of his wife dying in childbirth, adding pathos. The facts were much different: no child involved, Maryam blown to bloody shreds by a drone. But the factual version would not be as effective with Tawny. The proper emphasis needed to be on sorrow, not pity—or worse, horror.

Death, loss of family, abandonment—tools he knew intimately that wielded awesome emotional power. It had turned out to be elegantly simple to use her kindness, unlocking her vulnerability.

He had chosen well.

Chapter 3: The Joys of Technology

Over the next few days, Tawny and Kahlil met several times, always in public places, always too casual to be considered a date. At least, that's what she kept telling herself. He was too young, and she wasn't ready for romance yet, if ever. But a longing almost like hunger pulled her toward him.

Sunny mornings, they sat side by side on a bench in the park, where she posed more questions about the phone. He figured out the trumpeting noise came from the pedometer, signaling she had walked 10,000 steps. He demonstrated how to find businesses on the net. He playfully tested her skill with GPS directions as they wandered downtown streets, seeking out restaurants, sports shops, and bakeries.

She still struggled with mysterious screens that popped up without prompting, preventing her from making a phone call or directing her to a website she didn't mean to access.

"It does stuff automatically that I don't understand," she complained to Kahlil on Friday morning. "How can I make it stick to only the tasks I want?"

He smiled and patted her knee as they sat side by side near a low rock waterfall. "Be patient. Look how much you've learned in only a week."

"Ninety percent of what Lucifer does is no use to me," she exclaimed.

He gave her a puzzled look. "Lucifer?"

Tawny held up the smartphone. "This instrument of the devil. I named it Lucifer."

Kahlil chuckled, a deep throaty sound that made her tingle. "That's very funny. You are a delight."

She pulled down the pushed-up sleeves of her rust-colored hoodie, hoping he hadn't noticed the gooseflesh on her arms from the compliment.

A blue pinpoint of light blinked from the phone, reminding Tawny of more questions. "This light . . . sometimes it's blue, sometimes red or green. Sometimes it doesn't flash at all. What does it mean?"

"Red, it needs charging; green, the battery is full. Blue might mean a new voice mail or an update is available. Also it may mean the phone is searching for hot spots. Or it's pinging off a cell tower. Nothing to worry about."

"What about all the noises? It beeps, it trumpets, it clicks like a cricket."

He swiped until the clicking tone sounded. "That means you have a new text message."

She twisted her braid. "I'm scared to get the bill. It's got to cost a fortune to perform all these tricks."

Using his thumbs, Kahlil worked silently for a few moments. "You said your son sent this to you?"

She nodded.

He held the phone for her to see the display. "Well, it appears he already paid for the service a year in advance."

Tawny's throat swelled, and she blinked hard. That boy of hers. Neal had given her a gift any other mother would be thrilled with, and all she did was gripe about it. "I must sound horribly ungrateful."

Kahlil gave her a slight smile. "Not ungrateful. Just overwhelmed."

She shook her head. "That's the truth. There's too much to remember. Can't you disable all these extra tangents and just make it do the functions I need?"

"You think functions are useless only because you haven't learned what to do with them yet. Say you need to find out the balance in your checking account. Would you consider that useful?"

Tawny thought for a moment. In the back of her mind, a warning from Dwight echoed about potential dangers of banking online. "Yes, I suppose so. But what about hacking? I don't want thieves to access my account."

Kahlil grinned. "Excellent! I'm proud of you. You're thinking about security. Identity theft is the fastest growing crime."

"So why would anyone want to leave themselves open to theft?"

"Great question!" He beamed as if Tawny were a smart puppy mastering a new trick. "That's why you need strong passwords to protect your private information. Only *you* know the password, and only *you* can get into your account. Shall I show you?"

"I guess." Her doubts evaporated when his muscular thigh pressed against hers as he leaned closer to demonstrate.

"OK. What bank do you use?"

"United Bankcorp."

He flicked and tapped for a few seconds, then a screen appeared with United Bankcorp's logo. "I've downloaded their app to use as an example to walk you through the process. You do not want to perform financial functions unless you are at a secure Wi-Fi connection, like at your home. Please, do not ever do banking at a hot spot or unsecured connection."

She nodded. His advice rang familiar bells of Dwight's cautions about using her laptop in public places.

"Now I will enter a password. It's not real, just for demonstration." Tapered fingers touched the keyboard, and dots appeared across the screen. "This is fifteen characters long. That's a good length, with a combination of upper and lowercase letters, numbers, and symbols. You do not want to use your birthdate, phone number, or your children's names—anything a criminal could guess or find out about you online. Make the password as random as possible."

Tawny put on her readers. "How will I ever remember it? I barely know my PIN for the ATM."

"Write it down and lock it in a safe place, but definitely not in your wallet or beside your computer." He continued through the banking site. "Each institution will have different protocols, but the instructions are step-by-step and easy to follow."

"Hope they work better than my bank's phone system. You can't ever get a human to talk to."

"The nice feature of electronic banking is you do not need to talk to a human. All the information is at your fingertips."

Tawny made a mental note to look into the strange deposit. Neither the manager nor the Helena branch had ever called back, despite her many messages. Maybe she could access information online that she couldn't pry out of indifferent bank employees.

"Are you still with me?" Kahlil asked.

"Sorry, I was thinking about something else. Please, go on."

He wrapped up the lesson, then glanced at the time. "I must go to work now. But I want you to call me if you need help setting up your banking."

"All right. Thanks."

His green eyes twinkled. "And I will call you later, after you choose where you would like me to take you to dinner tonight." With a wink, he was gone, striding to his convertible.

A tickle of arousal startled her. A real date. Should she agree?

* * *

At home, Tawny tried out banking by smartphone as Kahlil had shown her. She invented a random password as he suggested, carefully writing down each character. To her amazement, almost instantly, Lucifer connected to her checking account.

No, that had to be wrong. Now the balance showed over $68,000. She backtracked to recent transactions during the past week. Her cash withdrawal of $41,500 appeared, along with several checks that had cleared.

Then another deposit three days ago.

$63,500.

What the hell?

How could the bank make two huge mistakes just days apart?

She tried to find additional details about the deposit, but the screen offered only the amount. Dammit! Not another trip to the bank. This was ridiculous.

Tawny stormed out to the garage and jumped in the Jeep. She drove to the bank, parked, and checked herself in the rearview mirror. Eyes snapping, she looked ready to do battle. "This ends right here, right now," she told her reflection.

She rushed through the lobby, past the surly operations supervisor with black horn-rims; Ms. Garza, the loan officer; and the tellers, feeling a pang that Margaret no longer stood at her window. Tawny sensed curious stares on her back and heard murmurs of annoyance as she climbed the stairs to the mezzanine.

The manager's office was in the corner, encased in glass. He appeared to be in his early sixties, wearing a charcoal suit of shimmery silk, custom tailored to his trim tennis player's physique. A pale-blue tie matched his pale-blue eyes that stared at a monitor through rimless readers halfway down his Roman nose. A nameplate read Branch Manager R. Hyslop. Snooty son of a bitch.

Tawny thumped on the glass door. He startled and straightened his coat. She turned the knob and entered. "Mr. Hyslop, today you are going to handle my problem, and I'm not leaving until it's resolved."

The manager reached under the lip of his desk, then slowly rose, shooting his cuffs, maybe to ensure she noticed the gold Piaget watch on his wrist. He was short, probably three inches under Tawny's five ten. "Why don't you sit down, and we'll talk about your issue."

She remained standing. "My issue is your bank has made two giant errors totaling more than one hundred thousand dollars. You don't answer my messages. Your employees blow me off. I keep getting passed down the line and ignored, and I've had enough."

Hyslop looked over Tawny's shoulder, held up one finger to someone behind her. Tawny turned to face a stout uniformed security guard standing in the door, hand on his gun.

Her stomach flip-flopped. What on earth? She'd never even bounced a check, and now an armed guard stood ready to draw down on her. Had these people gone nuts?

"Mrs. Lindholm," the manager said, "it happens I was just going to call you."

The man knew her name. How had he recognized her?

The guard shifted a foot closer.

A sour taste of anger rose in her throat. "Are you going to arrest me for being a dissatisfied customer?"

Where had that come from? It sounded like something Dwight might've said. He'd always handled trouble calmly and never caved to intimidation. How she missed him at this moment. He'd know exactly what to do. She tried to visualize him by her side.

Hyslop lowered himself into his chair. "Take a seat, Mrs. Lindholm. I have something to show you."

"What is it?"

The manager clicked his keyboard for several seconds, then rotated the monitor for Tawny to see. "This is a video recording of the deposit you claim you did not make. Please watch."

Grainy video began to play, showing the view of a drive-up window from a camera in the ceiling above a teller's head. A green Jeep Wrangler with a tan top pulled in. The drawer slid out. As the driver's window rolled down, Tawny gasped.

A woman in sunglasses, wearing a ball cap, placed four thick rubber-banded stacks of bills in the drawer without saying a word. The crackly audio of a teller's voice asked, "You want to deposit this into your account?"

The woman nodded. The drawer slid in, and the teller peered at a driver's license, made notations on a deposit slip, then gathered up the bills. She ran the cash through a counting machine. "Forty-one thousand five hundred. Correct, Mrs. Lindholm?"

The woman in the Jeep nodded.

The teller sent a paper out the window, which the woman signed and returned. The teller printed a receipt, then passed it out the drawer. The woman took it, rolled up the Jeep window, and drove off.

Tawny felt like she'd been kicked in the stomach. Her legs wobbled, and she sank into the chair she'd previously resisted.

She had just watched herself hand over a big wad of cash to the bank. The scene felt as real as the one a few days earlier when she'd withdrawn that same $41,500, now locked in her safe.

"And please examine this." Hyslop pulled up another screen, showing a bank form. He scrolled down the page. "Is this your signature, Mrs. Lindholm?"

Tawny stared at the handwriting. Hers. Stomach clenching, she nodded.

"So you agree you signed this form on the same day of this deposit."

"No!" Tawny grabbed her glasses and shoved them on. Hope sank as she studied the writing closely. "It looks like my signature, but I did not sign that. And I did not make that deposit."

"Well, Mrs. Lindholm." Hyslop folded his arms across his chest. "The video shows otherwise. You have harassed my employees repeatedly, claiming the bank made an error, but this recording makes it look as if you are the one in error."

"Th-that can't be me." Tawny felt the manager and the guard exchanging glances over her head. "Play it again. . . please."

Hyslop closed his pale eyes and stretched his brows high. Seconds passed, then he reopened his eyes and clicked on the keyboard. The video started once more.

Unable to breathe, Tawny watched as the sequence repeated. The car looked like an identical twin to Dwight's Jeep. The driver appeared to be *her* identical twin, a twin she didn't have. Who was this woman, this double, impersonating her?

She leaned closer to the screen and squinted, trying to find a flaw in the imposter. Although the ball cap was pulled low over her forehead and sunglasses masked her eyes, the profile matched hers: same mouth, nose, chin. An auburn braid fell forward over the woman's shoulder, just like hers did.

If Tawny didn't know better, she would have accepted the driver was her with a large stack of cash.

The manager clicked his mouse to stop the recording. "Are you satisfied?"

Tawny couldn't find her voice.

Hyslop rested his elbows on the desk and formed a steeple with manicured hands. "Mrs. Lindholm," his voice dripped sympathy, "if you're having trouble reconciling your account, I'd be happy to have someone assist you."

Through her numb shock, Tawny's temper flared. She wasn't a helpless ninny who couldn't balance a checkbook. Dammit, she'd kept their business's books for decades.

Hyslop pushed on. "I understand your husband passed away less than a year ago. Perhaps the strain of his death . . . well, maybe you're not remembering things you might have done."

"I'm a widow," Tawny snapped. "I'm not insane." But before her sharp denial faded in the quiet office, disturbing memories zinged through her head. The checkbook in the trash bin, her boots in the washer, the TV remote in the freezer. And finding herself fifty miles from home without knowing how or why she had driven there.

Virgie had suggested those lapses were caused by depression. But what if they meant a breakdown? Could she have committed a crime without even knowing it?

The manager's temporary attempt at sympathy evaporated as the cold mask again stiffened his face. "If there isn't anything else we can do for you . . ." He stood, indicating the door. The guard backed up, making way for Tawny to leave.

* * *

Kahlil sat on a picnic table, feet propped on the bench, near a boat launch ramp at the Hungry Horse Reservoir. He adjusted the hearing aid volume down after Tawny's argument with the banker and concentrated on the screen of a throwaway cell phone. After completing several transactions, he ate a sandwich he'd stuffed in his jacket pocket.

An old Ford pickup backed a boat and trailer down the ramp to the waterline. Kahlil recognized the man dismounting the truck as the tech who'd replaced a faulty hard drive in his computer at work. Kahlil had studied him for weeks. "Hi, Skipper."

The man looked over, lifted his chin in greeting. Under a John Deere cap, his nose glowed rosy and his steps wavered. "Hey, Kahlil." He jerked his head toward the water. "Gonna go drown some worms. Wanna come?"

"I would if I didn't need to get back to work."

"Aw, screw 'em. I took the rest of the day off." Skipper hauled a cooler from the pickup bed and hefted it into the boat. It landed with a loud thud.

While trying to launch the boat, the man stubbed his toes against a tire, smashed a finger, and cursed several times. Finally, Kahlil felt sorry enough for the drunk to walk over and help. Ten clumsy, fumbling minutes later, the boat finally floated in the blue water. Skipper stood in the rocking vessel, holding the wheel to keep his balance. If he didn't drown himself over the weekend, Kahlil expected he would call in sick as usual, with another case of Monday Flu.

"Want me to park your truck?" Kahlil gestured at the pickup and now-empty trailer.

Skipper blinked at the vehicle as if he'd forgotten it in his haste to go fishing. "Yeah, man, that'd be awesome." He pawed around in his down vest pockets for several seconds, wearing a puzzled expression.

"Are the keys still in it?" Kahlil prompted.

Relief washed over Skipper's ruddy face. "Yeah, yeah, I guess. Just leave 'em on top of the front tire inside the wheel well, OK?" He continued to fumble in his pocket.

"Sure." Kahlil moved toward the still-open driver's door, but Skipper hailed him.

"Hey, look at what I just won." He held up a smartphone exactly like Tawny's. "This thing costs five hundred bucks to buy. I don't even remember signing up for whatever the hell drawing it was, but damned if I didn't win the grand prize."

"You are a lucky man." *And about to become even luckier,* Kahlil thought.

Skipper dug in the cooler and pulled out a beer. "Hey, some of the guys are goin' to the Back Room later tonight for a couple of brewskis and ribs. Come along if you want."

Kahlil grinned. "I have a date."

Skipper grinned back, swaying. "She got any girlfriends?"

Kahlil waved him off. "If she did, I'd keep them for myself."

"Asshole." Still smiling, the drunken man turned over the engine, revved it, and sped across the reservoir.

After parking Skipper's truck, Kahlil returned to the picnic table, where he again went to work with the disposable cell, logging into the man's profile. Skipper was behind on his child support, and his divorce had stalled, not finalized because he owed his attorney. Yet he kept a separate account, one his wife knew nothing about, that automatically made his boat payments and probably kept his cooler stocked with Budweiser. Kahlil transferred $9,800 into that account.

Of the two dozen targets Kahlil had selected for the mission, only Tawny questioned the bounty from an unknown benefactor. Quite remarkable. All the rest simply accepted their good fortune as well-deserved luck. When Kahlil counted on greed, people rarely disappointed him.

One final task left to do on the throwaway phone. He texted a single word: *Withdraw.*

He removed the battery from the phone. Scanning the water and shoreline, he saw no one close enough to observe him fling the phone far into the reservoir. It landed with a faint splash. Fifty feet farther down the shore, he threw the battery in as well.

He hiked back up to the road that ran across the top of the dam, pausing for a moment to gaze into the rippling water of the reservoir. Dams always brought to mind his father, who had believed the future lay in hydroelectric power. Not just from rivers but also by harnessing ocean waves. He was a dreamer, a naïve idealist who believed problems could be solved. And that those in power wanted to solve them.

Poor Father.

Kahlil shook off the flash of melancholy before descending into the bowels of the dam.

Chapter 4: Being Neighborly

Tawny double-locked her front door and sank onto the brown velour living room couch, head in her hands. Despite the doubt swimming in her mind, she knew deep in her core that she still grasped reality. She might zone out, she might misplace things, but she had not gone around the bend.

The imposter was a *real person* who'd handed over *real cash*.

Why did a stranger who looked like her put money in her account? Had the second large deposit been made the same way?

Tawny wished she'd had the presence of mind to ask to see video for the second transaction, but she'd been too rattled. She hated herself for freezing, helpless and useless. Confrontations terrified her. Always before, Dwight had been the point man, taking the lead, going on the attack in disputes, while she lagged back, making excuses to herself that she played a supporting role. In reality, she was a coward, hiding behind his strength.

She should have stood her ground, but she'd been desperate to escape the suspicious glare of bank employees and the armed guard. Their knowing eyes condemned her. Someone wanted to make her appear to be a criminal or at least the perpetrator of questionable activities. Why?

Acid churned in her gut. She felt guilty but for what? Nothing she'd done was illegal.

Except maybe withdrawing the cash now locked in Dwight's gun safe.

Why had she followed Virgie's advice? It felt wrong, but she'd trusted her friend's judgment above her own. She shouldn't have.

If the bank hadn't already filed a "Suspicious Activity Report," surely they would now. Federal officers might even have Tawny under surveillance. During the drive home, she'd spotted a dark-blue sedan that might be following her.

Tawny realized the manager must have alerted the armed guard when he reached under the desk, probably hitting a silent alarm. Hyslop also recognized Tawny without her having to identify herself. From the moment she'd entered the lobby, she sensed that every employee in the bank knew exactly who she was and trained eyes on her, as if waiting for her to rob the place.

Where had that rapt attention been when she begged them over and over to look into her problem? They couldn't care less. She'd been invisible and inconsequential when she was simply a customer with a problem. Now they treated her like Pablo Escobar.

Fists clenched, she pounded the couch cushions. "I didn't do anything wrong!" She gripped a throw pillow, hugging it to her chest. "Dwight, I need you."

Except Dwight was gone.

Tawny was alone.

Twisting her wedding ring, she pulled it hard against her swollen knuckle. The pain felt reassuringly real in this unreal situation.

She crossed the living room to the pass-through window in the kitchen where the answering machine sat. She pushed the playback button to listen once again to the precious message she had saved for a year.

From out of the past, Dwight's voice, hoarse from chemo and radiation, spoke to her: "Hey, love, I'm done with the infusion. If you come pick me up, I *might* be persuaded to take you out for an ice-cream cone."

Swallowing a lump, Tawny remembered that day. By the time she'd arrived at the hospital, he was too sick for ice cream. But she'd saved the message, knowing soon this would be the only record she had of his voice.

She pulled on her braid. "Dwight, what am I going to do?" She tried to think of someone to call for help. The Slocums, her ex-banker neighbors? Sheryl, definitely no; Phil, maybe. But his parting expression had revealed doubt.

Virgie? A good friend, an educated doctor, but her well-meaning advice had already put Tawny in a worse situation.

Her children? Neal didn't answer her texts. Who knew where he might be, an unknown foreign base, out of touch, but hopefully—please, God—alive and healthy. Emma? Living in a van, moving from state to state, with a cell phone that sometimes worked, sometimes didn't, depending if she had enough money to buy more minutes. A good heart, but the judgment of a cantaloupe.

Dwight's old army buddies? Only a few survived, most dead from Agent Orange or alcohol, drugs, and suicides borne out of their tours in Vietnam. The remaining men would fly across the country at the slightest hint of need from a fellow veteran. All had come to say good-bye during Dwight's final week of life. Several might help her, but she felt reluctant to ask because they had given so much already.

She yearned to talk to the Roths, dear old friends who'd treated her like a daughter since she was a girl. They'd do anything for her. Except they'd been killed in a terror bombing during their vacation to Israel more than a year before Dwight died.

Other friends, couples they used to take trips together and share dinners with, had dropped off, one by one, during Dwight's long ordeal of declining health. When Tawny occasionally ran into them after his death, the wives linked arms through their husbands', as if to warn her away. As if she were on the prowl. What a laugh.

Phil Slocum's words came back to her: *Suspicious Activity Report*.

She needed to clear suspicion from her name. Whom should she ask for help? The FBI? An accountant? A lawyer? Where did you look in the *Yellow Pages* to prevent a bank from turning you in for crime you didn't commit?

If she went to the cops, they wouldn't believe her, not once they saw the bank's video. No, she needed a lawyer.

Kit Albritton might know how to untangle the mess. He'd written their wills and handled Dwight's probate. As a high school boy, Kit had worked in their diesel repair shop to earn college money. Now, she called his law office, but he was already gone for the weekend. She left a message.

Paranoia clutched Tawny's throat. Each breath felt like it might be her last. In the bedroom, she unlocked the safe. The paper sack of cash sat there like an accusation. She should turn it in. Would that make her look less guilty? Or more?

Dammit! She had no reason to feel guilty. She was an innocent victim being set up for unknown reasons.

The woman in the video clearly intended to impersonate Tawny, down to the same sunglasses and the braid falling over her shoulder. She'd forged a signature well enough to convince Tawny. Who was she?

She slammed the safe door and spun the dial. Virgie was right—better to be in trouble *with* money than *without* it. If the mess ever got straightened out, she'd give the cash back. Now, it served as her ace in the hole.

She hoped.

The phone trilled in her pocket. Caller ID read *Kahlil*, no doubt calling about the dinner date he'd mentioned earlier. Not now. She didn't feel like either food or company. She swiped his call off to voice mail.

To escape the turmoil swirling in her brain, she decided to take a walk. Fresh air and exercise always cleared her mind and usually helped her figure out a solution. But she had never before encountered such a complicated problem. She needed answers but didn't even know what questions to ask.

After changing into sneakers, she locked the door and walked the wide avenues, canopied by red maple and mountain ash. On the parkway, a few massive stumps remained from grand old trees cut down by Dutch elm disease. Roots had lifted the sidewalks. She picked past broken slabs of concrete—small hazards compared to the problem she now pondered.

With the school day over, children played in front yards, pumped their legs in tree swings, and bounced basketballs in the alley. Her neighborhood was a welcome throwback to a calmer era. When families went on vacation, neighbors fed each other's dogs and watered each other's houseplants. Many a kid had knocked on her door, needing a Band-Aid and a hug.

Tawny loved the security of her surroundings, where she strolled regularly without a thought to safety. Peacefulness eased her troubled mind now. *This* was normal, where neighbors waved, and no one suspected her of unlawful transactions.

No one except maybe the suspicious ex-bankers, the Slocums.

She walked the opposite direction from their house, avoiding a possible encounter. Rounding the corner, Tawny approached the Roths' old home. The tragedy of their violent deaths had left the narrow clapboard cottage vacant and mournful. A For Sale sign planted in the front yard made Tawny think of a marker on a grave. Her heart ached when she remembered the dear old couple who had shared many evenings of cribbage with her and Dwight over glasses of tea.

Except . . . now the house looked lived in, the single garage door partly raised, revealing the trunk of a silver sports car. And a light shone from the kitchen window, where a figure moved behind the miniblinds. Tawny paused, leaning against a horse-chestnut tree in the parkway, curious about the new occupant.

A covered breezeway connected the kitchen to the garage. She heard a door bang, then a dark man appeared.

Kahlil? Here in her neighborhood?

Tawny recalled the call from him that she'd ignored. Stepping behind the tree and out of sight, she checked Lucifer. A blue light blinked. She couldn't remember if that meant a new voice mail or it needed charging. Damn this complicated phone. Finally she hit on the correct icon to retrieve messages.

"Tawny," Kahlil's mellow voice said, "I hope I may take you to dinner this evening. Please call me when you can."

In passing conversation, he'd mentioned renting a place for the duration of his work project. Cautious of being a new widow living alone, she intentionally kept her address to herself. All their meetings had occurred in public places: the library, the coffee shop, the park.

Could he really be living a block and a half away, in the home of her old friends? What a weird coincidence. But that's how small towns were.

An incoming text clicked. Tawny swiped the screen and read: *R U all right? U seemed preoccupied this a.m. Dinner invitation still open. K.*

She sighed. It had been rude not to answer his earlier call, but the bank business put her in a tailspin of worry and paranoia.

A rumbling noise made her peek from behind the chestnut tree. Kahlil slid the garage door to full open. He backed the convertible into the driveway. Shutting down the engine, he got out and used a hose and a bucket of soapy water to wash the car. She watched the rhythmic roll and rotation of his muscular shoulders and biceps as he scrubbed. Even in a ratty T-shirt and jeans with holes in the knees, he looked dashing.

As he wiped down the gleaming finish with meticulous strokes, Tawny felt touched by his effort. It was something Dwight used to do—wash the car before taking his "best girl" out on the town. Emma would scoff at a boy who made that effort, but Dwight would have shared the suggestion with Neal. A sweet, old-fashioned gesture of respect to honor his date, a date Tawny now felt guilty about. Why hadn't she responded to Kahlil's messages?

Embarrassed, hiding behind a tree, like a teenage airhead. Ridiculous. She was a mature woman. This man had been unfailingly kind and patient with her. Only her silly vanity because of the ten-year age difference kept her from saying yes. That, and the irrational feeling she was somehow being unfaithful to Dwight.

Stop being stupid. It's only dinner.

She shook out the tension in her shoulders and strode down the sidewalk toward Kahlil. "Hello!"

He looked up from polishing the side mirror. A grin lit his face. "Hello! How did you find me?"

She stopped a few feet away. "I . . . wasn't actually looking for you. Do you live here?"

He hung the towel over the mirror and rubbed the rough shadow on his jawline. "Excuse my bad appearance. I need a shower and shave." He waved at the house. "Yes, this is where I'm renting. It belonged to an older couple who passed away."

She nodded. "The Roths. They were friends of my husband and me."

"Excuse me, would you like to come in? It's a bit messy, but . . ." He shrugged and smiled an apology. "Living alone, no one to impress." He swept his arm toward the door. "Please, come in. I'll make tea."

Tawny followed him through the breezeway and into the kitchen. The Roths' furniture still remained in place, the round oak table and four chairs, same gingham cushions. She moved to the arched doorway leading to the living room, knowing what she'd find. The familiar pair of recliners faced the TV, flanked by a plaid couch.

The hutch still held Ruth Roth's collection of Disney figurines, lovingly collected over the years for her granddaughter. A granddaughter who, as the Roths' sole heir, hadn't even bothered to attend their memorial service.

Last fall, Tawny recalled talking to the real estate agent as the man pounded the sign in the yard. He'd confided that the granddaughter only cared about whatever money she could pull out of the house and was pissed off it wasn't selling, as if she were the only one inconvenienced by the collapse of the housing market.

Sadness welled in Tawny's chest. The Roths gone, Dwight gone, no more visits full of laughter and bantering accusations of cheating at cribbage. No more long-winded stories Solly loved to tell, while Ruth heaved exaggerated sighs of impatience. Tawny imagined the echo of her voice: *Solly, puh-leeze, we've heard this a hundred times already.*

Kahlil touched her shoulder from behind. She hadn't heard him approach. He murmured, "Are you all right?"

Tawny swallowed. "They were sweet people. I miss them."

"Had they been ill?"

"No. Both were still sharp and active. He'd just retired. They went on a trip to the Holy Land. It was their dream. They lived in Israel years ago when they were students in a kibbutz. They wanted to go back one more time before they died." Her jaw clenched. "A terrorist blew up the café where they were eating lunch. Killed fourteen people." Bitterness pinched her.

"How terrible." Kahlil squeezed her shoulder.

"Senseless tragedy." Tawny faced him, eager to move away from the uncomfortable subject. "Maybe I shouldn't have told you. Are you superstitious or squeamish now about living in their house?"

He shook his head, gazing at her with a sad smile. "Not at all. I can tell this home was a happy place for them."

"It was." His perceptiveness touched her. What a sensitive, caring man. She found herself longing to sink in the depths of those beautiful, yet sorrowful, green eyes.

The kettle whistled. He made tea while she leaned against the archway, watching him. He moved with easy grace, as if he might be a good dancer. How would it feel to twirl in his arms? *Oh, for heaven's sake. Stop these fantasies. You're fifty years old.*

He brought her a mug and again rubbed the stubble on his face. "Please, sit down. Make yourself comfortable. I will not be long."

She eased into Ruth's recliner as Kahlil disappeared down the hallway leading to the bedrooms and bath. How like Dwight—didn't want her to see him until after a shower and shave, immaculate in clean clothes. With cancer, that fastidiousness had fallen away, and she knew how ashamed the odor of wasting and sickness had made him.

While she sipped fragrant jasmine tea, she noticed the few changes Kahlil had brought to the house. An open laptop sat on Solly's desk, the screensaver moving like ocean waves across the face. A card table had been set up to hold a combination printer/fax/scanner and a stack of external hard drives. The work area was orderly, without normal desk litter. A battery backup as large as a file cabinet hummed on the floor, barely squeezed under the card table. Looked like enough capacity to run the entire neighborhood, if not the whole town.

Other than the computer equipment, the interior appeared surprisingly unchanged, as if Kahlil treated the place like a motel room, setting up only what he needed without personalizing it into a home. Understandable, since his work involved frequent travel from place to place. Did he have a permanent home? He'd mentioned many different universities and countries where he'd lived, but all sounded temporary, not lasting.

Must be a lonely life, she mused. No roots, connections, lasting relationships—all values that Tawny cherished. Yet both her children had chosen nomadic existences, Neal with the army and Emma with her aimless, wandering ways. Maybe Tawny's emphasis on stability had stifled them, made them feel closed in and claustrophobic, instead of safe and wanted.

Her life had eroded away from underneath her. The children gone, Dwight gone, the Roths gone. Remaining friends deserting her. Even the local bank, where she now had to deal with indifferent, yet hostile, employees.

Only her neighborhood remained the same—safe, familiar, friendly. But without family and friends, a house wasn't really a home. Just four walls and a roof.

A clipping of yellowed newspaper caught her eye, lying on the floor half-hidden under the battery backup. Probably fell off the desk. She rose from the recliner, picked it up, and set it beside the laptop. Without her glasses, she could only make out the headline: "Child Still Missing After Father Kills Family." Just as well she didn't read about someone else's tragedy to add to her sorrow.

Kahlil reentered the living room, bringing with him a scent of soap and underlying masculinity. Freshly shaven, shaggy, damp hair combed, he wore his tweed sport coat over a button-down shirt and new jeans with knife-edge creases. His smile dazzled her with its brightness, instantly lifting her spirits. How happy he looked, like an eager child reunited with his best friend.

"Now that I am fit to be in polite company," he said, "may I take you to dinner?"

She glanced down at the jeggings and rust-colored hoodie she'd worn all day, wrangling with the bank, walking. "I'm not really dressed for . . . I don't even have lipstick."

He spread both hands. "You look amazing. I have yet to see you not look amazing. Please?"

She tucked loose strands of hair into her braid and wished she had a comb. "All right." Then she pointed to his desk. "Oh, that newspaper was on the floor."

Puzzlement crossed Kahlil's face. He picked up the clipping. "Oh." He immediately tossed it in the wastebasket. "I keep finding old bits and pieces tucked in odd corners around the house. Perhaps the Roths were, as you call them, 'hoarders.'" He placed his hand on her back. "Ready?"

Warmth flowed through her from his touch. His presence vibrated around her like an electrical charge. They left the house and climbed into the shiny, clean convertible.

The seat hugged her as she inhaled the new car smell. She ran one hand over the soft black leather, feeling its suppleness, so different from the scratchy, saddle-blanket seat covers in the Jeep. "This is beautiful," she murmured. Nothing like the big rigs their shop used to service. A Peterbilt or Freightliner might cost a hundred grand or more, but sitting in them never felt like this.

Kahlil reversed out of the driveway onto the street. "How did you find me?"

"Honestly, I wasn't looking for you," Tawny answered. "I had some things on my mind, so I went for a walk and there you were."

He pulled his head back. "Really?" Dark eyebrows lifted in amazement. "Do you live nearby?"

"A block and a half away."

He braked and swerved to the curb, eyes wide. "Really?" he repeated, staring at her as if she'd revealed the cure for cancer. After a moment, he smiled and put the car back in gear. "Then clearly it is destiny. Fate intended us to meet. The universe threw us together the first time at the library. In case we didn't receive that message, now it makes us neighbors. Fate has spoken."

Tawny watched his handsome profile as he downshifted at a corner. With his mystical talk of destiny and fate, a strange sensation crept over her. She had noticed the signs, too: First the postcard about the smartphone class in her mailbox. The shared loss of their spouses, even though neither was an age where widowhood was common. Their houses were practically next door. He even lived in the home of her old friends. "Maybe it's just coincidence."

He shook his head. "What is coincidence but destiny tipping its hand?"

Moments later, Kahlil turned into the parking lot of the restaurant where she and Dwight had always celebrated their anniversary.

"Well!" she exclaimed. "I guess that settles it. You chose my favorite restaurant."

* * *

The server greeted Tawny with a hug. "So good to see you again." He nodded at Kahlil. "Welcome, sir. What can I bring you to drink?" To Tawny, he asked, "Your usual—Moose Drool?"

"Please."

Kahlil ordered a bottle of pinot noir from the local winery on Flathead Lake.

After the server delivered their beverages, Tawny said, "Excuse me for asking, but I'm surprised you drink."

Kahlil lifted one shoulder and winked. "I drink, I dearly love barbecue ribs, and I fear I could not face Mecca without the guidance of GPS." He raised the wine glass. "I've lived many places and learned to partake of the pleasures in each culture." His mouth twitched to one side under the black mustache. "Although this evening, I do not need wine to feel intoxicated."

Heat flushed Tawny's cheeks. She hoped in the dim light he didn't notice, but the expression in his eyes showed he had.

Under the small round table, the sides of their feet pressed together. She wondered how electricity could pass through their shoes and tingle all the way up her legs.

"How much longer will your job here go on?" She tried to make the question sound like casual conversation, but the desire to know gripped her. If he left, she realized how much she'd miss him.

Kahlil leaned back in his chair. "The contract lasts another month."

"Then what?" Was her nosiness as obvious to him as it was to her? She took another sip to keep from talking.

"Then I will have an opportunity to enjoy the fruits of my labors." Green eyes fixed on her. "Would you have time to show me the mountains? I like to hike."

"So do I," she answered too eagerly. Three sips of beer on an empty stomach. Why the hell was she acting like this? By the time she finished the beer, she'd be running her bare foot up his leg. Dammit.

He gazed at her over the top of the menu. "I have developed an affinity for Montana beef. It's unlike other steak I've eaten."

"The owners of this place raise their own." She glanced at her menu. "Dwight's favorite is the T-bone."

The mention of his name jerked Tawny back to drown in a pool of memories. Like their twenty-fifth anniversary, sitting at that table over in the corner, when he gave her a diamond pendant.

It's too early, she'd protested. *Twenty-five is silver.*

When's the diamond anniversary?

Sixty, I think.

So I'm premature . . . in gifts, that is.

Do I get another one in thirty-five years?

We'll see if I put up with you that long.

This was her and Dwight's special place. She shouldn't be here with another man.

The server arrived to take their order. Kahlil chose the T-bone. Her hunger had vanished, so she ordered a dinner salad, but she held onto the menu to give her an excuse to stare at something besides the handsome man across the table.

Silence hung heavy for a few moments. What a mistake it was to let herself get carried away. She should leave now and never see this man again.

Light fingers touched her wrist, then traveled to brush her wedding ring. "I understand," Kahlil murmured. "It's all right."

The touch lasted only a second, but it was long enough to break through to her. She raised her eyes and saw the sorrow, the loss, the tenderness in his expression. "Thank you."

He shook his head. "No, thank *you*. You are a brave woman. After my wife died, I stayed in a hotel room for over a month. Wouldn't open the door to anyone. The manager finally called the police to throw me out." The side of his mouth quirked with a wry smile. "I think he was afraid I would kill myself and ruin his mattress."

She stifled a bitter laugh. "How understanding of him."

He shrugged. "Actually he did me a favor. My sorrow was not his problem. He had his own battles to fight. He made me realize the rest of the world did not care about my loss and would not stop turning while I wept. I needed to learn that lesson."

Tawny sighed. "It's not an easy one, is it?"

"That's why your friendship brings me such joy. You are wise without knowing it. You do what you must do. You are a lesson to me just by living."

Her gaze dropped to the menu again. "You have a knack for making me blush."

He rocked back in his chair and chuckled. "That's because you are even more beautiful when you blush."

The server rescued her by appearing with salads and bread.

The rest of the meal flew by. Conversation lost its earlier awkwardness. She described hikes and kayak trips to remote lakes she would show him. He leaned forward, eager with questions. She finished a second beer in a comfortable glow, then joined him in a glass of wine. And another.

As Tawny and Kahlil left the restaurant, she almost collided with the manager of the bank in the vestibule. He was entering with his wife, a thin, dark-haired woman whose plastic surgeon had tightened her skin till it looked ready to tear.

"Well!" Hyslop exclaimed. "Mrs. Lindholm, how nice to see you again." His underlying tone carried more than ice. It felt like a threat. He glared at Tawny, then Kahlil, and yanked his wife's elbow, pulling her into the restaurant.

Kahlil raised his eyebrows. "What an unpleasant man."

Tawny hurried outside and took a deep breath of cool night air, briefly shocking her back to sobriety. "The manager of my bank. We're having some issues."

"Ah."

He opened the convertible door for her. While he moved to the driver's side, Tawny felt a sudden impulse to check her bank balance. She flicked quickly through the log-on and, despite her alcoholic buzz, remembered the complicated password. Amazing.

The balance had jumped higher with another deposit of $40,000 the day before. "What the hell?"

Kahlil settled into the driver's seat and looked over at her exclamation. "Is something wrong?"

"Yes. Very wrong." She logged off and shut down. "I'll have to take care of it tomorrow." Then she realized the next day was Saturday, when the bank was closed. Could this mess wait till Monday? It seemed to worsen by the moment.

"Is it anything I can help you with?"

She forced a smile. "No, but thanks."

"Is Lucifer causing you grief?" he teased.

"Not this time. It's my bank. Something strange is going on, and they won't help me figure it out."

"Frustrating."

"Very."

He laid a reassuring hand on her shoulder. She ached with gratitude to have a friend to share her troubles with.

But not tonight. No more sharing troubles tonight.

Relaxed, in a light-headed haze from beer and wine, she ran the tips of her fingers across Kahlil's cheek, rough with new stubble despite his recent shave. She savored the light scratchiness, stroking his skin in small circles. He leaned close, tickling her ear with his mustache, the heat of his breath on her neck, the tightening of his arm around her shoulders. She melted against him, tasting his mouth, running her hand through his thick, coarse hair. A moan from deep in his throat vibrated against her lips.

A car door slammed next to them. A heavyset man with a drinker's veined nose peered through the convertible's windshield, grinned, and gave a thumbs-up sign.

Tawny and Kahlil looked at each other and laughed.

Then, at the far end of the parking lot, Tawny spotted a dark-blue sedan.

* * *

Progress on schedule.

Kahlil sent the encrypted text on another disposable cell phone. The screen on his laptop glowed, the only light in his dark living room. Leaning on the back legs of the chair, he reviewed the evening.

It had been difficult to leave Tawny at her front door when her willingness beckoned him inside. He hungered to unfasten her braided hair, let it fall loose, and imagined how it would look spread on her pillow.

But that was not on the schedule—not yet.

Her eyes had showed disappointment as he pulled away, holding her hands, stretching out their contact as he backed down the front porch steps.

"We're neighbors now," he'd reminded her. "I'll see you very soon. It's destiny."

How easily she accepted his fate and destiny explanation.

Perhaps destiny *had* played a role.

He tapped the keyboard to bring up the picture he'd first discovered two years earlier, the first time he felt that strange, startling jolt deep between his stomach and his groin.

An obscure internal newsletter for the Hungry Horse Dam contained the photo. It featured a short, stout old man whom Tawny towered over as she planted a kiss on his bald head. The old man beamed. A lively glint of mischief showed in her smiling brown eyes. The caption read: "At Solomon Roth's retirement party, longtime friend and coworker Tawny Lindholm congratulates Solly for thirty-five years of service at Hungry Horse Dam."

A month before, Kahlil recalled Maryam crowing with pride over the bombing in Jerusalem, showing him a news clipping that identified the dead and their home towns, including a Jew couple from Kalispell, Montana. That location had caught his attention because the Hungry Horse Dam was already on his list of possible targets. When he'd hacked into the dam's personnel files, he discovered the old man used to work there, prompting him to pursue the trail.

And then he saw the newsletter and the beautiful woman in the photograph.

Intuition urged him to dig deeper. He believed intuition was merely how the subconscious recognized threads in a snarled knot that could eventually be teased out and woven together. He followed Tawny's thread. Although she fell outside the statistical matrix he used to qualify subjects, she displayed qualities that intrigued him, so unlike the usual alcoholics, habitual debtors, and hard-luck cases he normally targeted.

Not only had she been friends with the Jews, but years before, the old man had secured a job giving tours of the dam for her. Decades later, her fresh young face still graced the brochures that were handed out to tourists.

For two patient years, Kahlil had watched and studied Tawny from afar as her husband's illness and death isolated her, leaving her lonely, depressed, and vulnerable. He accessed her email and learned that her son's position prevented regular contact with his mother. That offered the ideal opportunity to send Tawny the smartphone, ostensibly from her son.

Once Kahlil rented the Jews' house, it was only a matter of time before he connected with her.

The smartphone class had lured her in. Even if that tactic failed, the close proximity of their residences served the same purpose. The vital consideration: contact had to appear casual and unplanned but meant to be.

Taking her to that restaurant had been an uncertain judgment call. He'd debated the risk beforehand. Scanning through past years of their credit card charges confirmed the location's significance. Dinners there coincided with the dates of birthdays and anniversaries. He wondered if he could maintain the critical balance between her mourning and her attraction to him in an environment charged with memories. At one point that evening, she almost bolted, giving him a moment's doubt over his decision to take her there. But she had stayed.

The bank manager's appearance as they exited the restaurant had been a fortuitous accident. Tawny hadn't yet confided in Kahlil about her financial dilemma, but that would come soon.

The plan's many elements were converging nicely.

Chapter 5: *Pray 4 Me*

Saturday morning, when Tawny unplugged the smartphone from charging on the breakfast bar, the blue pinpoint light blinked. A text from Neal! After reading the message, her elation sank immediately to despair.

Mom, W/c if I can. In trouble. Pray 4 me.

What was wrong? Neal never wanted to worry her. What kind of trouble could he be in? Was he injured? Separated from his unit? Captured? Possibilities flashed through her mind, each one worse, more desperate, more terrifying. Sickness burned inside her.

The last she knew, he was in Afghanistan. With his classified work, even after missions were finished, he did not talk about them.

Neal was every bit as stoic and guarded as Dwight had been. That made this text all the more puzzling. Neal never admitted to problems, especially to her. He kept them to himself until he solved them.

If he'd been injured, a family liaison from the Rear Detachment was supposed to notify her. No word from them. Maybe she should call Rear D. But if Neal received a message through them that "your mommy is worried about you," he'd be furious.

Yet only a few weeks ago, TV news reported insurgents kidnapped two soldiers who'd been tortured before being executed. Danger lurked around every corner in that insane part of the world. A sergeant first class in intelligence made a tempting target, a valuable hostage . . .

She smacked her hands on the counter. *Slow down,* she ordered herself. *Stop letting worry run wild. Maybe it's a personal problem, not related to his service.*

As quickly as that thought came to her, she dismissed it. Neal wouldn't share his personal problems with her, either.

She reread the message until her eyes blurred. With trembling fingers, she texted back, *I'll do anything to help.*

Where was Neal? If she knew where he was, that might tell her something. Maybe the number where the text originated could be traced.

Kahlil!

He might know how to track the location of Neal's phone.

She tapped on his number, but instead of connecting, a screen popped up demanding she download a software update. She tried to back out and return to the contact list, but the update window stayed frozen in place. "Damn you! Why won't you let me make a simple phone call?" She shoved the device in her pocket and ran out the back door.

She hurried the block and a half to Kahlil's house and hammered on his front door. A minute later, he opened it, bare chested, wearing only lounge pants, eyes still heavy with sleep. "Tawny, what's the matter?" He pulled her inside, studying her face. "Are you all right?"

"M-my son texted me," she stammered and thrust the phone at him.

Kahlil quickly dispatched the intrusive update message and retrieved the text. After he read it, he wrapped his arms around her. "My treasure. My poor sweet," he murmured into her hair.

His skin still felt warm from his bed. She forced herself to pull away. "Can you help me find his location? With GPS or something? Like you showed me how to find landmarks."

He urged her to sit on the couch. "It's not through GPS. You see, each phone has a chip that identifies its location. Wherever the phone moves, its location pings off different cell towers. You are correct, it is possible to track where the phone is, but"—he frowned—"it will take me some time. Do you have any idea what country he's in?"

She shook her head, miserable in her ignorance. "Afghanistan, maybe. He's in army intelligence. I never know where he might be sent."

Kahlil swiped and tapped the screen, moving so quickly she couldn't follow.

Watching his deftness, she knew without a doubt she'd never master Lucifer. It tormented her with tantalizing bits of information she tried to follow but blocked her when she needed it most. She felt like a hostage to the shiny device that held a single fragile thread connecting her to Neal. With one wrong tap or swipe, she feared she might break that thread, destroying the only lifeline to her son.

Tawny hugged herself, trying to ward off the chill of fear.

Kahlil looked up from her phone. "Why don't you make us some coffee?"

Grateful to have a useful task, she went to the kitchen. The carafe held yesterday's dregs, so she washed it, filled the reservoir with fresh water, and opened a bag from Montana Coffee Traders. She scooped grounds into the machine, inhaling the aroma of the strong, dark blend. Yes, a stout cup of coffee was what she needed.

While the machine hissed, Tawny washed and dried a couple of glasses and plates that Kahlil had left in the sink. She opened cupboards until she found the right places to put them away. Still Ruth's dishes. A wave of sadness brimmed, yet the simple familiarity of the kitchen reassured her.

Tawny glanced at Kahlil, hunched over on the couch, elbows on his knees, brows drawn together with intense concentration as he continued to tap and flick. Dark hair covered his chest, with finer tufts reaching his shoulders and down his back. The intimacy of the scene struck her. This half-naked, unshaven man just risen from his bed, coffee gurgling in the background, her standing at the kitchen counter like the wife she'd been for so many years.

How many mornings exactly like this had she spent with Dwight? Worrying over one child or the other, sharing the trouble of life, supporting each other, together.

Could she find that togetherness again with this intense man, working hard to help her in time of need?

The brewing cycle finished. She poured two mugs, then rejoined Kahlil on the couch. He broke concentration briefly to smile his thanks for the coffee, then resumed his work.

By the time she finished her mug, his remained untouched and cold. When he at last looked up again at her, his expression made her hopes sink.

"I'm sorry. I tried all the techniques I know. But the location is blocked. I traced back the cell towers where the signal pinged, but the last hub dead-ends. The phone is somewhere in the Middle East, but I cannot pin it down more than that."

Tawny closed her eyes and leaned back on the couch. "Is there any other way to trace him? Can the army . . ."

He pressed her hand. "You said your son is in intelligence? The army may be the very ones blocking the signal."

Of course, that made sense. They didn't want enemies to find Neal's location. "I don't know what to do."

Kahlil's arm surrounded her shoulders and pulled her close. His lips moved against her forehead. "Do exactly what your son told you. Pray."

* * *

That afternoon, Kahlil insisted on taking Tawny for a picnic, driving with the top down on his convertible. "I must distract you from these troubles that distress you so terribly. When I cannot fathom the answer to a problem, I leave it behind on my desk and go away for a walk. When I return, poof! The solution appears to me. That is the mysterious way the subconscious mind works."

"What about when there isn't any solution?" she asked.

He squeezed her hand. "It will come to you if you have patience."

Tawny gazed at the mountains ahead, where blinding sunshine melted the snow into thready waterfalls that tumbled down gorges. The wind tasted fresh, tangy with spring. Kahlil handled the sporty car skillfully, although he tended to speed.

He meant well, trying to reassure her, but she recognized her powerlessness. She'd never found a solution to Dwight's cancer. Now she faced losing her son. On top of that, she was probably under suspicion for criminal activity. Even if she came up with a brilliant idea for Neal, if she wound up in jail, there'd be no way to help him.

The Hungry Horse Dam loomed, a massive arching concrete wall that held back miles of water in the reservoir. Kahlil turned onto the road that ran across the top of the dam.

"This is where I do my boring work," he said, but pride touched his tone.

She smiled. He wanted to show off for her. A childish but endearing effort.

He slowed as they approached one of the two elevator towers. "The bowels of the dam go down more than fifty stories. Would you like to see inside?"

She had to chuckle. "Not really. For years, my summer job was leading tours down there."

He looked momentarily chagrined. "Well, that makes me the fool. I thought I was offering you an adventure, but you probably know your way around better than I do."

She shrugged. "Solly—Mr. Roth got me the job when I was still in school. I worked here part time until last summer." She stopped before saying *when Dwight became too ill to leave*.

Kahlil stared quizzically at her for a long moment. Then he reached across, opened the glove compartment, and pulled out a trifold brochure. "I knew you looked familiar the first time I saw you. And here you are." He opened it for display.

Tawny recognized a photo of her young self, pointing out a turbine to a group of school children. The rest of the pamphlet described the dam's history and included long columns of specifications she'd had to memorize. "For goodness sake, I can't believe they're still giving out this old brochure. They really need to update."

Kahlil shook his head. "No, they don't. It is timeless and beautiful." He refolded the paper and started to put it back in the glove box, but a sudden gust of wind tore it from his grasp. It blew past Tawny out of the convertible. She opened the car door to go after it.

The brochure briefly dropped to the sidewalk, but, an instant before she reached it, another gust whipped it into the air, and it sailed onto the waist-high parapet. There, it settled again. She grabbed for it, only to miss a second time as it flew over the side, whirling in the air like a butterfly.

Kahlil joined her at the parapet. They bent forward, resting their forearms on the ledge, watching the brochure twirl in space. She felt him close, the current vibrating between them even without touching.

"I had planned to send that to my mother," he said. "I try to show her the various places where I work. I will have to pick up another one." He gave her a mischievous wink. "Now I can also tell her I know the famous tour guide pictured in it."

The breeze tousled his dark hair, blowing it across his forehead. She wanted to brush it out of his green eyes but stopped herself. "Not a very impressive accomplishment."

He grimaced. "Better than my pitiful, embarrassing attempt to impress you."

She liked that he made fun of himself. "Your work's probably more complicated and important than leading tourists around." She cocked her head to the side. "Although, I do know how many cubic tons of concrete it took to build the dam, how many men worked on it, and how many kilowatts are generated every year. Would you like me to bore you with a lot of statistics?"

He laughed. They returned to the car and drove across the remainder of the dam.

A few miles beyond, Tawny motioned to a trailhead. "There's a pretty spot to eat lunch up that trail."

Kahlil pulled over and parked. They strapped on two backpacks that Tawny had provisioned at home with water, sandwiches, a blanket, and coats. Kahlil didn't have hiking boots, so she planned to take an easy route.

She led the way. Although the spring sun beat down, when they moved into shaded sections, Kahlil shivered in the brisk air and pulled his tan canvas jacket tighter. He kept pace easily, but she heard his breathing—he was not used to high altitudes.

Two miles up the trail, they reached a rocky outcropping that overlooked the reservoir. Fishing boats dotted the water, eager anglers out after a long winter cooped up. Snow still coated the higher mountains in the distance, but nearby hills grew lush with new grass.

"How about here for lunch?" she asked.

Kahlil stood on a ridge, surveying the landscape, one hand shading his eyes. "It is very beautiful. So many trees, so much water."

Tawny smiled to herself. The scenery wasn't new to her, but she still felt the thrill of the wild vista, fold upon fold of mountains dense with trees, the clear blue dome of sky, the bright sun beating down on them. She dropped her pack and pulled out the blanket to spread on a flat rock warmed by the sun.

"The food is in your pack," she said.

Kahlil turned in a slow semicircle, still taking in the view. When he again faced her, a smile lit his expression. "Thank you for bringing me up here. I have never seen such beauty." He took a few steps toward her, cradled her face in his hands, and kissed her.

Her knees quivered. In a husky voice, she murmured, "Aren't you hungry?"

Warm lips moved across her cheek, along her jaw, mustache brushing her skin. One hand swept hair away from her ear so he could nibble the lobe. His breath sent shivers through her. He worked down her neck. She wanted to embrace him, but his pack was in the way.

She reluctantly stepped back. "Hey, let's get rid of this." She tugged on the shoulder straps until they slid down his arms. He set the pack down and looked at her with that intense, heavy-lidded green stare.

Bedroom eyes. That's what her mother used to say.

A movement to the side captured Tawny's attention. She caught a glimpse of a doe and a spotted fawn a few yards away. "Look," she whispered and pointed.

Kahlil turned with her. Together they watched the deer graze along the trail. The doe inspected them but didn't shoo the fawn to safety. Instead, she allowed the baby to come within twenty feet of them. It lifted its head, curious about the intruders, then returned to crop tender new grass. After several minutes, the doe changed direction and skipped down a steep embankment, hooves clattering on rock, the fawn frolicking behind.

"Wow," Kahlil said with a heavy breath. "I have never been so close to a wild animal. You have truly brought me to paradise."

Tawny unzipped his pack and took out sandwiches, apples, and bottles of water. They sat on the blanket, side by side, leaning into each other, and ate slowly.

Kahlil crunched on an apple, then said, "I have told you about my life, but you have not shared yours with me."

She shrugged. "Not much to tell. It's boring, compared with your travels."

"Tell me anyway." He playfully bumped her shoulder. "I will stop you if I get bored."

She snorted. "Born in Montana, lived here my whole life, will probably die here."

"There's more than that. What were you like as a little girl?"

"Stupid. I struggled with reading, couldn't even spell *cat*. My dad used to say, 'Thank God you're pretty, honey, cuz you sure are dumb.'"

Kahlil's brows furrowed with disapproval. "That's a dreadful message to give a child."

His comment made her pause. She'd heard her dad say it so many times, the words lost meaning long ago, a running family joke. But way back in the depths of her memory—maybe age seven—she recalled crawling under her bed to cry so he wouldn't hear how much he'd hurt her. For the first time, Kahlil made her realize the impact of the casual words from her childhood.

She shifted to a more comfortable position. "In any event, Dad was right. I was always on the edge of flunking out. I started modeling in high school because I got to skip classes. Did some TV commercials, local magazines, fashion shows, department store openings, that brochure for the dam. It was a lot better than school, where I was always behind, never caught up. When I graduated, I kissed books good-bye forever. At least that's what I thought. Then I met Dwight."

"Your husband?"

Tawny nodded. "He was fifteen years older. He'd finished his tour with the army and opened a diesel engine repair shop in Kalispell. Pretty successful. He was sponsoring a fundraiser for the community college to start a diesel mechanic training program. The college had hired me to model for its catalog. Pretty funny—*me*, pretending to be a student, modeling for a college I could never hope to get into. Anyway . . ."

She drifted backward in memories to the day she and Dwight had met. Everyone there for the photo shoot, student or professor, was smarter and more confident than she was. She'd felt horribly out of place, an imposter.

Then she'd spotted a big, square-jawed, barrel-chested man in a dark-blue mechanic's uniform, leaning against the block wall. He was watching the photo shoot. And watching her. The name patch on his shirt read Dwight, and his easy posture said he didn't have to prove anything to anyone. He looked too old to be a student—maybe he was an instructor but not one of the snobbish professors.

He'd ambled over to her and made a joke, which she couldn't even remember now, although she vividly remembered the crinkles of humor around his brown eyes. Despite her painful shyness, he'd put her at ease instantly. The rest of the crowd faded into the background, and they stood together, talking, the only two people in the universe . . .

Kahlil's voice brought her back to the present. "Then you married?"

She nodded, took a sip of cool water, which didn't quench the ache in her throat from remembering. "I told you I thought I was done with books. Well, I wound up keeping the books for our business. Had to learn payroll, general ledger, receivables, payables. But for some reason, the work was easier than school had been. Maybe because we were doing it together. Dwight always helped me when I'd get stuck. He didn't get mad or impatient, just kept telling me I could do it. Little by little, I learned."

"You are far from stupid if you can master accounting."

"It's not that hard. You just plug numbers in, and the computer does all the calculations."

"Tawny," Kahlil faced her, "you are not stupid. You are an extraordinarily intelligent woman. I know. I test intelligence in my work. Perhaps you had a learning disability, which is why you had difficulty in school. But you overcame it. You learned how to work around it, compensate, to figure out other methods that made more sense to your brain, your process of thinking. Not all people learn the same way. The important thing is that you learned."

She dropped her head low and murmured, "Dyslexia."

"I thought it might be," he answered softly, as if he understood her shame. "To overcome it, as you've done, requires great intelligence."

Gratitude welled like a warm spring flowing inside her heart.

Dwight had always tried to reassure her, but she never quite believed him. He was smart, but he was a mechanic, not a scholar.

But Kahlil was educated, really educated—a doctor. He had just explained the mystery of why her brain struggled with some things yet clicked easily with others. It finally made sense. She gazed at the reservoir, silently repeating his words like a mantra.

Kahlil fingered her ponytail. She hadn't bothered with her usual french braid that morning, distracted by Neal's text. His hand twined in the loose strands, stroking, gently pulling. When her head lolled to his shoulder, she noticed black clouds in the west.

"Tell me more," he asked. "What was life like after your marriage?"

She hugged her knees to her chest. "Good. Not exciting but steady. The business grew, eighteen guys working for us. After a few years, it was the biggest shop in northwest Montana. Paid our bills, raised our kids, lived the American dream." She paused, letting memories meander. Their life together *had* been good.

Kahlil waited, quiet, until she was ready to go on.

"Dwight wanted to retire while he was still young enough to travel, so we sold the business. Neal and Emma were on their own by then. We started looking at motor homes, figuring we'd drive around the country, catch up on all the vacations and weekends we'd missed while we were working six, seven days a week and me giving tours at the dam."

"Did you?"

A lump lodged in her throat. "No." Hoarseness roughened her voice. She blinked and swallowed, wishing he'd stop asking now that his questions veered into the time of their lives filled with so much pain.

Kahlil rubbed her back, comforting strokes that made no demand.

She felt torn between not wanting to talk and longing to share the burden of sorrow with him. "Agent Orange came back to haunt Dwight. He was diagnosed with aggressive prostate cancer." She pressed her lips tight together. "Never thought I'd have to learn to spell words like *prostatectomy* and *metastatic*. We spent the next eight years fighting it, but"—she had to swallow again—"it won. Finally took him last July."

Kahlil continued to rub her back, saying nothing. She was glad because she didn't want to answer any more questions or relive what she already relived, night after sleepless night, alone in their bed, clinging to Dwight's teddy bear.

She sensed Kahlil's quiet understanding. No further explanations necessary. He had lost his love, too.

A memory returned, unbidden. Hospice had been called in, spelling the end to false promises of remission, promises broken by cancer. One night in bed, Dwight had said, "You shouldn't have married such an old man."

She'd stroked the few remaining strands of his hair and tried to tease him. "I'm madly attracted to cradle robbers."

But for once he didn't want to joke. "You shouldn't be alone. You ought to find another man, OK? He'll be a lucky son of a bitch, just like I've been."

Was Dwight watching her now?

On the broad expanse of the reservoir, canoes and sailboats skimmed across the water. The sun warmed her face. The quiet felt peaceful—not lonely, as silence often did.

After a long time, Kahlil said, "I miss my wife. Every day. But once I met you, the pain became easier to bear." He twined his fingers in her hair.

Since meeting Kahlil, she'd found a reason to drag herself out of bed in the morning. She even looked forward to the unpredictable antics of Lucifer because that gave her an excuse to call him, to meet for coffee. He *had* made the pain easier to bear.

"In this most beautiful place on earth," he said, "I would like to make love to you."

She lifted her face to kiss him as he lowered her to recline on the blanket. *This is crazy. What am I doing?*

As his fingers opened her jacket, then slipped up under her blouse, she no longer cared about crazy.

* * *

The first big raindrops splattered on the blanket they had pulled over themselves to keep warm. Tawny felt the chill in the air and saw the clouds skidding rapidly across the sky. On top of her, Kahlil dozed, still inside her, his breathing soft and rhythmic. She shook his shoulder. "Wake up, a storm is coming."

He raised his head, kissing her before even opening his eyes. Then the raindrops fell faster, splashing on his back. He moved off her, pulling the blanket snug around her shoulders to cover her head. They quickly dressed as the rain increased. Clutching their packs, they raced down the trail, slipping as the downpour turned the path into a torrent of mud.

By the time they reached the convertible, they were soaked, just like the car since Kahlil had left the top down. Droplets streamed off the seats and drenched the plush rugs. While he raised the top, he began to laugh.

Using the side of her hand like a squeegee, Tawny scraped puddles off the beautiful leather, teeth chattering. Why was he laughing? She imagined Dwight's reaction to drowning a $50,000 BMW, and it wouldn't have been laughter.

Inside the shelter of the car, Kahlil continued to laugh, throwing his hair back, flinging drops like a wet dog. He turned on the heater and seat warmers and hugged Tawny close as they waited for the blowing air to warm up. "I'm freezing." His teeth chattered, but his voice sounded happy, almost giddy.

She marveled at his mood. "You're crazy."

His laughter resumed. "You are right. I am completely insanely crazy."

For Tawny, the afterglow had long since disappeared, lost on the muddy trail. Her joints felt as if ice stiffened inside them. Her ring finger throbbed, the knuckle swelling more than usual. With ten years' difference between them, Kahlil's bones probably didn't ache like hers.

"Is your seat getting warm?" he asked.

"Don't think so."

"The rain probably shorted out the wires."

Tawny wished they'd brought her Jeep. Not luxurious like Kahlil's convertible, but it was outfitted Montana-style, with emergency blankets and extra coats in the back.

They huddled together, shivering, until warm air finally filled the car. While they drove, raindrops changed to fat snowflakes that exploded on the windshield like water balloons. Heavy, wet globs of snow bent tree limbs and piled up on the road.

"So this is your springtime in the Rockies." A teasing smile played across Kahlil's face as he squinted through the slushy windshield, the wipers unable to keep up.

"All four seasons in twenty minutes," Tawny answered.

He turned on the radio, flicking through channels until he settled on the oldies station Dwight used to listen to. *How did he know?*

The Supremes sang "You Can't Hurry Love."

"Is this OK?" he asked.

Tawny nodded.

Her cold toes squished in mud that had slid inside her boots. More mud spackled her soaked jeans. The jacket she wore was drizzle resistant, not downpour proof. The heater blew some chill away but not all. She wished for the blanket they had made love on, but it was a sodden, dripping mess, flung in the back.

Kahlil hummed along with Diana Ross. The clamminess of his clothes didn't appear to bother him.

A perverse desire to taunt him came over Tawny. "You weren't even born when this song came out."

"I was when Phil Collins sang it."

She stared at him.

He chuckled, as if refusing to let her make an issue out of their age difference. The conversation reminded her of the good-natured debates she and Dwight used to engage in. Dwight swore Sam Cooke's version of "Don't Know Much About History" was the best, while she argued for James Taylor's. Now Tawny felt like the old fogy in the music debate.

As they drove through Columbia Falls, a billboard advertising United Bankcorp shifted her mind back to real problems. Who kept depositing big wads of cash into her account? An imposter was hell-bent on making her appear to be a criminal. She just wanted to live her ordinary, law-abiding, low-profile life, but the bank mess prevented it.

Neal's desperate message returned to haunt her. She had to find a way to help her son. Problems piled deeper like the heavy snow outside.

She longed to return to those sweet moments in the mountains; to Kahlil's tender kisses, his sensual caresses, the heated press of his body against hers. For a little while, he'd allowed her to forget about the real world. She wanted to tell him about the bank and the imposter. But that would only ruin his day, too. He looked so content. She decided to keep the trouble to herself.

Back in cell-tower range, Tawny checked for texts from Neal. No messages, no calls. She scrolled to read her son's plea again as tightness squeezed her heart.

"Tawny." Kahlil's voice came softly.

She realized she had stayed quiet for a long time while she studied the phone. "Mm-hm?"

"I have been thinking about how to find your son. There is a colleague of mine who is very skilled in matters of locating and tracking. May I ask her for help?"

Hope rose in Tawny's heart. "Oh yes, please ask her. I'll do anything to find Neal." She leaned back in the seat as a question edged into her mind. "Why would a psychologist know a tracking expert?"

He pulled close on the tail of a tractor–trailer rig. She wanted to warn him truckers never drove slowly without a good reason, but before she could speak, he answered, "Sometimes I need to follow up at a later time with subjects in case studies. If they've changed employment or moved, I ask my colleague to find them."

"Oh. Like a private detective?"

"Similar." He steered too fast around the creeping semitruck. The BMW's rear tires broke loose in a quick fishtail.

Tawny sucked in air, feeling a thrill of fear.

Kahlil slid in the icy slush but regained control, then glanced sideways at her intake of breath. His slight smile reminded her of Neal when *he* drove fast, the overconfidence of being young, male, and bullet proof.

"Tomorrow," Kahlil said, "I must fly to Houston for a conference. I will speak to my colleague there."

Apprehension undermined Tawny's gratitude for his offer a moment before. "Houston? You didn't say anything . . . how long will you be gone?" As quickly as she had blurted out the question, she immediately hated herself for sounding needy. Just because they'd made love once didn't require Kahlil to report to her.

As if he read her thoughts, he said, "I did not want to spoil our perfect day." He gave her an apologetic smile. "I will miss you, too, my treasure. But it is less than a week."

If she couldn't take back her outburst, she wanted to diffuse it. "Perfect day? We could have died from hypothermia."

He reached over and slid the backs of his fingers along her cheek. "Then death would come with my heart full of joy."

How did he always know the right words? Words she didn't even know she longed to hear, yet when he spoke them, they wrapped her in serenity and peace. He was a poet, like Emma's book, *The Prophet*.

* * *

Back at Tawny's home, they hurried up the walk, past the front flowerbed, where daffodils bent under snow. The white cloak smothered new grass. She unlocked the door and led Kahlil to the bathroom. They stripped off their damp clothes. Together they climbed into the bathtub. Steamy water from the showerhead beat down on them.

Head thrown back, he groaned with pleasure from the heat. Seeing him fully naked for the first time, she ran her hands over his sinewy shoulders, the lean muscles in his thighs and buttocks, the black thicket of hair framing his erection. Unlike Dwight, he wasn't circumcised. With soap-slick hands, she explored the difference, which intensified his moans to climax.

He gathered her in his arms. "Now you have made me useless."

"You'll think of something else," she teased.

He did.

* * *

Kahlil returned to his house that evening with a stomach full of Tawny's delectable homemade soup and sexually spent. She'd let him know he would be welcome to stay the night, but he resisted, claiming an early flight to Houston the next morning.

There was no conference in Houston.

The desire to be with her tugged at him. He longed to again taste her nipples, hardening into pink pebbles between his lips, to feel the arching of her back, to watch the rosy flush bloom across her chest when he brought her to climax. But spending the night, in the bed she shared for many years with her husband, was too risky. Her emotions hovered close to the surface, threatening to spill over at any moment. Taking her husband's place in their bed could trigger a backlash of guilt. He had half expected regretful tears following their initial lovemaking, but she proved stronger than anticipated.

Strong, yet with a soft, gentle way about her. So unlike Maryam, with whom sex meant a ferocious challenge. In the early years, his wife's demands had excited him, her passion great but her rage greater. As he'd grown older, the relentless pressure to perform weighed heavily on him. Entering her always meant a competition he feared he might fail.

He fell asleep, thinking of Tawny's silky welcome.

Early Sunday morning, he turned in the rain-damaged convertible to the rental agency and chose a Subaru SUV, its commonness rendering it nearly invisible on Montana roads.

Invisible and anonymous.

Chapter 6: NSF

On Sunday morning, Tawny called Virgie Belmonte to have breakfast.

"Love to," her friend replied. "Just let me kick David out of here, and I'll meet you at eleven." David was Virgie's third ex who sometimes spent the night.

At the restaurant, buzzing with the after-church crowd, the aroma of sausage and warm maple syrup filled the air. The hostess hugged Virgie. "Great to see you, Dr. Belmonte."

"How's your dad?" Virgie asked.

"Good, thanks to you."

"Give him a big kiss for me."

When they were seated in a booth, Tawny said, "We can't go anywhere without running into your fans."

Virgie flicked her bangs back and scanned the menu. "Cancer's everywhere. I'll always have a job . . . unfortunately."

"Or fortunately, according to that young lady's father."

Virgie's eyes misted. "I just wish I could have done more for Dwight. Doctors aren't supposed to have favorite patients, but he was mine. Such a kind, decent, good man." She wiggled her shoulders as if to shake off sadness and grinned. "He didn't have any eligible brothers, did he? I'd like to find one just like him."

"Last of the family. And our son is too young for you."

Virgie raised one eyebrow with a sly grin. "Are you sure?"

She forced a smile, although worry settled like boulder on her chest. "You couldn't stand him for long. Smelly socks everywhere." She put on glasses to study the menu. "Besides, he's gone all the time, stationed God knows where."

"That could be a benefit. Enjoy the hell out of him while he's around, then ship him off so I'd have some peace and quiet. I'm not long-term marriage material. Not like you and Dwight."

After they ordered, Tawny's need to confide in her friend couldn't wait any longer.

Fear returned over Neal's plea. "Virg, Neal's in trouble. He sent me this text." She displayed the message.

Virgie whistled. "That doesn't sound good. What did you do?"

"Texted him back. Then I asked Kahlil if he could track Neal's location through the phone."

"Kahlil?"

"Dr. Zhivago."

"Ah." Virgie nodded. "Did he?"

"Said he couldn't, but he knows someone who might be able to. Meanwhile, I'm half-sick with worry. You can't imagine where my mind has been going with this. He's been kidnapped, held for ransom, tortured, on and on. I'm even thinking about drawing the rest of that weird money out of the bank so I'll have a war chest in case my fears come true."

"What about that screw-up with the bank? Did you get it straightened out?"

Tawny shook her head. "I took out the cash, like you suggested. But more money keeps appearing. Get this: there's a woman who looks exactly like me who deposited that first batch of cash. The bank has it on video. I saw it. It's . . . spooky."

Virgie's brown eyes widened. "Wait a sec. Someone is impersonating you and sticking money in your account?"

"Yes. There have been three different deposits, more than one hundred forty thousand dollars. I only saw the video for the first incident. But I'm guessing the same woman did the others, too."

Virgie leaned back in the booth, lines deepening across her forehead. "You're being set up. Why?"

"Damned if I know. Every time I go in the bank, they treat me like a felon. The manager called a security guard on me. I thought he was going to pull his gun. On *me*! *Me*, who's so devious, I couldn't even keep my five-year-old daughter from finding out about her surprise birthday party." Tawny dropped her head into her hands. "I don't know what to do."

"Has anyone in law enforcement contacted you? The sheriff, FBI, Homeland Security, IRS?"

Tawny shook her head, fingers pressing over her scalp, wishing she could squeeze a solution from her brain.

"I'm betting they will," Virgie said. "Hate to tell you, but you're probably already under surveillance."

"I figured that. In fact, I keep seeing this dark-blue Crown Vic." Tawny stared out the restaurant window, scanning the parking lot and street for the possible tail. "I tried to get in touch with our lawyer, but he was out. I'm scared to talk to anyone without him." She twirled her coffee mug, spreading a spill. "The imposter drove a Jeep that looks just like Dwight's. This is *big time*."

Concern deepened the brackets around Virgie's mouth. "You say you took out some of the money?"

"Yeah, on the advice of a *friend*." Tawny punctuated the last word with finger quotes.

Virgie grimaced. "Well, I hope you learned your lesson not to listen to friends who have their head up their ass."

"You couldn't know. I didn't know. Who would have guessed this would morph into a sinister conspiracy? When it started, I thought it was just a stupid computer error."

Virgie grasped Tawny's hand. "All the same, I hope I haven't made it worse."

"So do I."

Their breakfasts arrived, and the server refilled their coffees. Virgie sprinkled Tabasco over her scrambled eggs while Tawny cut into her omelet and twirled melted cheddar around her fork. They ate in silence, mulling over the problem, occasionally exchanging glances:

Think of anything yet?

Nope, you?

Virgie finished off her last bite of toast. "How's Dr. Zhivago?"

Tawny felt her cheeks redden. "He's sweet. Very sweet."

"Really." Virgie's tone sounded less than surprised. "I thought you looked especially glowing when you came in."

"Stop it."

Virgie's lopsided smile carried a taunt. "Tell me it isn't true."

Tawny picked up the orange slice garnish and nibbled it to avoid answering.

"Well?" Virgie persisted.

"OK, yesterday. We went on a picnic up past the dam."

"Nice romantic setting."

"He tells me things that make me feel all warm inside. He's a psychologist, a doctor, but he tells me *I'm* smart. Miss Almost Drop-Out."

Virgie huffed with exasperation, blowing her bangs up. "Quit selling yourself short, Tawny. You're a very intelligent woman. When I think of how you handled Dwight's different specialists, with all those complicated protocols and meds, yet you kept track of contraindications and interactions . . . well, I just wish all my patients had an advocate like you. In fact, why don't you come to work for me?"

"Oh, stop." But Virgie's compliment reassured Tawny.

"Go on about Dr. Zhivago."

Tawny felt blood rising in her neck again. She glanced at surrounding diners, but all appeared preoccupied with their own conversations. Even so, she dropped her voice. "Dwight's the only man I've ever been with . . . till yesterday. It was . . ." She searched for the right word to describe Kahlil but gave up. " . . . nice. Actually, way beyond nice." A twinge of guilt pinched her. "But something just doesn't feel right. It's too soon."

Virgie snorted. "It's too soon to put him on your credit cards. It's too soon to buy a house together. But"—she rapped a spoon on the table—"it's not too soon for a little taste of honey after the eight crappy years you've been through." She shoved her plate to the side. "Look, Tawny, you're not being unfaithful to Dwight. He's gone. Besides, he'd want you to enjoy life. He told me that."

So Virgie and Dwight had talked about her future. Not surprising. They both loved her and were concerned about her being alone.

Virgie leaned forward. "You're here, and you're still young." She winked. "Although not so young you have to worry about getting pregnant."

"Thank goodness for menopause."

"As long as you're practicing safe sex, and I assume you were . . ."

Tawny nodded. Kahlil had been prepared with condoms. He'd known beforehand that they'd make love that day. To be honest, so did she, she thought with another tweak of guilt.

Virgie continued. "Then who's getting hurt? He isn't married, is he?"

"His wife died."

"Well, fine, then. You're home free. Although you might Google him and make sure *he* didn't bump her off."

Tawny stifled a laugh. "You're terrible."

"That's why you hang around with me."

Virgie was right, though. Tawny made a mental note to search out Kahlil online. "It just seems weird." She blew out a sigh. "I mean, you're used to dating, but I haven't gone out with a guy since high school." She sipped her coffee, now cold. "Sometimes I don't know how to react, but he always knows the right thing to do or say. Like last night, I asked him if he wanted to stay over. He said no, very nicely and gentlemanly, but it kind of hurt my feelings. Then later on, I realized I didn't really want to wake up this morning with him in our house—Dwight's and mine—in our bedroom. Somehow he must have known I'd feel that way, even before I did."

"Didn't you say he's a psychologist? He certainly ought to recognize the stages of grief and how uneven and unpredictable they are. He anticipated your very normal reaction, that's all."

"It's more than that. He understands me, like he's known me for a long time, almost like he's inside my head. He keeps talking about how fate and destiny meant for us to meet."

"Oh, crap." Virgie threw up her hands in mock despair. "He sounded pretty hot until he dragged out a pickup line from the 1980s." She slapped the table. "Look, sweetheart, just enjoy it while it lasts. Don't try to build it up into something it's not. You're alone and horny, he's charming and sexy. End of story."

Dear Virgie, always earthy, never beating around the bush. "I guess you're right. Besides, he's only here temporarily. His work contract runs out in a month. He'll probably be gone soon after that."

"So have a fabulous lust-filled month. OK?"

Tawny chuckled. "You sure know how to reduce a big old kettle of soup down to a bouillon cube."

"OK, now that we've solved that, back to serious matters—the bank mess and who's setting you up. Listen, one of my patients is retired FBI. Let me talk to him and see if he can make some calls, find out what's in the air."

Tawny exhaled. "That would be terrific. Thank you."

* * *

Too restless to go home after breakfast, Tawny drove around, as she and Dwight used to do on Sundays while he still had the strength. During the building boom, a subdivision had started up on the west side of town. They'd toyed with the idea of moving to a new house and walked through the models but decided to stay put. Their home was old, but paid for.

When the 2008 crash hit, Tawny thanked God they didn't have the burden of a big mortgage as Dwight's medical bills mounted. Now, she drove through the nearly deserted streets of that subdivision, past a scattering of houses abandoned in various stages of construction. Weathered studs of partly framed shells poked at the sky like spindly fingers. Torn insulation wrap fluttered in the breeze.

She spotted a hand-lettered Moving Sale sign in front of a house ringed by bare dirt, out of money for landscaping. She slowed as she passed. An open garage door revealed a clutter of household goods and furniture. A silver-haired woman in a baggy pink sweatshirt and gray lounge pants stepped outside in the sunshine. She shaded her eyes with one hand, probably hoping to wave Tawny down, as she was the only possible customer in sight.

Tawny started to accelerate, not wanting to feel like a buzzard picking the bones of another family's misfortune. Then she recognized the woman—Margaret, the friendly teller from the bank. Tawny parked and got out of the Jeep, then couldn't think of anything to say. The surroundings told the story.

Margaret's normally cheerful face now sagged with fatigue and worry. "Hi, Tawny, how are you?"

"You're moving?"

The woman tossed a glance over her shoulder. "Have to. The bank canned me. We're upside down in this place. My husband's disabled, can't work anymore, even if there were any construction jobs to be had. Going to Wolf Point, live with our kids. Our son's got a job over in the Bakken oil fields."

Tawny shook her head slowly. "I'm sorry, Margaret. I don't know what to say."

Margaret lifted one shoulder. "Got stuck in one of those damn adjustable-rate mortgages. Back in '06, my husband figured he'd get the house built and sell it before the five-year balloon came due. Then the economy tanked. I went to Hyslop, see if he'd renegotiate the loan. You'd have thought I was asking for Buckingham Palace." Her mouth drew into a tight hard line.

Tawny caught movement in the dimness of the garage. A stooped, balding man leaning on a cane hobbled toward them, a hopeful smile on his drawn face. "Margie, make this lady a good deal on whatever she wants to buy."

The woman waved backward at her husband. "I got it, hon. Go back inside."

Tawny's heart broke for them.

Margaret pulled her sweatshirt, stretching it down over her thighs. "Wasn't enough for that prick Hyslop to turn me down flat. Next, he says to me it's a new bank, moving in new directions, and I wasn't keeping up." In a sardonic singsong, she flicked air quotes and said, "My 'services were no longer needed.'" She hugged herself. "Just a crooked excuse to save them from paying my retirement. Well, they're getting their damn house back, and I'll gladly shove it up Hyslop's ass." Angry tears glinted behind her bifocals.

Tawny wanted to hug her, but the woman's pride threw up an invisible wall, warding off sympathy. "Well, I'm glad you'll be with your kids. Good luck." Tawny climbed into the Jeep, feeling guilty gratitude that, despite her problems, at least she wasn't at risk of losing her home.

* * *

Neal's text message continued to bother Tawny like an eyelash stuck under her lid. He'd always prided himself on his ability to solve problems. To admit trouble was like admitting failure. Whatever he now faced that caused him to reach out to her must go way beyond ordinary. How could she help?

Before his last deployment, because of his sensitive work, he'd asked her not to call unless it was urgent. After a sleepless night, she decided on Monday morning this *was* urgent. She tapped his number and counted to fifteen rings before the connection went dead. *For heaven's sake, Neal, why haven't you set up voice mail?*

Next she scrolled to the Rear D number. Should she contact the family liaison? If his buddies kidded him about his worried mommy, dammit, he was a big boy—he'd just have to deal with it.

She tapped the number. A female voice answered on the second ring. "Rear Detachment, Sergeant Stuart speaking." The woman had a husky voice with an accent Tawny couldn't place. Not Scottish, so maybe Stuart was a married name.

Tawny recited Neal's identifying information to her and explained the text she'd received. "My son gave me your number in case I needed to get in touch with him. I was hoping you could help me."

Stuart didn't answer right away, and through the connection, Tawny heard sounds of typing on a keyboard. "Very well, Mrs. Lindholm, I'm trying to ascertain Sergeant Lindholm's location at the moment, but I don't seem to be having much luck. It's possible he's on a mission and out of touch."

Sounded like the standard nonanswer the army gave when they didn't know or care. Tawny took a deep breath. "That's why I'm concerned. He wouldn't say he's in trouble unless something very bad has happened to him."

Stuart's whiskey voice lost the official tone and sounded more sympathetic, calming. "I can understand why you're disturbed. That must be a frightening message to receive. But I'm sure everything's fine. Let me do some checking, and I'll get back to you, all right?"

Tawny felt herself being verbally patted on the head but said, "I appreciate your help," and disconnected.

Would Sergeant Stuart get back to her? Tawny feared another empty promise.

* * *

Tawny called the Rear Detachment the next two days but received only repeated reassurances from Sergeant Stuart. She claimed to have been in touch with Neal's unit commander, who promised Neal would call soon.

To distract herself from worrying, Tawny followed Virgie's suggestion to Google *Kahlil Shahrivar*. Many pages referred to Kahlil Gibran and *The Prophet*. She learned "Shahrivar" was the sixth month of the Persian calendar. It meant "desirable power" and was the name of a god of metal and a protector of the weak.

His elegant formal website described him as a *Consultant in Industrial/Occupational Psychology*. Besides his PhD, long strings of additional credentials were listed as well as universities where he'd done research, fellowships he'd been awarded, references from his clients, and links to publications in various scholarly journals. All impressive, professional information but nothing personal.

She found several academic papers, studies he'd previously described to her as long and boring. After sampling part of a page, she had to agree. The drudgery of reading slowed her to a crawl. Too much jargon she didn't understand, too many long, complicated sentences where the point got lost somewhere in a muddle of big words.

Confused, frustrated, and overwhelmed after fifteen minutes, she gave up, satisfied at least she hadn't found any headlines about Virgie's joking concern that he'd killed his wife. What a hoot.

Then she tried something she'd never done before: Googling herself.

For someone who shied away from social media and kept her business private, the amount of personal information online stunned her. References to *Tawny Lindholm, Kalispell, Montana* filled several pages.

Dwight's obituary listed her as his surviving spouse of thirty-two years. More documents included business licenses and permits for the diesel shop; registrations for their vehicles, including the commercial trucks Dwight used to drive; property tax filings; the reconveyance deed when they paid off their mortgage; contributions to political candidates; probate court filings for her parents' estates, including her signature as executor; a mention in Neal's high school newsletter about baseball equipment their business had donated.

When she clicked on *Images*, a line of photos showed up, including older magazine shots from her modeling days. A picture of Dwight appeared in the hospital magazine as the first patient to receive treatment from a new linear accelerator, while Tawny stood by, holding his hand. An illustration on a travel agency website showed her bidding *bon voyage* to the Roths as they left on the Bible Comes Alive Tour to the Holy Land. The trip they never returned from.

Who put all this stuff online? It was visible to anyone who tapped in her name.

Then anger started to swell.

Where was her privacy? What gave total strangers the right to be Peeping Toms in *her* life?

She didn't have dark secrets to hide, yet she felt as if her home had been ransacked, her life strewn all over the front lawn for anyone passing by to stare at.

Queasiness merged with anger.

When Kahlil first called her, he'd admitted he looked her up online. How deeply had he dug? Probably down to the bedrock of her existence. Since he worked with computers all the time, he undoubtedly knew far more places to search than she could ever imagine.

The back of her neck prickled. She felt naked, exposed, vulnerable. Fingers of paranoia probed her thoughts—the cash deposits, the video of the imposter, someone setting her up . . .

But . . . no . . . she couldn't imagine any reason for Kahlil to harm her. He'd always been a gentleman, unfailingly patient about her fumbles with the smartphone, tender with his understanding of her grief. His aching loneliness matched hers. They'd both lost their mates too soon. They'd both been cheated of the chance to grow old with their first love. They lived in totally different worlds yet had come together. The heaviness weighing down her heart had lightened since they met.

She'd watched plenty of crime shows about con men who preyed on widows. Predators always wanted something: a small investment that promised a ridiculous return, or a loan for their sick mother's operation, or other phony nonsense.

Kahlil asked nothing from her. He'd been respectful of her reticence, stepping back to avoid pressuring her, understanding her need for space before she recognized it herself. Offering comfort but never pushing.

Besides, he'd given her advice that had saved her from being scammed by Lucifer.

She felt ashamed to suspect him.

She didn't quite trust his driving, though. He liked speed and took chances on the narrow, winding Montana roads, treacherous with ice and suicidal deer. Fortunately, with spring coming, at least ice wouldn't be a worry for much longer.

Dragging her concentration back to the laptop, Tawny suspected whoever caused her banking problems had also dug deep into her identity online.

Deep enough to know where she banked. What kind of car she drove. How to find her signature.

Deep enough to set her up as a pawn for an illegal enterprise.

Too much about her life, habits, and finances was available to anyone with Internet access. No wonder identity theft was rampant. Damn this miserable technology.

Mind whirling, Tawny headed to the gym, eager for the release of a workout. At the front desk, she ran her card through the check-in scanner. The clerk didn't greet her with his usual grin. His mouth a stiff line, eyes downcast, he muttered, "Mrs. Lindholm, the accounting office needs to speak to you."

Mrs. Lindholm? Everyone at the gym called her by her first name.

"What do they want?" she asked.

The man stared intently at the computer screen before him. His ears had turned red. "You'll have to ask them."

"OK, I'll go after Zumba. The class is starting." She headed toward the locker room.

He called to her, "They said they needed to see you as soon as you came in."

What the hell?

Annoyed, Tawny walked down the hall to the admin offices. At the door, she glanced back at the front desk and caught the clerk staring after her like a mournful dog before he whipped his head to focus on the computer again. She knocked and a bookkeeper let her in, closing the door behind her with a click that sounded like an automatic lock.

"Hi, what do you need?" Tawny gestured at the wall clock. "I'd like to make the ten o'clock Zumba class."

The bookkeeper's rolling chair squeaked. "Just a minute." She tapped her keyboard and didn't meet Tawny's eyes, either.

What was up? Everyone who worked there knew her. Why suddenly treat her like she had typhoid fever?

The bookkeeper rotated the screen for Tawny to see. "We're having a problem with your check. It was returned. Insufficient funds."

"What?" Tawny pulled her readers out of her gym bag. "That's impossible." She studied the monitor. An image of the check for her monthly dues showed on the screen, stamped *NSF*. "There's plenty of money in the account. It's a mistake." She faced the bookkeeper. "That bank has been making all sorts of mistakes lately. Let me call them right now." She yanked the phone from her pocket and tapped through the bank log-in sequence. And waited. Why was it taking so long? Other times, the connection had been instant.

The bookkeeper sucked in her cheeks. "Mrs. Lindholm, out of courtesy for your long-term membership, we put the check through a second time." She gnawed on her lip, staring down at her desk. "It bounced again. There is a thirty-five-dollar charge each time a check is returned."

"That's crazy. I'll make it good, of course." Why didn't the log-on connect? Fuming, Tawny pulled her wallet out.

"Sorry, but I can't accept any checks," the bookkeeper said. "I'll take a credit card for the dues and the returned check charges."

A message appeared on Lucifer's screen: *Unable to verify*.

Tawny handed the woman her MasterCard. As soon as she finished here, she'd go straight to that damned United Bankcorp, close the account, and find a different bank.

She paced the cramped room, impatient.

Mortified. That had been her mom's favorite word when Tawny did something embarrassing in front of other people. Now she felt mortified even though she hadn't done anything wrong. The bank's incompetence had hurt her reputation. Employees at the gym, people she saw every day, thought she was a deadbeat. After this, she could kiss any chance of being hired as a substitute Zumba instructor good-bye.

"Declined."

Tawny whirled to face the bookkeeper. "What?"

"Your card's declined." The woman's mouth puckered.

Dammit! The accounts were tied together. The bank must have fouled up her credit card, too.

She unzipped the cash pocket of her wallet. "I only have sixty dollars on me." She handed over three twenties.

The bookkeeper accepted the bills. "I need to give you a receipt. When do you think you can pay the balance?"

Dammit to hell! "As soon as I sell a kidney." Tawny immediately felt bad for snapping at the bookkeeper. The bank was at fault, not this poor woman just trying to do her job. "Sorry," she muttered. Chafing with impatience, she tugged on the door handle. Locked. She faced the bookkeeper who remained intent on typing. "Open the door, please."

The woman finished her task and then waited for the printer to spit out a receipt. She handed it to Tawny and released the lock from under her desk. "Have a good rest of your day."

Yeah, right.

* * *

When Tawny banged through the bank's entrance, she didn't care if the security guard tackled her. She rushed up the stairs to the mezzanine and strode into the manager's office, where emperor-of-the-branch Hyslop sat in conversation with Guadalupe Garza, the loan officer. Without knocking, Tawny pushed the door open.

"What is going on with my account?"

The bankers exchanged glances. Garza looked as if she'd like to slither under the desk. Hyslop, on the other hand, drew himself up to his full five seven, chin lifted, nostrils flared.

"Mrs. Lindholm, your accounts are frozen, as you well know."

"What? Frozen? What right do you have? That money is mine. I demand you give it to me now. I've had enough of this bank's screw-ups."

"I'm afraid it's not possible to give you anything."

"Why not?"

"I said, the accounts are frozen."

"What the hell does that mean?"

"It's out of my control."

"Whose control is it in? I want to talk to them."

"The Department of Homeland Security."

An invisible fist punched the air from Tawny's lungs. She and Virgie had talked about federal scrutiny, but until this minute, the possibility didn't quite seem real.

Tremors worked their way up through her torso, down her arms, into her hands. She clenched her fists, trying to stop the helpless quivering. Her head wagged back and forth between Hyslop and Garza, like a surreal tennis match, searching for reasons, for clues, for explanations.

Hyslop's pale eyes blinked slowly, like a snake's.

Garza cowered in her chair, looking everywhere in the cubicle except at Tawny.

Think! Don't let them intimidate you.

Finally, her lungs overcame paralysis, and she took several deep breaths. "This is because of those deposits, isn't it?"

"Banks are governed by the Bank Secrecy Act and the Patriot Act," Hyslop said. "We must follow those protocols to protect our customers and our country."

"But most of all, your own asses," Tawny blurted.

His tight lips twitched. "When certain triggers occur that show a sudden change in behavior that's inconsistent with normal customer activity, we are required to be vigilant. When a customer makes frequent large currency deposits without the source of those funds being known, we monitor activity. When a customer uses a branch that is geographically distant from that customer's home or business, we monitor activity. When a customer makes high-value transactions not commensurate with the customer's known income, we monitor activity."

He removed his rimless glasses and carefully wiped them with a pocket square, taking his time.

Tawny's knees wobbled. She locked them tight to keep from swaying.

Hyslop replaced the glasses on his nose and stared at her like a judge pronouncing a prison sentence. "Mrs. Lindholm, your recent banking patterns meet those standards of suspicious activity."

Her heartbeat throbbed in her ears, making it hard to hear. "I don't care what your video shows. I did not make those deposits. When they started, I came in here time and again, trying to get you to look into them." She glared at Hyslop. "I left messages that you didn't return. I talked to different people. I called your useless phone merry-go-round. I talked to *you*." She pointed at Garza. "I did my damnedest to get to the bottom of the mistakes. I raised so much hell, your security guard almost threw me out."

Tawny sucked in more air as buzzing roared in her ears. *Don't get dizzy. Don't faint,* she ordered herself. "If I'm a criminal trying to launder money or whatever you think I'm doing, what kind of sense does it make to draw all this attention to myself? If I was guilty of whatever you think I've done, I'd be lying low, not shaking things up."

She grasped the hard wooden back of the visitor chair for support, spent from making her defense.

Hyslop again adjusted his glasses. "Mrs. Lindholm, I have no idea why you engage in suspicious behavior. You may leave now. Our business is concluded."

Tawny shoved the chair aside, planted both hands on the desk, and leaned into Hyslop's face. "Our business is *not* concluded. You have my money, and I want it."

"I am unable to release any money to you. It has been seized by Homeland Security."

"Seized?" What the hell?

Hyslop nodded with a triumphant curl in his lower lip.

"How can they seize my money without telling me?" What were those legal words she'd heard on TV shows? "Don't they need a warrant? What about due process?"

Hyslop glanced down at his desk and plucked up a paper. "Oh dear, my administrative assistant was supposed to mail this to you. Here is the official notice." His reptilian eyes fixed on Tawny as if he planned to swallow her like a mouse. "It will tell you everything you need to know." He handed the government letterhead to Tawny. "I'm afraid *I* can do nothing more to help you. It's out of my hands."

* * *

Numb with shock, Tawny didn't remember the drive home. In the kitchen, she played new messages on the answering machine. Through still-buzzing ears, she heard complaints that more checks had bounced at the electric co-op, the water company, and her dentist.

Just like the gym dues. How many other payments would bounce?

She picked up the letter that asshole at the bank had given her. She tried to plow through the bureaucratic language and legal terms but ended up even more confused. It was signed by Maximillion Grosvenor, with several initials after his name.

How could Homeland Security seize her money when she hadn't even been charged with a crime, let alone convicted? This was the United States of America, not some corrupt third-world dictatorship. You were supposed to be innocent until proven guilty. What the hell had happened? The justice system she'd taken for granted had slipped away, a bedrock belief swallowed in an earthquake fault.

Squeezing her temples, Tawny took stock. With the checking and savings accounts frozen and her MasterCard shut off, she was broke.

The cash in the safe floated into her mind.

Why had she taken money that wasn't hers? The act pricked her conscience, but, at the time, there didn't seem to be any other way to get the bank to pay attention. Did that trigger the seizure? One thing was for sure, she would not give it back now. She couldn't. It was all she had.

Her mother's childhood advice echoed: *Two wrongs don't make a right*. But she had no choice.

The home phone rang. Probably another unhappy supplier with a bounced check. She couldn't bear to pick up the receiver.

A woman's hesitant voice stuttered through the answering machine. "Mrs. Lindholm ... Tawny ... this is Lupe ... Lupe Garza ... from the bank. I have to talk to you. It's important. Please call me ..."

Tawny snatched up the receiver. "Hello?"

Garza sucked in a surprised breath. "Oh, good, you're there. Listen, can you meet me?"

Should she even talk to the banker? Was this a trap? Maybe she needed to get a lawyer first, but Kit hadn't called her back. "What do you want?"

"I must talk to you but not on the phone or at the bank. I could lose my job."

Intuition urged Tawny to follow the woman's lead. It might be another bank double cross, but it might also mean more information, information she desperately needed. "All right, I'll meet you. When and where?"

"The Glacier Peaks medical building, second-floor lobby, in an hour."

* * *

Fifty-five minutes later, Tawny took the elevator to the second floor, a large open room that served as a central waiting area for different medical offices, shooting off like spokes of a wheel. The lobby buzzed with clients. Outside the optometrist's suite, rotating displays of eyeglass frames occupied floor space. In the pediatric suite, children climbed on a curving plastic caterpillar in a play area cluttered with blocks and toy trucks. The medical equipment supply area stocked crutches, orthopedic braces, and walkers. Tawny remembered renting a wheelchair there for Dwight.

After a quarter of an hour of pretending to read a magazine, she wondered how much longer she should wait for Lupe Garza. Minutes later, the elevator doors opened, and the loan officer stepped out. She glanced at Tawny but quickly looked away. Her already rounded shoulders drooped even more than before, and her lank gray-brown hair hung over her face. She walked to the eyeglass frames and spun the display wheel.

Tawny continued to hold the magazine, watching, waiting for a signal. From between the tall racks, Lupe checked around the lobby, then lifted her chin, pointing to the restroom. She disappeared inside. A moment later, Tawny closed the magazine and followed.

In the restroom, a pregnant mother was changing a baby boy on a fold-down shelf. Two stalls were empty, but the door to the third was closed. Lupe must be inside it. Tawny exchanged smiles with the mother, who looked familiar. She washed her hands, then put on lipstick, and fussed with her hair, dawdling. She watched the baby's chubby legs kicking the air. "What a cutie. How old is he?"

The mom taped the diaper snug. "Thirteen months. His baby sister is due in four months."

"You'll be a busy mommy."

"That's a fact." The mother sat the baby up on the shelf and appraised Tawny for a brief instant. "I know you, don't I?"

Recognition clicked. "You used to check at the supermarket."

The woman nodded. "Quit when I got pregnant with him. Couldn't stand on my feet that long."

"Hadn't seen you for a while," Tawny said.

The woman shifted and patted her belly. "Now I wish I hadn't quit 'cause my husband just got laid off. It sucks having a baby in this lousy economy."

Tawny tried to make her smile reassuring but shuddered inside for the young family. "The recession can't last forever."

With a sigh, the mom nodded, then asked, "Hey, would you mind watching him for a second? Every fifteen minutes, either he needs changing, I need to pee, or both."

"Sure," Tawny agreed, taking the toddler's waving hand. He gurgled, squeezed her finger, and gave her a delighted smile. Before his mother had time to close the stall door, he reached both arms out to Tawny, asking to be held.

She gathered him up and nuzzled his soft baby hair, instantly transported back in time to when Neal was that age. Inhaling his sweet smell, she held him close. He melted into her, nestling his head into her neck, making contented little grunts.

Her heart almost broke with longing for Neal. Would she ever see her son again?

When the mom came out of the stall, she washed her hands, retrieved the diaper bag, and took the baby back. "Thanks."

"He's a sweetheart." Tawny opened the door for them to leave and swallowed a lump, forcing her awareness back to the problem at hand.

With the restroom empty, she said softly, "Lupe?"

The loan officer immediately came out of the stall, eyes darting. "Here." She thrust a business card and thumb drive at Tawny. "Mr. Hyslop has been stonewalling you. He's had that notice from Homeland Security for several days. I told him he should call you, but he didn't. He was supposed to give you this card, too. It's from the guy that ordered the freeze on your accounts."

"Everything? Even my credit card?"

Lupe nodded. "The thumb drive has video of a woman— you—making a withdrawal from the Helena branch last Friday. A cashier's check for a hundred thousand. That's what triggered the seizure."

"It wasn't me. It's someone impersonating me."

Lupe held up her hands. "I don't know if it's you or not. But I know you did try to tell us those transactions were a mistake. What you said to Mr. Hyslop—that a criminal wouldn't draw attention to themselves like you have—well, it made me realize you're right. I don't know what's going on, but it doesn't make sense. And it isn't right what they've done to you."

Tawny fingered the thumb drive. "What you said about losing your job . . ."

Fear flashed in the woman's eyes. "Please, don't tell anyone I gave this to you. I'm supposed to retire in eighteen months. The bank is canning older employees right and left. If they fire me, I lose my retirement, everything. If anyone sees me talking to you, I could be arrested. They'd say I interfered with their investigation by tipping you off." Her rounded shoulders hunched, like an abused dog waiting for the next kick.

Tawny remembered her favorite teller, Margaret, who'd been ruthlessly axed by the cold-blooded manager. Lupe's fear was no exaggeration. "Thank you. I promise I won't say anything."

Lupe checked her watch. "I have to go. The bank thinks I'm at the eye doctor. I hope you find out who's doing this to you." She fled the restroom.

Tawny leaned against the counter and studied the business card: Maximillion Grosvenor, Division of Financial Investigations, Department of Homeland Security. A phone number and email but no physical address. Same guy who'd signed the incomprehensible letter. She slipped the card and thumb drive into her pocket and walked out.

Chapter 7: Identity Theft

Four videos with four different dates played from the thumb drive on Tawny's laptop at home. Hyslop had shown her the first one that day in his office. The second and third were virtual repeats: the imposter in a Jeep Wrangler, stacking bundles of cash in the bank drive-up drawer, signing a form, and receiving a receipt without speaking a word. All appeared to have occurred at the same drive-up window in Helena.

According to Lupe, the fourth video took place inside the lobby of the Helena branch.

The imposter handed the teller a note and driver's license, speaking a few words in a hoarse whisper Tawny couldn't make out. The teller took the ID and showed the supervisor the note. Muffled audio of their conversation indicated the note said the customer had throat surgery and had difficulty talking. She requested a cashier's check payable to Tawny Lindholm for $100,000 for a piece of property she intended to purchase. After a short discussion, the supervisor approved the request. The teller keyed in the transaction on her computer, and a printer produced the cashier's check. The imposter signed a receipt, took the check, and departed.

Tawny replayed the video, studying the woman carefully. Same height, same sunglasses, same figure as Tawny. The close-fitting, belted leather coat looked just like one she used to have. Stovepipe pants, calf-high boots, nothing out of keeping with her normal way of dressing. A patterned scarf was artistically knotted around the imposter's head and neck. The fabric covered her forehead and jawline. It might pass for a style statement rather than a disguise, but Tawny felt sure its true intent was to mask identity. The overall effect reminded her of tabloid photos of Jacqueline Kennedy Onassis in later years, trying to remain incognito in public.

This was real identity theft. Someone had stolen Tawny's actual appearance.

She hurried to the bathroom off the hall. Under bright lights, she pushed her cheeks with her palms and turned side to side, examining her profile in the triple mirrors. Her face hadn't changed. Yet someone had taken it away from her and used it to frame her. Her lip trembled and she bit down to make it stop.

Why?

The Jeep that the imposter drove was a twin to Dwight's. The identification must have appeared genuine enough to convince the supervisor to approve the withdrawal. And she had forged Tawny's signature on the form well enough to fool Tawny herself.

She flashed back to the Internet search she'd done, remembering court papers she signed for her parents' estates. Maybe the forger found those documents and used them to copy her handwriting.

That coat. A few months before, when she finally forced herself to go through the closet to give away Dwight's clothes, she'd included her old leather coat in the bundle for the veterans' thrift store. The imposter could have bought it from there.

According to Lupe, it was the last transaction on the video, the $100,000 withdrawal, that caused the feds to seize her checking and savings accounts.

Tawny went back to her office and picked up the business card. Her first impulse was to call Maximillion Grosvenor and raise hell. If they suspected the cash deposits were from illegal activity, let *them* figure out where they came from. She sure couldn't.

But they couldn't deprive her of what she and Dwight spent their whole lives working hard to earn, could they? They'd paid their taxes. How could the government steal her money without even telling her?

She *had* to see Kit Albritton. She called his office again and set up an appointment for later that afternoon.

* * *

Tawny drove downtown to the parking lot of a restored mansion built in the 1920s by one of the town's early fathers. A sign listed a dozen attorneys, with Kit's name in the middle. The walls of the reception area seemed to contain even more books than the library—heavy leather-bound volumes with gold lettering. She shuddered at the thought that Kit probably needed to read all of them to become a lawyer.

His footsteps thumped down a wide thickly carpeted staircase from his second-floor office. His navy three-piece suit fit tighter over his paunch, and his blond hair had receded a little farther since Dwight's funeral. But the mischievous blue eyes hadn't changed since he was a high school kid working in their shop.

He hugged her tightly. "Great to see you, Tawny. Come on up." They climbed the stairs arm in arm. His walnut-paneled office smelled fragrant with lemon oil. He sat behind his desk while she settled into a stiff leather chair accented with hobnails.

"How's Neal doing?" Kit asked.

Tawny hesitated. "Wish I knew. He's somewhere in the Middle East, but he can't talk about where he is or what he's doing."

"He'll always land on his feet. He's smart and sneaky—good combination for a soldier."

"Kit, I wanted to thank you again for the donation to the college in Dwight's name."

"Hey, no problem. Dwight started that training program, and it was only right to honor him." He leaned his elbows on the desk. "So what brings you here today?"

Tawny slid the business card and the letter from Homeland Security across the desk to Kit. "I'm in trouble with the government. They've seized my bank accounts and shut off my credit card."

"Whoa, Tawny, what have you been up to?"

She offered him the thumb drive. While the video played on his computer monitor, she explained how she had tried but failed to get the bank to correct the transactions, how she came under scrutiny by Homeland Security, and the final freeze.

"Where'd you get these videos?" Kit asked.

"I can't say without getting someone in trouble."

He fingered the card. "Have you contacted this Maximillion Grosvenor?"

She shook her head. "I figured I better have a lawyer first."

"Good thinking. The bad news is I don't handle criminal cases."

"But I'm not a criminal."

"What counts is the feds think you are, and sad to say, but they're the ones in charge here. You've got to prove your innocence."

The cash in the safe jabbed Tawny's conscience. "Kit, there's one more thing. When I couldn't get the bank to help, I withdrew the amount of the first deposit, forty-one thousand five hundred dollars in cash, and put it in Dwight's gun safe. I thought that might get their attention."

His lips creased into a line. "Frankly, Tawny, that wasn't the best idea you've ever had. In law, there's the doctrine of clean hands. You knew and freely acknowledged that money wasn't yours, so once you took it, your hands weren't clean anymore." He rocked back in his chair and stared at the ornate tin ceiling for several minutes.

Tawny hoped he believed she hadn't done anything wrong . . . except withdraw the cash. She knew now that had been stupid, but she couldn't undo her mistake. Massaging her aching ring finger, she prayed Kit could find a way to help her.

Finally he leaned forward and accessed a new screen on his monitor. It looked like a list of names and contact information. "Let me make some calls. As I said, we're not a criminal firm. Estates, real property, business—those are our areas. But I'll see if I can find someone specializing in government seizures. I don't know anyone locally but maybe in Great Falls, Helena, or Billings. I'll let you know."

"Kit, I'm sorry I took the money. I never intended to keep it. I just wanted them to find out what was going on." She licked her lips. "But now that's all I have. My checks are bouncing all over town. I have to make it right to the people I owe. And I need something to live on. They've cut me off at the knees. I have to use that cash."

Kit heaved a weary sigh. The mischief in his blue eyes had vanished during their conversation, replaced by concern. "Tawny, I can't advise you to do something illegal. You have to use your best judgment." He handed her the thumb drive, letter, and Grosvenor's card, then added his own business card. "If Homeland Security or anyone from law enforcement contacts you, refer them to me. Whatever you do, don't talk to them without legal counsel present, either me or someone else. OK?"

She nodded as he rose to walk her out.

At the office door, she grasped his sleeve. "I'm not a thief, Kit. This morning, a woman I barely know handed me her baby while she used the restroom. She trusted me, a stranger, with the most precious thing in the world to her. And she was right. I would never have betrayed her trust. Why is someone doing this to me?"

Kit gave her a smile that looked oddly sad. "Maybe that's exactly why they chose you. You're the last person anyone would suspect of wrongdoing. The perfect cover."

As she padded down the stairs, she wondered about his parting words. What did he mean? The perfect cover. Cover for what?

She sat in the Jeep, thinking. Normally she'd go to the gym, sweat off the stress and worry, but she couldn't now. Not unless she paid the rest of her dues in cash.

What about Virgie? Had she talked to her FBI patient? Tawny called her. The receptionist put her on hold and came back a minute later. "Dr. Belmonte's with patients the rest of the day, but she said to tell you the person she spoke about is out of town on an extended vacation. She'll call you tonight."

Tawny thanked her and hung up. Another dead end.

Lucifer rang, startling her so much that she fumbled the phone, which dropped to the floor under the steering wheel. She picked it up and saw Kahlil's name on the screen. "Hello, Kahlil."

"Tawny!" His voice sounded eager with excitement. "I am so sorry I have not been able to call. The meetings go late into the night, and I did not want to wake you. But my heart is singing to hear your voice. I miss you."

She looked out the Jeep window at passing traffic, wondering how to answer. He wanted her to say she missed him, but he had not even crossed her mind in the day's chaos. "How are you?"

"Tired, but we accomplished a great deal. How are *you*, my treasure?"

His treasure. The endearment made her realize how long ago their lovemaking seemed. She struggled to move her focus away from the present ugly reality to the sweet, caring man on the phone. "I've had better days."

"What is it? Is your son all right?" Concern colored his tone. She could almost feel him leaning forward to comfort her.

"I haven't heard any more. Did your friend know how to track him?"

A silent hesitation. Had he forgotten to ask the tracking expert? Or was it bad news? "She was not able to help. I am sorry."

Well, if that wasn't the icing on a perfect day.

"Tawny, your voice sounds very . . . sad. I am worried about you."

"Just a bad day. I'm all right." Yeah, sure. "When are you coming back?"

"Tomorrow afternoon." A long pause. "Are you really OK? I want to help you if you will allow me."

What could *he* do? But she didn't want to sound ungrateful for his offer.

Voices mumbled in the background. Kahlil spoke to someone away from the phone, then came back. "Tawny, please be safe. I will see you tomorrow."

After talking with him, she felt even more out of sorts than before, though that hardly seemed possible. Kahlil was a temporary interlude, full of passion and ecstasy. They came together in a beautiful, impossible fantasy, a fleeting romantic escape.

But in real life, dire problems threatened to crush her. She had to concentrate on defending herself from Homeland Security, clearing her name, and getting her money back.

Or else she might wind up in prison, unable to save her son.

And Lucifer was the only tool available to help her locate Neal.

* * *

Tawny parked the Jeep in the garage and slid her key into the dead bolt on the back door. When she turned the key, she realized the bolt wasn't latched. *Strange,* she thought, *did I forget to lock it?* Another damn memory lapse.

Inside the mudroom, something felt odd, a different smell, like a faint hint of perfume, hanging in the air. She passed through the kitchen, dining area, and living room. Nothing appeared out of place. In Neal's old bedroom, her laptop was open, as she'd left it.

But the mouse appeared to have been moved.

She woke the computer from sleep mode and the screen lit up. Before she'd left for the appointment with Kit, she'd been playing the video Lupe had given her. When she removed the thumb drive, she hadn't closed out the video player. But now the screen instead showed the desktop opening mode.

A chill gripped her. Someone had been inside her home, inside her computer.

She backed away, as if the laptop now harbored a contagious disease. A burn started in her stomach. She raced to her bedroom. The closet door was cracked a couple of inches. She always closed it.

She yanked open the drawer in the bedside table. Her revolver lay in its place in a soft oiled cloth. Grabbing it, she found the cloth folded differently from the way she normally wrapped it. She opened the cylinder and checked the cartridges. Someone had handled the revolver but left it loaded. Thank goodness! She clicked it closed.

She gripped the gun in both hands. From now on, she would keep it on her at all times.

Her stomach felt on fire, acid creeping up to her throat. Was the intruder still in the house?

Should she leave? Call 9-1-1? No, dammit, she was armed, and this was her home. Anger galvanized her.

She swept aside the clothes in the closet, looked under the bed, checked behind the shower curtain across the tub in the master bath. When she left her bedroom, she closed the door. She searched Neal's and Emma's rooms, the second bath in the hallway, the guest closet, securing each door after verifying the rooms were empty. The main floor was clear.

At the top of the stairs leading to the basement, Tawny hesitated, listening. If the intruder was down there, he was trapped without egress windows. But a search of the downstairs laundry room, pantry, and Dwight's man cave yielded nothing.

Slightly relieved, she climbed the stairs and closed the door at the top, locking it.

Back in her bedroom, she poked inside the closet for further signs of disturbance. The intruder had rearranged her shoes, maybe to reach the gun safe. She tested the handle. Still locked. With fumbling fingers, she tried to dial in the combination. It took three attempts before she finally succeeded and swung the door open.

Dwight's rifles and shotguns stood in their notched rack as they were supposed to. On the top shelf, the diamond pendant from Dwight, her grandmother's pearls, and a few other pieces of nice jewelry sat neatly in their boxes. The second shelf held three pistols, apparently untouched, beside the paper sack of cash. Hands trembling, she removed the sack and spread the bundles of bills on the bed to count. Still $41,500. She repacked the bag and replaced it on the shelf.

They—whoever *they* were—didn't get inside the safe, thank goodness.

Who had broken into her house? The feds? Or the people hell-bent on setting her up?

When she opened the dresser drawers, her underwear and folded clothes appeared rearranged. The searcher had not been a ransacker but careless enough that Tawny knew, without a doubt, that he or she did a thorough job of snooping.

Tawny almost wished they *had* ransacked the house. For some reason, this sneaky surveillance felt like more of an intrusion than a regular burglary. At least normal thieves grabbed what they wanted and got the hell out with the loot. The lack of disturbance made her afraid that they meant to come back. She fingered the smooth grip of the revolver.

Should she call the cops to report the break-in? If they'd stolen something, she wouldn't hesitate. But this . . . no forced entry, nothing missing, only a faint scent of cologne.

Nine-one-one, what is your emergency?

I want to report someone moved my mouse and rumpled my underwear.

The operator would fall on the floor laughing.

Besides, the intruders might have been the feds. After all, they'd seized her money, and that had to be against the law. What prevented them from entering her home? Maybe they wanted to set up surveillance.

New fear twisted her insides. She started to search for hidden cameras and microphones but soon gave up. With the government's sophisticated tiny equipment, she could tear the house down to the foundation and never find the bugs. From now on, she had to assume they watched and heard everything she did in her home.

Her roiling stomach rebelled this final insult, forcing her to race into the bathroom to throw up in the toilet. When she finished heaving, she rinsed her mouth and squeezed her pounding head.

She wandered through the house, lost, torn between a desire to flee and an angry determination to defend her home, her property, her life from the intruders. In the kitchen, she glanced out the window and noticed her next-door neighbor, Starshine, in her backyard, tending her marijuana plants.

Dwight always said Starshine must have dropped acid one too many times in the sixties. If he ever saw her heading for their house, he usually ducked downstairs to the den, whistling. *"This is the dawning of the Age of Aquarius . . ."*

Starshine didn't believe in money. When her old beater car broke down, she used to come over, begging Dwight to fix it, offering to barter with oral sex. He politely declined and worked on her car anyway while she hung over the fender, instructing him on what to do. When he came in the house afterward, he ran a greasy hand across his sweaty forehead and cursed. "That woman never shuts up. She thinks she knows all about engines and gave me a long lecture about what I was doing wrong. Hell, I only own a repair shop! What do *I* know? I finally asked her if she's such an expert, why doesn't she fix her own damn car?"

Tawny had giggled. "Maybe you *should* have let her *pay* you. She can't talk with her mouth full."

Dwight lost his frown and broke into a grin. "I'd rather cut it off."

"Please don't."

He hugged her.

She tried to push away. "You're covered with oil."

"Since we're both greasy now, let's go slip and slide around in the tub." And they had.

Why did that dear, silly memory come back to her at this moment?

Tawny watched Starshine, on her hands and knees cultivating the young plants, her frizzy cloud of gray hair held out of her eyes with an Indian-style headband. A long tied-dyed smock puddled on the ground around her.

Could *she* have seen the intruders?

Tawny put the revolver out of sight in a kitchen drawer. She clipped down the back steps and approached the fence between their properties. "Starshine, can I ask you a question?"

"Oh, hi, Tawny." She heaved herself up, wiping dirt-covered hands on her dress. "I just made some new earrings for you. Out of bottle caps and can tabs with little seed pearls. And they don't match, each one is different. They'll look great on you—"

"No, thank you. I already have more earrings than I'll ever wear." *Besides, I'm not accepting any more "gifts" that you expect a "donation" for.* "Did you see anyone going in or out of my house today?"

"Just you. And weren't *you* a busy girl, coming and going, coming and going? What have you been up to?"

Tawny steeled herself. "It's important, Starshine. I think someone's been in my house."

"Well, I didn't see anyone. Who do you think it is? Couldn't it be the people who work on your water softener? You know, drinking soft water is very bad for your health—all those chemicals. That poison water is what gave Dwight cancer, you know—"

"Never mind, thanks." Tawny turned away and headed for her door.

Starshine added, "What did you forget? When you left the first time, you weren't gone five minutes, then you came back. I'm always doing that, starting out for someplace and having to backtrack—"

Tawny froze midstep. "What do you mean I 'came back'?"

Starshine puffed her cheeks out at regaining Tawny's attention. "You went out, drove away in the Jeep. Then you were back just a few minutes later, left the Jeep in the alley, and went inside. But why on earth were you wearing a coat on such a warm day?" She flapped her loose smock. "I'm roasting. Aren't you feeling well? I can make you rose hip and kale tea that will mend your immune system. It's high in vitamin C, and the kale binds with bile acids . . ."

The imposter driving the twin Jeep, wearing the leather coat. That's who'd broken into her home.

She hurried inside, leaving Starshine babbling to thin air.

In front of the laptop, Tawny studied the screen. She knew experts could track where users had been in a computer, but the technology mystified her as much as the damn smartphone did.

The phone chirped in her pocket. She pulled it out and saw a text from Virgie: *Stuck at hospital. Patient emergency. Call U tomorrow.*

Damn. She longed to confide in her friend, seek advice, figure out what to do. Should she stay home, try to defend her space? Or run? But where to? If she were gone, what kept the intruder from coming back, next time, maybe to crack the safe?

At least if she needed to make a break for it, over $40,000 meant a running start. Thank goodness she had the cash, even if it gave her what Kit called "unclean hands." Better to beg forgiveness.

She retrieved the gun from the kitchen drawer and noticed the light on the answering machine flashing. Another three calls about her checks bouncing at the supermarket, the pharmacy, and the cable company. Shame burned inside. Never in her life had she tried to cheat anyone.

In her office, she scanned the check register and added up how much money she owed so far. Five hundred thirty-nine dollars, not including bounced check penalties. Thank goodness the dentist visit had only been a cleaning, not a crown.

She leaned back in the desk chair and tried to fight down the swelling powerlessness from circumstances she couldn't control or understand. The imposter who looked just like her had broken into the house. Why?

To plant evidence to incriminate her with Homeland Security or the IRS?

To steal something? What did Tawny have to steal? With her bank accounts and credit card frozen, they couldn't make her more helpless than they already had.

Why impersonate her? Why set her up to take a fall?

What should she do to save herself?

When an insurmountable problem faced them, Dwight always used to say, "If you have to eat an elephant, do it bite by bite."

Bite by bite.

She went to the safe and removed the sack of cash. She counted out enough to make good on the bounced checks, then locked up the rest. Tucking the cash and gun in her bag, she headed toward the garage, intending to go to the post office to buy money orders. Almost five p.m. She might just make it before they closed.

The front doorbell rang.

Tawny's heart leaped to her throat. She clutched the revolver and dropped her bag on the breakfast bar.

She tiptoed to Emma's bedroom, hugging the wall beside the window that looked out on the front porch. The mirror on the dresser faced the window at an angle. In its reflection, Tawny saw two men standing at the door.

They had to be feds. Brush-cut hair, dark suits, white shirts, regimental ties, the posture of importance, authority, and power.

Power over her fate.

One man turned toward Emma's window. Tawny shrank and dropped to the floor behind the bed, praying it blocked his view.

The bell rang again several times.

From her cowering position, she heard footsteps approach the window. He must be peering inside. Could he see her? She hoped she was hidden far enough out of sight that he couldn't use the mirror to spot her the same way she had watched him. She didn't dare look up.

More ringing, then a fist hammered the door.

Would they break it down? Arrest her and haul her to jail?

She remembered Kit's advice: *Don't talk to them without a lawyer present.*

In her pocket, the phone trilled. Dammit! She snatched it to silence the ringer. Had the feds heard?

The caller ID read *Kit*. Exactly who she needed to talk to.

She crawled on the floor out of Emma's room and hurried into the second bathroom off the hall, the one without a window. Silently closing the door, she answered the phone.

"Kit, I think the feds are outside," she whispered. "They've been ringing the bell and banging on the door."

There was a pause. "Do they know you're there?"

"I'm not sure. I've been hiding."

"OK, take this down." He started to rattle off a number.

"Wait, let me get something to write with." She pawed through the drawers in the vanity and found an eyeliner pencil. "OK, I'm ready."

He repeated the numbers, office and cell, which she scrawled on the tile counter. "His name is Tillman Rosenbaum. He's in Billings, specializes in government seizures and forfeiture. I want you to call him as soon possible and make arrangements to surrender. It'll be better if they don't have to bust in on you."

"Surrender?"

"That's what I said. Take care, Tawny." He clicked off.

She slid to the floor and stared at the phone. She couldn't live like this—hunted, watched, waiting for someone to take her down. Maybe Kit was right. If she surrendered, she'd explain what had gone on, show them the videos, and let them find the imposter and figure out why the woman was pretending to be her.

Except . . . when she tried to explain to her own bank, they hadn't believed her. Why should the feds treat her any differently? Her ex-banker neighbors, the Slocums, whom she'd known for years, didn't believe her.

Besides, she couldn't out Lupe Garza, who'd risked her job and arrest to give Tawny the thumb drive.

She swiped the phone's screen to life and tapped into her online banking. A gong sounded. *Access not available.*

They'd locked her out of there, too.

Next, she called the office number for the Billings lawyer. "This is Tawny Lindholm. Kit Albritton referred me to Tillman Rosenbaum. It's urgent I talk to him."

"Mr. Rosenbaum is in trial. May I take a message?"

Tawny's insides twisted. She gave her number to the receptionist, then tried his cell. Voice mail. Not surprising, if he was in court. She left a message and disconnected. What good was an attorney if she couldn't reach him?

If there had been anything left in her stomach, she would have thrown up again. Pressure inside her head made it feel like her eyeballs might burst from their sockets.

What a coward I am. Cowering on the bathroom floor like a cockroach. Dwight, I need you.

The doorbell and knocking had stopped. Had they given up? They might be in an unmarked car—maybe that dark-blue Crown

Vic she'd been seeing—waiting for her to emerge like a quivering rabbit from a hole.

Tawny tiptoed into the hall. Silence rested over the house. Hugging the wall, she peeked out Emma's window again. No one was on the front porch now. She slipped into the kitchen and checked the backyard. Clear. But the garage blocked her view of the alley. They might be parked out there.

Next door, Starshine held a hose, soaking her marijuana plants. What if the feds talked to *her*? Heaven only knew what she'd tell them.

The sun dropped behind the trees and houses across the street. Soon darkness would cover the neighborhood. Did they want her badly enough for an all-night stakeout? She moved from room to room, closing drapes, lowering window blinds, leaving lights off.

Her muscles screamed for the release of exercise, writhing like irritated snakes beneath her skin. Trapped. In her own home. Her sanctuary had now become her prison.

A soft but irritating buzz caught her attention, leading her to the office bedroom. A fat fly, newly awakened from winter hibernation, batted itself against the window overlooking the side yard. She picked up a sheaf of papers to swat it, then stopped. Instead, she opened the window and set it free into the dusky night. *How dumb,* she thought. *I'm reduced to feeling sorry for a fly.*

Would anyone open a window for her?

Back in the living room, she sank into Dwight's recliner, longing for its soft cushions to fold her into a hug as he would have done. How many times when she passed by his chair had he dragged her down onto his lap? How often had she pulled away and scrambled to her feet, claiming a more urgent task? What could have been more urgent? So what if the clothes wrinkled in the dryer? So what if the steaks cooked to well done or even burned to ashes? She damned herself for placing more importance on petty nuisances than a moment never to be recaptured, now lost forever. A sob caught in her throat.

The hard shape of the revolver bit into her thigh. She removed the gun from her pocket, opened it to recheck the cartridges, then rolled the cylinder around and around. If the feds busted in, what would she do?

Shoot? A guaranteed bad ending, like Ruby Ridge or Waco.

Drop the gun and raise her hands?
Turn the gun on herself? Join Dwight?

Chapter 8: Hiding Out

The doorbell rang.

Tawny startled from sleep, fighting for breath, grasping for familiar surroundings in the blackness. Her hands found the padded arms of the recliner. A weight pressed on her lap. The revolver. The clock on the mantel glowed. 12:03. Just after midnight.

The feds again? Trying to catch her by surprise?

Or the burglar returning? Maybe this time to attack her.

Gripping the gun in both hands, she crept to the living room window. The porch light glowed through closed drapes. She didn't dare look out. If they saw the drapes move, they'd know she was inside.

Lucifer jangled like a manic alarm clock. She jumped at the sound, fumbling the phone from her pocket.

Kahlil!

She whispered, "Hello?"

His mellow voice comforted her. "Tawny, I do not mean to frighten you. I am at your door."

On tiptoe, she peeked out the high window. Kahlil stood in the pool of the porch light. Alone.

Thank God. A friend in need.

She set the phone on the end table beside the door. Still holding the revolver, she unfastened the dead bolt and opened the door, crouching behind it.

Kahlil stepped inside. She quickly closed and locked the door behind him. He blinked in the darkness of the living room, holding out a hand toward her as if blind. She grasped it. Then his arms folded around her, warm, close, safe.

"You're shaking, my treasure." His lips moved in her hair. "I am sorry I frightened you. It was not thoughtful to come to your door in the middle of the night."

She clung tight to him, feeling foolish to be gripping the gun but unable to let go of him long enough to put it down.

"When I called this afternoon," he murmured, "your voice sounded strained. I knew something had gone terribly wrong. I left the conference early and caught the first plane back here." He moved toward the couch, reaching to turn on a lamp.

She caught his hand. "No!"

They sat side by side, his arm around her shoulders. He didn't press her with questions. Gratitude welled in her for his patience. She tried to pull her thoughts together, still struggling out of sleep, disoriented, not knowing where to begin.

Kahlil stiffened. Tawny realized he'd noticed the gun in her lap, illuminated by the dim light through the high window. She set the revolver on the coffee table, pointing the barrel away from them.

Were there bugs, hidden cameras watching them? Did she dare talk? Who might be listening?

She put her lips to his ear, touched the small hearing aid. "Will you take me out of here?"

He nodded.

She stood, slid the gun into her jeans, grabbed a jacket and her bag. He followed her through the dining area to the kitchen. From the glass-enclosed mudroom, she looked out into the backyard. The security light that Starshine always complained about lit the breezeway connecting to the garage. A flagstone path led to the rear gate that opened on the alley. Beyond the fence, shadows deepened. She flicked the switch off, and blackness shrouded the backyard.

They went out the rear door, which she locked behind them. *For all the good* that *did,* she thought. Dead bolts hadn't stopped the intruder before. They crept silently along the pathway, opened the gate, and reached the alley behind the house. She turned in the direction of the Roths' house, now Kahlil's. Hand in hand, they moved quietly through the dark, emerging on the cross street. A dog barked. They walked faster. Another block and a half, and they reached his place.

Thankfully, no porch light lit the entrance. He unlocked the door, and they went inside. Apparently picking up on her paranoia, he closed the miniblinds before turning on a light in the kitchen.

They blinked, staring at each other, while their eyes adjusted, a mystified expression on his face. She didn't want to imagine how she must appear to him: tear-streaked cheeks, puffy eyes, a gun bulging in her jeans.

He turned a kettle on to boil and took tea from the cupboard. The sweet aroma of peppermint filled her nostrils. Her mouth tasted like the bottom of a trash can. He pushed her down in a chair at the kitchen table and made little gestures to put her at ease, massaging her tense shoulders, rinsing mugs, unwrapping teabags. So often she'd sat at this same table, comfortable, relaxed, laughing with the Roths.

When the kettle whistled, Kahlil poured hot water and set a mug before her, sitting across the table. Worried green eyes took stock. He reached to hold her hand, gently, not demanding, but reassuring. Somehow he knew what she needed to calm down.

Away from surveillance, temporarily safe from arrest, she sighed, blowing steam up from her tea, inhaling the fresh scent, eager to wash the sour taste of fear from her mouth. She closed her eyes for a long moment. "Thank you," she murmured.

An answering squeeze reassured her.

Taking a deep breath, she started her story. "This is going to sound crazy, but someone is setting me up, making it look like I'm involved in criminal acts. I'm probably going to be arrested." She paused, gauging his reaction, expecting him to recoil.

His lips parted. "What?" He leaned forward, dark brows drawn together. "Who would do such a horrible thing to you?"

She'd feared she might see doubt in his eyes, but she didn't. Instead of pulling away, he moved closer. Her tense muscles loosened a tiny fraction. He wasn't going to desert her. Thank goodness. She shook her head. "I don't know, but they've gone to a lot of trouble. A woman who's a dead ringer for me has been making suspicious transactions at my bank, over in Helena. She's forging my signature, using my account. She even drives the same type of Jeep. I've seen a video of her. If I didn't know better, I'd swear it was me. When I first saw it, I thought I was losing my mind. Wondering if I'd blacked out and done things I didn't remember."

He didn't appear shocked or disbelieving but rather ready for more of her strange tale.

She sipped the tea. It burned her tongue, but the pain reassured her—a normal sensation in the unreal events swirling around.

"These suspicious transactions caused the Department of Homeland Security to monitor my account. Now they've frozen it, seized all my money, and shut off my credit card. Then someone broke into my house while I was gone and searched my computer."

Kahlil's brow furrowed. "Did you call the police?"

Tawny shook her head. "No sign of forced entry. They must have used a key or picked the lock. Nothing missing. But I *knew* someone had been inside. Then my neighbor verified my suspicion. She saw a woman she thought was me, but it was the imposter."

"No wonder you're terrified." He gestured to the gun in her pocket. "You felt you needed protection."

She took another sip, again burning her tongue. "That's not even the worst. A little later, two men who looked like federal agents showed up, pounding on my door. I . . .." She lowered her head, ashamed to admit her cowardly behavior. "I hid. Wouldn't answer the door. Eventually they went away, but they may be watching the house. That's why I had to get out of there."

He rose and came to her, pressing her head into his taut abdomen, stroking her hair, rubbing her knotted neck, rocking her gently. "You're safe here."

She put her arms around his waist and clung tightly.

After a few minutes, he pulled her to stand and led her to the bathroom. He turned on the shower to warm up, while he carefully undressed her, pulling the T-shirt over her head, unhooking the bra, unzipping jeans. His eyes asked about the gun. She took it from her pocket and set it on the counter. Then he peeled off the rest of her clothes, wrapped a towel into a turban around her hair, and guided her into the shower.

A moment later, he had stripped and joined her. She felt too weak and exhausted to lift her arms or hold her head up any longer. He soaped her body, turned her around to massage her back, hot water sluicing down, bubbles frothing over her shoulders. She closed her eyes and let him bathe her like a baby, swaying under the gentle pressure of his palms.

After rinsing off, he wrapped her in a towel and rubbed her dry, removing the turban that covered her hair. He took a moment to dry himself, then put his arm around her waist and led her into the bedroom. They slipped under the blankets, and she curled her back into the curve of his body, legs intertwined, his arms cradling her as she drifted off.

* * *

Kahlil stared at the ceiling, one hand under his head, while Tawny slept in the crook of his other arm, her breathing finally even and peaceful. An hour earlier, she'd thrashed, moaned, and called out her son's name. He expected her to have nightmares under the strain—even wanted her to. He had soothed her, whispering reassurance, pulling her closer, and she settled down. Good. She felt safe with him. That was the whole point. She had to trust him, feel bound to him, for the plan to work.

Goal accomplished.

* * *

Dawn light woke Tawny. Kahlil lay on his back, snoring softly. His morning erection tented the blanket, which made her smile. She stroked the black hair on his chest, wondering at the unexpected feeling of hope in her heart.

Yesterday had been one of the worst of her life, second only to the day Dwight died. Somehow Kahlil had known she was in crisis. Not that she was all that hard to read—the Roths used to jokingly warn her against playing poker for money because, as Solly used to say, a blind man could guess what kind of hand she held.

How trapped and alone she'd felt, unable to reach Virgie or the Billings lawyer. Yet Kahlil had raced back from Houston to help her. He didn't think she was crazy. And most of all, he hadn't run the other way when she explained the jeopardy she was in. She hoped her problems wouldn't bring him down, too.

She slid out of bed quietly. He shifted, tossing an arm above his head, but didn't wake. She padded barefoot into the bathroom. Her revolver still sat on a shelf. She picked up her jeans from the floor, feeling in the pocket for the thumb drive, reassured it was there. She needed to play the video of the imposter for him. Her evil twin, she thought grimly.

Where was Lucifer?

Not in her pockets. She tiptoed to the living room where she'd left her jacket and bag. Not there. Then she remembered setting the phone down when she'd opened the door for Kahlil. She needed to go home to retrieve it in case the lawyer, Virgie, or Sergeant Stuart from the Rear Detachment called.

Home. Did she dare go back? At some point, she had to, for the cash in the safe, a toothbrush, fresh clothes.

Yet the prospect of being arrested didn't seem as terrifying today with Kahlil by her side.

She returned to the bedroom. He still slept, and the tent still stood straight up. *Be a shame to waste it,* she thought as she slipped under the covers to wake him.

* * *

They ate breakfast at the Roths' table, drinking coffee and trading contented smiles in the afterglow. But Tawny needed to return to reality. "I have to go home, but I don't want to put you at risk if cops are there to arrest me."

Kahlil suggested, "I will go first. My car is parked on the street. I'll walk around the block and see if anyone is watching. If anyone approaches me, I will tell a story. If it is clear, I will drive back and pick you up. If not, we can disguise you, or you can give me your key, and I'll get what you need."

She thought for a moment. Seemed sensible, safe. "OK. Look for a dark-blue Ford sedan. But be careful. I don't want you in danger because of me."

He cocked his head to the side and gave her an odd, crooked smile. "Do not worry about me." He kissed her. "I will walk there now. Back very quickly."

In less than ten minutes, an Audi convertible pulled into the Roths' driveway, and Kahlil beckoned. Tawny hurried out to meet him. "Different car?"

He grimaced. "Took the rain-soaked one back to the rental company. I must learn never to leave a top down in Montana." He backed onto the street. "I saw no one. I believe all is well."

At home, Tawny threw necessities into an overnight bag, including a box of ammo and the phone charger. While Kahlil carried the bag to his car, she opened the safe and grabbed the money, transferring it from the paper sack to a zippered tote. She touched the diamond pendant, wondering if she should take it, but decided it was probably more secure locked up, even though she didn't know if she might ever see it again.

As she spun the dial to lock the safe, Kahlil's voice came from the hall. "Are you ready?" She quickly closed the closet door and faced him. A lifetime of caution about valuables prickled her. The fewer people who knew about a safe containing money, guns, or jewelry, the better.

"Yes. Let's go."

On the way out the front door, she picked up the phone and slipped it in her jacket pocket. The revolver already made her jeans bulge. She felt weighted down.

Kahlil glanced at the weapon in her pocket. "Do you know how to use that?"

She tossed her braid over her shoulder. "If you meet a woman in Montana who doesn't know how to handle a gun, she's probably from California."

He looked puzzled.

She shook her head. "Never mind."

They drove out of the neighborhood toward Main Street. Kahlil asked, "What comes next?"

"I should find somewhere to stay, away from this area."

He glanced sideways at her. "You are welcome with me."

"Too close. The neighbors all know me."

He nodded. "You are correct." He straightened in the seat. "There are several motels near the dam where I work. They are far enough away that you won't run into your neighbors. And I will be close."

Sounded all right. At least until she got her bearings, met the lawyer, and found out where she stood. "OK."

Once they were out of town, on the highway, he lowered the convertible top. Wind whipped loose wisps of her hair. The sun warmed her face. With her hand resting on Kahlil's muscular shoulder, she again marveled how quickly her world had changed from bleak to hopeful because of him. Why had she ever worried about a petty concern like the ten-year difference in age? The important thing was his kindness, his unfailing understanding, his willingness to help her in time of trouble. Those things mattered. The rest was superficial.

But his driving . . . her toes curled as he tailgated a van, then whipped around it on a blind curve through Bad Rock Canyon. Heavy timber crowded one side of the road, the river on the other.

Seconds later, a deer burst from the trees. Brakes squealing, Kahlil swerved but clipped it with the front fender on his side. He veered to the narrow shoulder and stopped, his arm flung across Tawny in a feeble attempt to hold her back.

They faced each other, eyes wide, breathing ragged, seatbelts taut against their chests. He gasped. "Are you all right?"

She clutched his hand and nodded. "You?"

"Yes." He swiveled in the seat, looking back to where the deer lay on its side, front legs flailing in a futile effort to escape. He undid his seatbelt and turned again to her, pulling her close. "I am so sorry."

She watched over his shoulder as the deer tried to rise but fell back. It lay in the lane of oncoming traffic.

Behind them, the van that Kahlil had passed pulled over. The driver jumped out and ran to the convertible. "Holy crap, mister, what the hell do you think were you doing?" Thirtyish, his face white with shock, stubbly beard, coveralls, baseball cap on backward. To Tawny, he said, "You OK, lady?"

She nodded. A wave of dizziness passed through her. She felt the revolver in her pocket and knew what she needed to do but didn't want to think about it.

The van driver slapped his thighs. "Damn, I can't believe your airbags didn't go off! You're one righteous lucky son of a bitch. Hit a deer with a damn convertible and not a scratch on you." Despite his cursing, he sounded more frightened than angry.

Kahlil got out and extended his hand. "I must apologize for my foolishness."

While the two men shook hands and then checked the fender damage, Tawny climbed from the car, crossed the road, and approached the deer. A splintered rear leg bone jutted through the hide. Its hips twisted unnaturally. Front hooves pawed the air. She moved behind its head, out of striking distance. "We've got to get her off the road."

"Watch yourself, lady," the van driver said. "Don't let it kick you."

Tawny pulled the revolver out, dropped to one knee, and cocked the hammer. "Easy, now," she murmured to the stricken animal. "It's going to be all right." She aimed inside the ear, took a deep breath, and pulled the trigger. The gun leaped in her hand, the deer spasmed but seconds later went still. She straightened, revolver hanging by her side, staring down at the pitiful creature. At least it didn't suffer for long.

Then she felt Kahlil behind her, squeezing her arms, pulling her out of the traffic lane to the shoulder.

A truck approached, slowed, and steered around the carcass.

"The lady's right," the van driver said. "Let's get this out of the way." He and Kahlil each grabbed a leg and dragged the deer off the road.

With a shake of his head and a wave, the man climbed in his van and drove away.

Back in the convertible, Tawny said, "We ought to report this."

Kahlil pursed his lips. "Do you really think that is a good idea, with your situation?"

Oh yeah, she was on the run from the feds. How could she forget? "You're right. Let's get out of here."

Despite the crumpled fender, the car handled all right. Tawny felt relieved that Kahlil now drove much slower, keeping a long distance from vehicles ahead of him.

In Hungry Horse, they pulled into a motel parking lot. Kahlil had not spoken a word since they left the dead deer. After turning off the engine, he sat for a long moment, head down.

Was he shocked, scared, embarrassed? Or maybe horrified by her action?

What was done was done. She couldn't let the animal suffer. She reached in the back for her bag.

He faced her, green eyes brimming with regret. "I cannot tell you how sorry I am. I should never have put you in such a situation. I damn myself for making you go through . . . that." His glance dropped to the butt of the revolver, now back in her pocket. "What a brave woman you are, to end the misery of another being."

She tried to shrug off his words, but they hit deep in her heart. "You do what you have to do."

He kissed her, gently, tenderly, then reached for his wallet. "Do you need money for the motel?"

She shook her head. "No, I'm OK." But his offer warmed her.

He ran his fingers across her cheek. "I must check in at work, and I should turn the car in and see about the damage. But I will be back as soon as I can."

Tawny got out, lugging her bag. With a glance at the fender and a wry smile, she asked, "Who would be crazy enough to rent *you* another car?"

He threw back his head and laughed as he drove away.

The motel was old, rickety, but clean. In the office, she started to fill out the registration form but realized she needed an alias, something that had never occurred to her before. Pretending to drop the pen, she bent to the floor, racking her brain.

Her mother's maiden name. Louisa Ellen Dent. She added the address of a house where they'd lived briefly in Butte when she was in first grade.

When the clerk asked for a credit card, she almost panicked but quickly counted out enough cash for a week's rent. That satisfied him, and he gave her the key.

The room was located in a rear building, out of sight from the highway, with a queen bed and kitchenette containing a bar fridge, microwave, and coffee maker. She immediately searched for a safe hiding place for the tote bag of cash and spotted a ceiling vent. Not a good solution, but it would have to do for the time being. She used a dime to unscrew the fasteners and pulled the grille down. A cloud of dust came with it, making her sneeze. But there was enough space in the duct, just barely, to stash the bag. She refastened the grille.

Sitting on the bed, she checked her phone and found a voice mail from Virgie: "Sorry to leave you hanging. Patient needed emergency surgery. He made it, but I didn't get home till three in the morning. Ah, the glamorous life of a physician. Anyway, call me when you can. Love ya, sweetheart."

Tawny put on her readers and texted a response: *Big problems, but I'm OK. Call when U have LOTS of time 2 talk.*

She ejected the spent shell from her revolver and reloaded. Then she unpacked toiletries in the bathroom, realizing she'd forgotten deodorant. After counting the cash in her wallet, she hiked a short distance down the highway to the supermarket. There, she bought coffee, milk, a few apples and oranges, deodorant, several bandannas, and a sewing kit.

Back at the motel, Tawny retrieved the tote bag from the vent. Using the sewing kit and bandannas from the store, she fashioned several pouches and sewed them inside the flannel lining of her denim jacket. Each pouch held five thousand without making obvious lumps. Satisfied, she stitched the hidden pockets closed. Like the revolver, from now on, she needed to keep the money with her at all times.

At nine o'clock, she called the lawyer's office in Billings again and received the same excuse as yesterday. "He's in trial. May I take a message?" Tawny repeated her urgent plea for a call back and hung up, discouraged.

Good thing she was away from home where the feds couldn't easily intercept her since the lawyer seemed impossible to contact. What help was he?

Then she recalled the tracking capability on the smartphone. The feds might find her through that. When Kahlil returned, she needed to ask him to disable that feature.

A pinpoint of light flashed red. Putting on readers, she checked the battery—only 7 percent left. She plugged it in to charge. A moment later, it vibrated on the bedside table like a nervous hamster and lit up, showing a new text.

From Neal!

Her heart stopped.

Abducted. Need help bad. W/s details soon.

Dear God, no!

Neal kidnapped. The worst case she'd imagined had come true. Her maternal intuition was right, too damn right.

A collage of memories cascaded through her mind: Neal immediately after birth, crusty, purplish, skull elongated like an alien being but so unbelievably beautiful. His smile of delight when, at seven months, he pulled himself up on wobbly legs and stood without help. His pinched scowl during dentist visits. The softness of his eyes when he gazed at a little blonde girl he had a crush on in sixth grade. So many snapshots through his twenty-nine years of life, growing into a mature, accomplished army sergeant with erect posture, firm mouth, and many ribbons on his uniform.

No!

She'd lost her husband. She couldn't lose her son, too.

She forced fear to the back of her thoughts and focused instead on how to save Neal. The army *had* to take action now. She flicked through the contact list on the phone to the number for Rear Detachment.

To her great relief, the same husky-voiced woman answered.

"Sergeant Stuart, this is Tawny Lindholm. We've talked several times about my son, Sergeant Neal Lindholm."

"Yes, ma'am, I remember." Noise rustled in the background, then Stuart came back on the line. "Mrs. Lindholm, I'm sorry there's no easy way to tell you this. Your son has been taken prisoner by insurgents."

God, no.

Army confirmation made it official. Tawny squeezed her eyes tight. Pinwheels of light whirled behind her lids. "Yes, I know. I was calling to tell you I received a text message from him."

"Ma'am, could you read the message to me, please, and the number it originated from?"

Tawny repeated the terrifying words, recited the number, then asked, "What does he mean about details? Will they ask for a ransom?"

The sergeant remained silent long enough that Tawny thought the connection must have dropped. Finally, Stuart spoke, "Mrs. Lindholm, are you aware of the official US policy about negotiations with terrorists?"

She gripped the phone tightly. "Yes."

"The government does not pay ransom. But be assured, we are on it. I will keep you informed. Can you be reached at the number you're calling from?"

"Yes, yes, any time, day or night." She disconnected and let her pounding head rest in her hands.

What did "on it" mean? A rescue attempt? Maybe. They wouldn't share details with her. But she feared Neal might sink into the swirling whirlpool of secrecy that surrounded his work only to come home in a coffin.

Tawny had to be prepared to act on her own, not depend on the army.

She ran through her options. Only $40,000 left of the cash after paying for the motel and bounced checks. They—whoever *they* were—would surely demand more than that for ransom. How could she get enough money? The feds had seized her bank accounts.

The house was free and clear, but getting a loan against it would take time. How long would the kidnappers allow before they hurt Neal?

She knew better than to ask the treacherous bank for help. Lupe Garza, the loan officer, had sneaked the thumb drive to her at risk of her job and arrest, but Tawny knew the woman dared not take even greater chances by lending her money. Besides, considering how the coldblooded manager, Hyslop, had treated poor Margaret, he would never approve a loan. Worse, he'd turn Tawny in to the feds and enjoy doing it.

She racked her brain to think of someone, anyone she could borrow money from.

Other banks wouldn't touch her—not with frozen accounts and the specter of probable arrest hanging over her.

Virgie?

Even after working fifteen years as a doctor, Virgie complained about still paying down her student-loan debt. She owned a condo with a hefty mortgage against it, and a nice SUV, whose payments sucked out a lot of her income. She was the poorest doctor Tawny had ever known.

Still, there was no one else to ask.

Tawny tapped Virgie's cell number. It instantly went to voice mail. Probably she turned it off at work. Next, Tawny tried the office number and told the receptionist it was an emergency.

Virgie came on the line within moments. "What's the matter, baby?"

"Virg, I may need a lot of money, fast. To save Neal. Can you help me?"

"How much?"

"I don't know yet. He's been abducted."

"Jesus! Have you called the FBI?"

Tawny gritted her teeth till her jaw ached. "I can't. He's somewhere in the Middle East."

"Won't the army do anything?"

"I've called them, but they refuse to pay ransoms. Virgie, please, I need money."

A heavy silence followed. "Sweetheart, I'll give you what I can, but it isn't much. Maybe a few grand. My credit cards are all maxed out. I've been spending too much on retail therapy."

If the situation hadn't been so dire, Tawny would have laughed out loud. Instead, she tried to swallow the boulder stuck in her throat. "OK. Thanks."

"Tawny, what is going on?"

She shook her head in defeat, as if Virgie could see her through the phone. "I wish I knew." She broke the connection.

Dead end.

Kit?

He appeared to be making a good living at the law firm. He'd loved Dwight like a father and treated Neal like a younger brother. She called his office and got through to him immediately, thank goodness.

"Kit, Neal sent me a text. He's been abducted. I may need money to pay a ransom, and the bank froze my accounts. Can you help me? Please?"

Silence dragged out for a long time. When Kit finally spoke, he asked, "Did you talk with the attorney I referred you to?"

"No! I've tried, but he's in court and not returning my calls. Kit, I'm desperate. I don't know how much the kidnappers will demand, but I'm damn near broke with the feds tying up my money. I need help."

Another long pause. Too long. "Tawny, I told you this is out of my area of expertise. I don't want to advise you about a sensitive legal matter that I don't have proper knowledge of."

She pounded the mattress. Didn't he understand? Neal's life was at stake. She didn't care about his legal expertise. She needed help. "Can you lend me money, Kit? I wouldn't ask if I wasn't desperate. I've got to save Neal."

Why didn't he answer? What was he thinking? Why the hesitation?

"Look, Kit, if you're worried about getting the money back, I promise I'll find a way to pay you. I'll sign over the deed to my house. I'll get a job, six jobs, whatever it takes."

He heaved a weary sigh. "Tawny, it's more complicated than that. Don't you know that kidnappers rarely let a victim go, at least not alive? That's why the government refuses to ransom captured Americans. Neal knew that risk when he joined the army."

His words felt like another kick in the stomach. A sob choked her. "No!" She let the phone fall to the bed and doubled over in anguish. Not Neal. Not her child. They couldn't kill her son. Somehow she had to find a way to save him.

Kit's faint voice sounded tinny out of the dropped cell. "Tawny, are you still there? Talk to me."

She picked up the phone. "I'm here."

"Listen to me. You need help. You're in deeper than I can handle. You may even be in a worse situation than my colleague in Billings can handle. You need to turn yourself in. Do you still have the card from that guy with Homeland Security, Maximillion Grosvenor? I think you should get a hold of him and tell him the whole story, including about Neal. Federal agencies cooperate with each other better than they used to. He'll interface with the State Department, the CIA, the big guns. Let the pros handle it."

Was Kit crazy? "You can't be serious. You expect me to throw myself on the mercy of the same people that already found me guilty of a crime they didn't even bother to tell me about? They've stolen my money, money Dwight and I worked hard for and paid taxes on. I'm supposed to trust government thugs to get my son back safe?" Her desperation changed to rage. "Forget it, Kit. I'm sorry I bothered you."

She disconnected, jumped up from the bed, and paced, fists clenched, teeth grinding.

Struck out. The only two people who might lend her money were unable or unwilling. She might have to rob the damn bank to get her money back.

The revolver chafed against her hip bone.

Rob a bank?

If that was the only way to pay the ransom, maybe she should think about it. What did she have to lose? They already treated her like a criminal. She'd probably end up in prison anyway since they were so sure she was guilty.

But if that helped Neal, so what? If she lost her son, life was useless.

She hugged herself, trying to stop the shaking. On legs stiff as boards, she stalked to the bathroom to blow her nose and splash water on her blotchy face. To the reflection in the mirror, she hissed, "Get a grip on yourself! You're losing it. You can't help Neal if you go off the rails."

She couldn't shortchange a vending machine, let alone rob a bank. Her shooting skill was limited to punching tiny holes in the black circle of a paper target. She couldn't hold a gun on a human being. Kit was right—she was in over her head.

A knock on the door. She grabbed the revolver from under the pillow, hurried across the room, and looked out the peephole.

Kahlil stood there, holding a bouquet of daffodils and tulips.

She opened the door. As soon as he saw her expression, he dropped the flowers and gripped her arms.

"What is it? What has happened?"

She pulled back and pointed at the phone lying on the bed. "Neal."

He picked it up, then looked at her with a silent question.

"Read the text."

He studied the message with a deepening frown. "This is very bad."

She sank to the bed and he sat beside her, arms and thighs touching. "I don't know what to do. How can I help my son?"

"Let us think this through logically. We do not know for certain what they want. He said he will call with 'details.'"

"*Details* has to mean a ransom demand. They'll want money. What else could they want?"

"You are probably correct." He squeezed her leg. "But we must have patience. We will not know until they contact you again."

She scrubbed her hands together. "I tried to raise cash, but I'm hitting dead ends. My house is free and clear, but I'm afraid that with the seizure, the feds will tie it up, too. No bank will make me a loan if I'm arrested."

"Is money all?"

"What do you mean?" She studied the concerned furrow of his brow, the pursed lips under his mustache.

One shoulder lifted. "If all you require is money, I make an excellent living. I have a good deal of money. I will give it to you."

His open expression made her think of the simplistic way a young child solved problems, naively unaware of adult complications and consequences. His willingness made her heart swell to bursting. "Oh, Kahlil, that is unbelievably generous of you. But you hardly know me. You can't just give me . . ." Then she started choking.

"Shh, shh," he whispered, rubbing her back. "Listen to me, my treasure." He cupped her face. "If money would have made the difference to save my wife and daughter, do you not think I would have thrown it at the doctor with both hands? If money will rescue your son and save you from a broken heart, I will throw it with both hands. Please accept it. If you do not, my heart will break again."

She gazed into his green eyes—tender, compassionate, full of love.

Destiny, fate, whatever it was, brought this man into her life during her most desperate hours. How could she feel so tortured yet so blessed in the same instant?

Her voice quavered. "I'll pay you back, I promise."

He closed his eyes and waved her off, shaking his head. "Let us not worry about that now. Let us take care of this moment's problems, OK? I thought of something I should do to keep anyone from tracking you."

Her earlier idea came back. "Disable the GPS?"

He smiled. "Very good. You are becoming more conversant with Lucifer." He took the phone and swiped various screens, changing settings. "When you do make calls," he cautioned, "move several miles away from the motel so cell towers do not triangulate on this location."

"I'll need my car."

"Later we will drive back to town and pick it up."

He continued to fiddle with the phone, making more adjustments Tawny didn't follow. No matter how he tried to reassure her, the damn smartphone still baffled her. Why did strange screens pop up, asking her to activate apps she didn't recognize or want? Why did bizarre tones—gongs, chirps, jingles—sound off without apparent reason?

"I don't know how you do it," she lamented as he flicked from one function to another so quickly her eyes couldn't keep up. "I'll never figure it out."

He gave her a lopsided smile. "Yes, you will. You are not accustomed to technology, that is all. Besides, I am here to rescue you from Lucifer's antics." He stroked her cheek. "Do not worry."

She sighed. "I can't help it. That instrument of the devil is my only lifeline to Neal. If it does something I don't understand, or I screw up an urgent message, I could cause him to be killed."

"You must not think that way. The most important functions are call and text. You know how to do those. I will help you with anything else."

"What if you're at work when he contacts me?"

"I will be close by. Do not worry."

* * *

The irony of naming the phone Lucifer amused Kahlil. If only she knew.

He admired Tawny's graceful sway as she crossed the room to the window. She stared out at the mountains while he worked on her phone.

The device transmitted video and audio that he remotely activated. The video camera had proved less useful than anticipated because the phone usually stayed in her pocket or pointed at her kitchen ceiling while it charged. In the future, he would not bother with the video option.

Besides, the audio had been more than adequate for tracking her activities as well as her mood. When she talked on the phone, or face-to-face, he heard conversations perfectly, played through the hearing aid device he wore. When she cried, or sang along with the car radio, or cursed, or talked to her dead husband, he knew. The monitoring of her mood cued him to the optimal times to withdraw and be unavailable or appear when she was most desperate.

Her early conversations about him with her physician friend had been endearing, a charming diversion from his serious preparatory work. How many men, he mused, enjoyed the rare opportunity of secretly listening to a woman's honest opinion of them?

For a brief moment, he allowed himself to open the compartment in his mind where he contained his growing affection for Tawny. Her helplessness touched his heart. Maryam had never been dependent on him. He'd never felt the protective instinct toward his wife that he did for Tawny. Even as he maneuvered her into peril, he longed to shield her from pain.

But it could not be. He closed the compartment and returned to the task at hand.

With his phone, he sent a text: *Tamper now*.

Then he returned to Lucifer. Skimming the hidden call log, he noticed four attempted calls from Tillman Rosenbaum, the Billings attorney. Kahlil had already blocked incoming contact from those numbers. The longer the delay until Tawny received legal counsel, the more the noose tightened around her. To authorities, her actions appeared increasingly erratic and indicative of guilt.

"Kahlil." Tawny's voice pulled him from his reverie back to the motel room.

She stood silhouetted against the window with the backdrop of towering mountains. What a vision she was: slender, willowy, glossy braid tumbled over her shoulder, soft brown eyes, and a sweet expression.

A needle of regret pricked him.

Chapter 9: *Ojo*

Tawny stood at the window watching Kahlil, who was absorbed in thought, sitting on the bed, holding her smartphone. It was noon, and her stomach growled. Courts adjourned for lunch, and she hoped to get a hold of the Billings lawyer during recess. But to prevent her location from being tracked, she needed to leave the motel.

When she spoke his name, he looked up, startled, as if from a faraway planet. Then he smiled. "Yes?"

"I'd like to make a call, and I'm hungry."

He popped up off the bed. "Let us go, then." He handed the phone back to her. She donned her jacket to cover the revolver in her pocket. Outside the room, a Cadillac Escalade sat in the parking slot.

Tawny shook her head. "I can't believe they rented you another car."

A sheepish expression crossed Kahlil's face. "I had to go to a different agency." Once on the highway, he asked, "Where shall we go?"

"Back toward town. There are lots of places to eat between here and there. Do you think it would be OK to pick up the Jeep, too?"

He turned sideways. "You no longer trust my driving."

She chuckled. "I never did. But that's not why. You have to work, and I need to get around."

"You are welcome to use this car."

"That's not very handy for you."

He faced forward, frowning. "I'm thinking of the people who want to arrest you. They may have a bulletin out on the Jeep."

He was right. Should she rent a car? But that meant showing identification and using a credit card. Even if the agency accepted cash, she had to conserve money for Neal.

She needed advice on how to proceed. Slipping on her readers, she pulled the phone from her pocket and tapped the lawyer's number. "This is Tawny Lindholm. It's urgent I talk with Tillman Rosenbaum."

"Mrs. Lindholm!" the secretary exclaimed. "I've been trying to reach you. Mr. Rosenbaum wants to see you. He's making a trip to Helena tomorrow. Could you meet him there?"

A four-hour drive, but finally a chance to talk to him face-to-face. "Yes, I can do that. Tell me where and what time."

The secretary named a hotel near Fort Harrison and suggested eleven in the morning.

"I'll be there." Tawny hung up. For the first time in days, she'd made progress. Then she felt Kahlil staring at her. "I have to go to Helena tomorrow to meet a lawyer."

An odd expression crossed his face. "Helena? That is a long way."

She shrugged. "It's the only way to see him. The secretary said she's been trying to call me." She skimmed Lucifer's call log. No messages from Tillman Rosenbaum's number. Was the secretary lying, trying to cover for a boss who didn't return calls? Or maybe she'd called the home phone, and Tawny hadn't been there. Oh well, it didn't make any difference now that she had an appointment to meet him.

Kahlil's mouth pulled tight.

Why did he look so strange? He knew she needed help. "Kahlil, I have to find out where I stand, whether I'm going to be arrested, if he can get my money released. I can't stay in limbo like this. Not with Neal in danger."

Kahlil said nothing, but Tawny got the strong feeling he didn't approve. She waited several minutes, thinking he'd explain. When he remained silent, she asked, "What is it?"

He focused on driving. Finally he answered, "I have a great fear your hope will be disappointed."

"What hope?"

"That this attorney will be able to help you. Your son's situation is . . . precarious. Your own situation is grave. I do not wish to dash your hope, but I do not see a way this attorney can do anything to change these circumstances."

She huddled in the seat, pondering his words. For her whole life, she'd revered people with education: lawyers, doctors, accountants, professionals. They held the secret keys that unlocked knowledge she could never possibly gain. They knew the unseen powers behind the system. They had answers.

Yet when cancer struck Dwight, the specialists with many letters after their names had failed to find answers.

Now, beside her sat a man of education—a psychologist—who expressed doubt about her faith in another man of education—a lawyer. Whom should she believe?

She laid her hand on his shoulder. "I have to try. He's a specialist in government seizures and forfeitures. Even if he doesn't have all the answers, maybe he can tell me what my rights are, what the government can or can't do to me. I need to know."

He pressed her hand, then returned to steering the curves. "You will make the right decision."

* * *

So close. Kahlil had tried to postpone her contact with the Billings attorney. If only the delay could last one more day. Should he move up the timetable to prevent her from going to Helena? No, too many details still to complete. Not worth the risk of failure by rushing. Better to finish the job properly. After years of preparation, a day or two did not matter. Focus on the overall mission, not the minutia.

Should he shadow her to Helena? Not really necessary, as long as she kept the smartphone with her at all times, which he knew she would while waiting to hear from her son. Yet Kahlil hated to think of her away from his physical control with the plan this close to fruition. Unforeseen circumstances might arise. He had observed that phenomenon too often. No matter how well planned the plot, things went awry. A person took a shortcut and arrived at a meeting early . . . as Maryam had done, an instant before the drone strike.

If only she'd waited for him, she would have lived.

"Are you all right?"

* * *

Tawny studied the drawn line of Kahlil's mouth, the tightness of his jaw, his fingers clenched around the steering wheel. His color was strange. Under dark-olive skin, he looked ill.

"Are you all right?" she repeated.

His head jerked to face her. Even his beautiful green eyes looked glazed and flat. Then he blinked several times and smiled, his normal expression returning. "Forgive me for losing focus. A memory of my wife . . ."

Of course. Tawny supposed her own face sometimes underwent changes like that when she remembered Dwight. The pain inside breaking through to the surface. She squeezed his arm and smiled back in understanding.

They stopped for sandwiches, then continued to town. Kahlil drove around several blocks, circling Tawny's house. She recognized a few neighbors' cars, but most people were working at midday. No strangers stood out on the quiet streets. "Looks OK," she said.

Kahlil nodded. "I need to go home for a bit. After you get your car, text me and we will drive back to the motel. I will lag behind to see if anyone follows you."

"Good idea." She kissed him and got out of the big SUV in the alley behind her garage. She hurried through the gate toward the back door, hoping Starshine didn't spot her.

With Tawny's key in the lock, her neighbor's voice rang out. "Hi, Tawny!"

Damn. She half turned and waved, hoping to duck inside without interference, but Starshine had already trotted up behind her, stopping at the foot of the steps.

"Look what I brought you!" Starshine held out several ugly, misshapen pieces of metal that looked like beer cans a car had driven over. "It's my new design for a necklace and bracelet collection. Here, I want you to be the one to debut them." She thrust the junk toward Tawny.

"Starshine, I'm in a real hurry, I can't talk now. Later, OK?" She slipped inside the mudroom and closed the door in Starshine's face. The woman peered in, leaving greasy nose prints on the glass. Tawny closed the secondary door between the mudroom and kitchen, pulling curtains to block Starshine's view.

The feds didn't need to set up surveillance. They could just hire Starshine.

The house felt strange, as if she'd returned from a long trip. Was it only this morning she had packed to leave? Seemed like weeks ago.

In the bedroom closet, Tawny considered her one dressy suit, a navy-blue pinstripe with a cropped jacket and skintight pencil skirt, still in the dry cleaner's bag since Dwight's funeral. Emma had insisted Tawny buy it for the service, despite the outrageous cost, because "Daddy would want to see you looking this hot." *Hot* wasn't Tawny's idea of mourning attire, but if that comforted Emma, fine.

Now, meeting the lawyer, Tawny wanted to make a good impression. She pulled out the suit, with a lace silk camisole and navy pumps, to take with her.

She unplugged her laptop and stuffed it in a bag. The answering machine blinked, and she hit "Play." Two more calls about bounced checks. But no message from Tillman Rosenbaum. So his secretary had lied when she'd claimed he tried to call back. Oh well, Tawny would see him tomorrow.

Ready to leave, she checked for Starshine, lurking to pounce. The neighbor appeared to have given up. Tawny texted Kahlil and hurried to the garage with her bags and the suit, which she hung on the roll bar. She backed the Jeep out and drove down the alley. In the rearview mirror, she spotted Starshine staring after her.

At Kahlil's house, she slowed. He already waited in the Escalade and waved her on.

The trip went fine until she stopped for gas. Without a credit card, she needed to go inside the convenience store and pay cash. She handed the attendant forty dollars, then returned to the Jeep. A highway patrol cruiser pulled into the station and parked across the lot, facing her. Was he watching her? She debated whether to take the time to pump gas or just drive off, leaving behind the forty dollars. With money scarce, she decided to fill the tank. She peered between the pumps, trying to see the trooper, but sunlight glared on his windshield, blocking her view.

A short distance away, Kahlil's SUV idled on the shoulder while he used his phone.

"Hurry up, hurry up," she urged the pump under her breath. At $38.75, it clicked off. She jumped in the car and left without retrieving the change. Back on the highway, she watched her mirrors to see if the cruiser followed.

He did.

Within a quarter mile, he lit her up.

"Dammit to hell!" She immediately pulled to the shoulder and stopped. Was this the end? Would he arrest her, or worse, confiscate the smartphone, severing her only link to Neal?

Mouth sticky-dry and heart thudding against her ribs, she pulled the registration and insurance from the glove box and took her license out of her wallet. Two car lengths behind, the cruiser sat canted diagonally, half on the shoulder, half still in the lane, flashing strobes brighter than the Fourth of July. Seconds dragged to minutes. What was he waiting for?

The revolver! She quickly removed it from the pocket of her jacket and put it in the glove box, where it was legal. Not that it made any difference if he arrested her.

She flicked through the phone contact list, highlighting Tillman Rosenbaum's number. She knew she had the constitutional right to a phone call. Although, with the seizure of her money, she seemed to be coming up short on rights lately.

From the limited view of the Jeep's mirrors, Tawny couldn't see Kahlil. She didn't dare turn around for fear the trooper might interpret that as aggressive behavior.

At last, the man got out of his car. He was built like a weight lifter, sleeves tight over bulging biceps, shaven bald with sunglasses propped on his shiny forehead, about thirty, Neal's age. It was a small town; maybe he'd been one of her son's classmates.

"Afternoon, ma'am." He peered in the window, giving the once-over to both her and the interior.

She offered the paperwork. "Hi, how you doing?" She tried to sound casual but couldn't prevent the quiver in her voice.

His name tag read J. Yarborough, a name she didn't recognize as a friend of Neal's. The trooper accepted the documents, studied them, then returned to his car without a word.

Damn. She'd stayed just under the speed limit, signaled lane changes, drove like a little old lady on her way to church. She must have done something wrong to capture his attention . . . unless the feds had ordered an alert to pick her up. She should have rented a car or taken Kahlil up on the offer to borrow his.

Guilt had to be broadcasting from her like the cruiser's strobes. Not answering the door to the feds, hiding out at a motel, concealing money, packing a pistol. All these were the acts of a guilty person. She hadn't sought out the insane situation she found herself in, yet running away made her look suspicious at best, guilty at worst. The trooper's inner radar had to sense that.

The waiting, the suspense, her unknown fate was almost worse than being dragged out of the driver's seat and cuffed. Well, maybe not quite.

The trooper approached again, handing her paperwork back. "Mrs. Lindholm, the reason I stopped you is your right taillight is burned out."

"What?" Relief flushed through her like spring runoff. "Really? I didn't know."

He handed her a paper. "This is a warning for equipment violation, not a citation. As long as you get it fixed soon, there's no problem." Yet, even relating good news, his face remained stony. She sensed the warning covered far more than a taillight.

She accepted the paper. "I'll fix it right away. Thank you." *Thank you for not taking me to jail. Thank you for not searching till you found my gun. Thank you for not preventing me from trying to rescue my son.*

"You're welcome. Afternoon, Mrs. Lindholm." His voice sounded as chilly as his expression. No matter, as long as he let her go.

While she put the documents back, she watched the rearview mirror. The cruiser sat parked, strobes still beaming. *Go away, man. Catch speeders and drunks.*

The phone rang. Kahlil. She answered, "It's OK. Just a warning. I'm going to stop at an auto-parts store up ahead and get a replacement bulb."

"Good. I will stay behind and watch. Do not lead him to the motel. Keep driving around until he's no longer following you."

"Right." She disconnected.

Tawny started the Jeep, turned on the signal, and cautiously pulled into the lane. The trooper followed.

Her churning stomach screamed that this was more than a polite warning.

A memory flicked in her brain, from years before when she and Dwight still owned the repair shop. Two Spanish-speaking mechanics had squared off in the yard while other employees ringed them. Dwight had galloped out of the office, Tawny following. Fighting on the property was a firing offense he took seriously. Stepping between the men, he spoke Spanish in a low menacing voice, then touched the side of his eye with an index finger: *Ojo. I'm watching you.*

Looking in the rearview mirror at the highway patrol cruiser, she felt the warning heavy on her shoulders. *Ojo.*

Only she suspected this warning came from the feds, delivered courtesy of a state cop. *We know where you are. We can pick you up whenever we want.*

At any moment, an unmarked dark-blue Crown Vic might light her up.

Staying two miles under the speed limit, she drove to a nearby Napa store and pulled into the parking lot. The trooper continued on the highway, still regarding her as he passed by.

From under the rear seat of the Jeep, she dragged out Dwight's toolbox, found a Phillips screwdriver, and removed the red plastic lens cover.

The bulb wasn't burned out—it was missing.

She stared at the empty socket. Someone had purposely removed the bulb. To give cops an excuse to pull her over.

Her evil twin or the feds.

Feeling even sicker, she went inside the store and bought a replacement bulb. She installed it, screwed the lens cover back on, and stared out at passing cars. The Jeep might have more problems, invisible ones. They—whoever *they* were—might have put in a tracking device. Paranoia gnawed at her raw stomach.

She drove through Columbia Falls, spotting Kahlil's car parked at a bank. He fell in behind, leaving a couple of blocks between them. No cops or unmarked sedans in sight. They continued through Columbia Heights into Bad Rock Canyon.

On the shoulder, ravens pecked at the insides of the dead deer Kahlil had hit. Tawny shuddered at the memory of shooting it.

She crossed the river bridge into Hungry Horse and passed the motel, keeping a constant look out. At the supermarket, she turned in, waiting and watching for several minutes before backtracking. Instead of parking in front of her room, she went around behind the motel, out of sight of the highway, and stopped near a dumpster.

Kahlil parked beside her and got out. "Good idea." He nodded in approval.

She gripped his arm. "Someone removed the taillight. I think it was intentional. To get the cops to stop me."

He frowned. "I do not want to leave you like this, but I must go to work. Unforeseen problem. Will you be all right?"

She nodded.

"I may not be back until quite late. Call me if you hear from your son." He kissed her, a lingering one that made her tingle in spite of her tension. Then he left.

In the motel room, Tawny hung up the denim jacket with the cash sewn inside. To prepare for the trip to Helena, she packed her laptop and the thumb drive in the now-empty tote bag. She pulled the plastic bag from her dressy suit, ready for the morning. Jeep gassed. New taillight working. But what other unpredictable dangers lurked ahead? The spinning hamster wheel of her brain went into overdrive.

She lay on the bed and clicked through TV channels, seeking a mindless respite from nagging fear. Instead, she spotted a news ticker on the bottom of the screen: "Five soldiers missing in Afghanistan."

Heart pounding, she grabbed the phone and hit the Rear Detachment number. It rang eight times until a recording came on. "We apologize for the inconvenience, but a communication blackout has been ordered. Designated family members will be updated as soon as confirmations are available. At the tone, please leave your name and number and your service member's identifying information."

Communication blackout. Tawny knew what that meant. When a soldier died, all information was shut down until families were notified in person. Death notifications never came by phone. A bereavement team might be ringing her doorbell at this very minute. Should she rush home?

Voice quavering, she stammered out the required information, adding, "I am away from my home. If my son has been . . ." She couldn't say the word. "Please, please call me at this number."

Tawny ripped through TV channels, seeking more details. Except for the cryptic ticker line, news anchors kept busy debating fashion trends for the royal wedding. Enraged, she threw the remote across the room. It smacked against the wall, fell in two pieces, and clattered to the floor. Double A batteries rolled loose.

Dammit, now she'd owe the motel for a new remote.

The clicking signal for an incoming text startled her. She grabbed her readers and peered at the screen. From Neal!

Ransom 250K. Details to follow 48 hours.

A quarter of a million dollars.

An impossible amount of money, but . . . the ransom demand meant Neal was still alive! Captured, but gloriously alive. Thank you, God!

But . . . not necessarily. Horror rising inside her, she realized anyone could type a text on his phone. There was no way to confirm that Neal was alive unless she actually spoke to him. She might be ransoming his corpse.

No! She couldn't allow herself to think like that. He had to be alive. She had to move forward with that belief. But before she turned over any money, she would insist on hearing his voice. If she found a way to raise the money . . .

Forty-eight hours.

She remembered Kahlil's offer. But he might not have that much. Even rich people would be hard-pressed to come up with a mountain of cash so fast. If he was that wealthy, could he collect it in forty-eight hours?

Her conscience chafed at the idea of taking money from him, as kind and generous as he'd been, when she had no way of paying it back. At age fifty, with her pathetic job prospects, she'd never live long enough to earn $250,000.

The only way to be fair was signing over her house to him. She had to pray the feds couldn't attach it. More than ever, she needed to talk to Tillman Rosenbaum. Tomorrow.

She checked the time. Seven thirty, dusk outside. She tapped Kahlil's number and listened to ringing. More ringing. He had always answered her before. Finally an automated voice offered to take a message.

"Kahlil, I got another text from Neal." She hesitated. Should she tell him the ransom amount? He might need every minute in the next two days to gather the funds. Yet she couldn't bring herself to make such an outrageous request to a recording. *Hi, this is Tawny, I need a quarter million dollars in forty-eight hours. See ya.* She decided no. "Please call me."

The room shrank with each step she paced.

She called the Rear Detachment number again and listened to the same message about the communication blackout. "Sergeant Stuart, this is Tawny Lindholm. I just received another text from Neal. The kidnappers are demanding two hundred fifty thousand dollars in forty-eight hours. Please call me."

Kit's and Stuart's warnings came back to her about the government's policy of refusing to negotiate with terrorists. The call to the family liaison was probably a waste of time. Even more foreboding, Kit had said kidnappers usually killed their victims anyway.

Utter helplessness made her legs weak. No way could she reach her son, rescue him, and destroy the bastards. Nothing to do but pray.

And answer the text. Neal and the kidnappers waited for her response. She rehearsed answers in her head.

I'm trying.

Too wishy-washy. Needed to sound positive, that she *would* pay, that his life *would* be spared.

Working on it.

Better but vague, indefinite.

I will do anything.

More positive, but it sounded too desperate, begging. The kidnappers might even increase the amount if they believed she had given in to their demands too easily.

She couldn't negotiate worth a damn. That had been Dwight's forte. Why wasn't he here with her? She flopped facedown on the mattress, pounding the pillows till her arms ached with fatigue.

Finally the right words came to her. She tapped out the return message: *I will have it in 48 hours. Hang in there, son.*

* * *

Tawny's anguish played over the audio monitor to Kahlil's earpiece. Her plaintive cries to her husband, her son, to the kidnappers, to God, wrenched his chest. When she'd called him, he longed to answer but resisted. Unavailability at a crucial time played a vital part of the plan.

Tawny's panicked state of mind needed to be maintained, with desperation at a maximum. The traffic stop by the trooper ratcheted up her paranoia, as Kahlil had intended when he gave the instruction to tamper with her car. He could not allow her rationality to raise questions or doubts. She needed to be completely malleable and suggestible. When he stepped in with the solution, her gratitude would overwhelm all judgment.

The kidnapping was a hoax. The author of the pleading texts was not her son, but himself, as he increased the pressure with each new message. Her calls to the army had been redirected to his colleague, posing as the family liaison.

The surveillance report he'd received yesterday confirmed Tawny's son lay relaxing on a beach in Dubai, entertaining beautiful young women during his leave, perfectly safe and quite content.

Tawny's worry was based solely on an illusion.

But he'd underestimated the difficulty of monitoring her pain. He could not bear to listen any longer to the keening sound of a mother's heart breaking. He removed the earpiece.

Chapter 10: Ransom

A soft knock on the motel room door woke Tawny from fitful nightmares. Four fifteen in the morning. She slipped the revolver from under her pillow, put on a robe, and peered through the peephole.

Kahlil.

She replaced the gun before opening the door. He hadn't said anything, but the weapon seemed to worry him.

He looked weary, eyes sunken in dark shadows, stubble thick, vertical lines cutting his cheeks, but his smile radiated with joy at seeing her. He kissed her deeply. "I am sorry to wake you."

"Doesn't matter. I wasn't sleeping much anyway." She closed and double-locked the door behind him.

He took her hand. "Your son?"

She sank onto the bed and handed him the phone with Neal's text. Somehow she couldn't bring herself to speak the ransom amount to his face any more than she'd been able to leave it on his voice mail.

He read the screen. "Forty-eight hours," he murmured.

"Less than forty left." As she waited for his reaction to the amount, her heart jolted with erratic beats.

He encircled her shoulders with one arm, pulling her close. "My poor darling."

The question caught in her throat. It must be too much. Why doesn't he say so? *No, I don't have two hundred fifty thousand dollars to give you.*

He pulled his own phone from his pocket. Removing his arm from her, he swiped, tapped, and flicked through various screens. Without her glasses, she couldn't follow, but the blurry images appeared completely different from her phone. Using only his thumbs, he typed so quickly she marveled at his dexterity. She would never operate Lucifer with such ease.

The question hung between them. She longed for his answer yet dreaded it.

She forced herself to sit still while every fiber, every nerve, jumped under her skin. One eyelid began to twitch. The colored lights of his screen twirled like a kaleidoscope in her flickering vision. Her stomach spasmed, threatening to revolt. She fought back nausea.

Several minutes later, he shut down the phone. "There," he said, setting it on the bedside table.

The suspense tortured her. She had to ask, but all that came out was a croak. "What?"

He turned to her with a casual air, as if he'd spent the last minutes playing a video game. "It is done."

"What is?" she choked.

"I have put the wheels in motion to marshal various accounts with different banks. The money will be available quite soon."

She stared at him, disbelief nearly slapping her to the floor. "You mean, you're going to pay the ransom?"

"Of course."

"But it's so much. I didn't expect you to . . ."

He regarded her with his head slightly cocked, frowning. "Did I not tell you I would? Do you think I would break my promise to you?" He put his arms around her, pulling her to his chest. "My treasure, if your son can be saved, I will do anything in my power to make it happen."

Tears gushed from her eyes. Her heart, so constricted seconds before, felt ready to burst with joy. She sobbed until his wet shirt clung to his skin.

"Shh, shh," he whispered. "You must stop crying so I can take a shower and shave off these terrible whiskers." He rubbed his jaw.

She clasped his prickly face between her hands. "They are not terrible. They're beautiful whiskers." And she kissed them all over until her lips were raw. Pain didn't matter. Only saving Neal mattered.

Chapter 11: Kid, I'm Gonna Make You a Star

Tillman Rosenbaum swept into the hotel lobby like a swash-buckling actor from a Cecil B. DeMille spectacular. Tight black curls crowned his head. Well over six and a half feet tall. His jaw jutted forward, lower teeth in front of the upper ones, like a narrow-faced bulldog. A three-piece suit fit his lanky frame flawlessly, the color a garish shade of gold. The only wardrobe accessory missing was a cape.

An underling trailed after him, taking notes on an electronic tablet.

The lawyer's baritone voice boomed and long arms gestured as he reeled off requirements for a conference room. "Seating for a hundred, minimum, check? You verified gluten-free options with the caterer, right? Are the badges ready for prepays? Is credit card processing available for walk-ins? I don't want another screw-up like that bar luncheon. Two screens for PowerPoint . . ."

Tawny watched from an inconspicuous table in a quiet corner, nursing a latte. When she'd arrived at ten thirty, she spotted Rosenbaum's name and photo on a scrolling video sign as the keynote speaker for a CLE luncheon—whatever *CLE* meant.

People clotted in groups, chatting, chins lifted with confidence, wearing name tags with lots of initials, like *JD*, *LLM*, *JSD*. Most of their outfits looked as if they'd just finished a tennis set or nine holes at the country club.

Tawny had worn her elegant funeral suit and heels, hoping to make a good impression on the lawyer, but now she felt conspicuously overdressed among the casual–chic crowd in snake-print sneakers and designer jeans. She'd stuffed her cash-laden denim jacket in the tote bag with her laptop and wished she could change into it to blend better with the surroundings.

In the midst of such a high-powered group, Rosenbaum held a place at the top of the food chain. How could Tawny afford him? If the lawyer's fees gobbled up all the money the feds had seized from her, how did that help? She'd be broke either way. Was this a wasted trip?

Rosenbaum finished with the assistant and made his way across the lobby, stopping for a few words with several groups before striding straight toward her. How had he recognized her?

She rose from the table and held out her hand, looking up at him . . . way, way up. Being tall herself and wearing heels, she rarely needed to crane her neck back this far. "Mr. Rosenbaum–"

Nearly black eyes snapped in his long, thin face. "Mrs. Lindholm, why are you blocking my calls?"

"Sorry?"

"I'm squeezing you in as an accommodation to Kit Albritton, who, by the way, holds you in very high regard. If you're my client, I need to get in touch with you at all times. If you don't accept my calls, I can't assist you."

"Mr. Rosenbaum, I'm not sure what you mean. I called you and left messages, but I never received any calls *from* you."

"My point exactly."

His rapid-fire accusations unnerved her. Had this trip been a big mistake? "I have my phone with me at all times. My son has been kidnapped. The phone is my only link to him. If you or anyone else calls, I answer."

"Very well. Make sure my number is unblocked."

"I will." What a jerk. No wonder people hated lawyers. But unfortunately she needed this guy's help.

"Let's find somewhere private." He strode away while Tawny rushed to gather her tote bag, following him down a hall to a small annex. When they were inside, he closed the door. "Now, Albritton brought me up to speed on your situation. Sizeable cash deposits started to appear in your bank account, and you claim you don't know where they came from. However, the bank has video showing a woman who looks exactly like you making those deposits. Is that correct so far?"

"I didn't make those deposits, and the woman isn't me." She hurried to unpack her laptop, but he flicked his fingers, *don't bother*.

The man hardly paused to breathe. "A few days ago, this woman who looks like you withdrew one hundred thousand dollars in a cashier's check payable to you. At that point, FinCEN froze the account due to suspicious activity. In addition, your unrelated assets and a credit card were also frozen. Correct?"

"Who's FinCEN?"

"Financial Crimes Enforcement Network."

"I don't know who froze everything."

"Did you receive notice beforehand that your accounts were going to be seized?"

Tawny pulled the official, but incomprehensible, letter from her bag. "The bank manager was supposed to give this to me but held onto it for several days. Long enough for my checks to bounce all over town. If I hadn't gone to the bank, I don't know how long he would have kept it without telling me."

Rosenbaum gave it a quick glance, then resumed his machine-gun questions. "Did you contact Maximillion Grosvenor?"

"No."

"Any contact from any federal or state law enforcement entity?"

"No. Uh, well, I got stopped by a highway patrolman yesterday."

"Why?"

"He claimed it was a burned-out taillight, but he kept checking me out and following me. I had a strong feeling it was more—"

"All right, so no contact at all—"

"Wait a minute, please." Tawny felt breathless, intimidated by the impatient, towering lawyer. "The bulb was gone. Someone must have taken it out so I'd get stopped. Also, someone broke into my house, searching, getting into my computer."

"Did they take the cash you withdrew?"

Tawny's tote bag suddenly felt weighted with lead and guilt. She shook her head. "I took that money to get the bank's attention because they weren't taking my complaint seriously. But now that I'm dead broke because of the seizure, I'm damn glad I have that cash."

"Fine, fine, but what about any contact from—"

Tawny held up her hand, trying to push back against his tidal wave of questions. "Please . . . wait."

He beckoned impatiently, head thrusting forward. "Yeah?"

"Two men came to my house a couple of days ago. I think they might have been feds."

"Yeah, yeah, so what happened?"

Heat flushed her cheeks, and she looked at her navy pumps.

"What? Come on, dammit!" he snapped.

She swallowed. "I hid. Didn't answer the door."

Her cowardice shamed her but didn't appear to bother Rosenbaum. He grunted. "Wish some of my other clients hadn't answered *their* doors." Then he rushed forward again. "You said your son has been kidnapped?"

"He's a sergeant in army intelligence. Last I knew, he was in Afghanistan. He's been abducted and is being held for a quarter million dollars' ransom."

"Who contacted you?"

"He did, by text on the phone."

"Have you spoken with him?"

"No, just the texts."

"No contact from the kidnappers? Or the army? His commanding officer? The State Department?"

"I called the family liaison emergency number. She confirmed his abduction, but when I called again, a recording said there was a communication blackout in place. The army does that when a soldier is"—she bit her lip and forced out the word—"is k-killed until family is notified."

Rosenbaum yanked a cell phone from his vest. "What's that number?"

Tawny scrolled through her contact list and read it off to him.

He placed the call, thumping the heel of a Gucci loafer while it rang. A frown bunched his forehead. "Listen." He tapped the speaker on.

A recording said the number was not in service. She stared at the lawyer in disbelief. "Are you sure you dialed the right—"

He grabbed her phone and compared it with his. Same number.

"What . . ." Her question trailed off into bewilderment.

He glared at her. "Mrs. Lindholm, you're being shaken down."

"What do you mean?"

"You. Are. Being. Shaken. Down." His tone rasped with exasperation. "Your son may or may not be kidnapped. Someone may be posing as your son. In fact, your son may be the one trying to extort money from you. Right now, what you have is bupkes."

"I don't understand."

"You are a patsy, a dupe, a mark, a pigeon."

Each insult felt like a slap across Tawny's face. "I'm scared for my child. Someone is setting me up to look like a criminal, but

I'm not. I don't deal drugs or launder money or cheat on my taxes. I'm an innocent victim."

"Isn't that what I just said?"

She slumped against the wall. If this lawyer was supposed to be on her side, why did she feel like she'd been worked over by a thug? "Can you help me?"

"About your son's supposed abduction? No. In fact, hell no. Emphatically, hell no. About the seizure of your property without due process? Maybe. I'll call Max and get back to you."

"Max?"

He flicked the business card. "We're old buddies. I've defended damn near every asset forfeiture case he's prosecuted since the Patriot Act."

"Mr. Rosenbaum—"

"Call me Tilly."

If not for the critical circumstances, Tawny would have burst out laughing. A better nickname would be Attila the Hun. "I don't know how I'm going to pay you. All my money is tied up, except for forty thousand dollars in cash I withdrew—"

"For God's sake, don't talk to me about that."

She recalled Kit's point about unclean hands and how he'd refused to advise her to do something illegal. Maybe Rosenbaum didn't want to know the source of his fee. "All right. But I'm not rich. I haven't worked in years, but I'll get a job. I'll make payments. I just want you to know up front."

Again, the dismissive flick of his hand.

She noticed a gold wedding band, and a fleeting question occurred to her: What kind of woman could put up with *him*?

"If all this takes is a few phone calls, forget it. If it turns into a federal case"—he cracked a wry grin at his joke—"I'll do it pro bono. If you're as squeaky clean as Albritton says you are, if you really are the innocent victim of overzealous prosecution, you could be my poster-child case for the Supreme Court to overturn the Patriot Act."

What the hell was he talking about? Poster child? Supreme Court? She had the uncomfortable feeling his proclamations were the lawyer's version of a promise from a scummy modeling agent. *Kid, I'm gonna make you a star.*

He started toward the door.

"Mr. Rosenbaum—Tilly, one more question?"

"Yeah?"

"Can they take my house? It's free and clear, worth about two hundred fifty thousand dollars."

He paused. "The same amount as the ransom?"

"Yes?" What was his point?

Dark eyes bored into her. "You aren't going to pay the ransom, are you?"

He didn't understand being a mother. Otherwise, he wouldn't hurl insults like *pigeon* and *mark*. "Neal is my son. End of story."

For the first time, Rosenbaum's harsh, aggressive expression softened. "You're a very nice lady, Mrs. Lindholm, but don't be a stupid one." He started through the door but turned abruptly. "Hey, why don't you stay for lunch? My talk happens to be on seizures and forfeitures. You might find it interesting."

Tawny hesitated. The last place she wanted to be was in a room full of lawyers. "Uh, how much does it cost?"

He pulled a face and waved his hand. "You're my guest."

"Well, OK. Thank you."

Back in the lobby, she returned to the same secluded table, trying to sort out the rude, abrupt conversation. Kit was a lawyer, but he sure didn't act like this guy. In less than five minutes, Rosenbaum had insulted her, accused her son of extorting money from his mother, offered to drag her in front of the Supreme Court, and invited her to lunch. What the hell?

But Kit, whom she knew and trusted, had also said don't pay the ransom. Both were so emphatic about it. They were smart, educated, and certainly more experienced in such matters than she was. She needed to consider their advice carefully.

Tawny put on her readers and pulled the smartphone from her pocket, tapping the number for "Rear D." The same communication blackout message played as before. Something weird was going on. The army didn't shut down emergency contact lines. So why had Rosenbaum gotten a disconnect recording from *his* cell?

Next, she brought up the screen that showed Neal's three texts.

Mom, W/c if I can. In trouble. Pray 4 me.

Abducted. Need help bad. W/s details soon.

Ransom 250K. Details to follow 48 hours.

Three short messages that had turned her world upside down.

She tried to suppress her emotions, her mother's instincts, and analyze the texts logically. How would Kit or Rosenbaum assess them? Rosenbaum suggested the messages might not even be from Neal.

Was he right?

Someone posing as Neal could be targeting her for money.

She needed to hear his voice. Then she'd know. She tapped his number. It rang fifteen times, then clicked off again, dead. Still no voice mail option.

She reread the texts. Would Neal ask her to pray for him? She and Dwight had raised him with the Ten Commandments and the Golden Rule, although they didn't attend church. In college, he'd actively questioned the existence of God and decided to be an atheist. One night at the dinner table, when he'd come home on leave after his first tour, he blew up. He'd shouted there was no God because, if there was, he would never allow the evil that Neal had witnessed. Dwight had slung his arm around Neal's shoulder and guided him downstairs to the den, where they talked for hours with the door closed, and both got roaring drunk on Canadian Club.

Asking her to pray for him didn't sound like Neal. Yet Dwight always said there were no atheists in foxholes. In crisis, Neal might have changed his mind.

Need help bad. Did that sound like Neal? Not really, but communicating by text created new abbreviations, clipped phrases, and slang. With Tawny's dyslexia, she liked texting's shorthand. But Neal had graduated from college with a minor in journalism, so he spoke and wrote with precision. She remembered struggling to read one of his published essays, thirteen pages long, but became bogged down after only two pages, embarrassed because she didn't understand what her son was writing about. Somehow *need help bad* didn't sound like Neal.

The last message resembled a terse, no-nonsense business demand that a creditor might send. Neal knew her assets were pretty slim after Dwight's death. He would know the value of the house matched the ransom, as Rosenbaum had pointed out. But

Neal wasn't aware of her troubles with the feds or that even the ownership of her house could be in jeopardy.

Maybe Rosenbaum was right—someone had to be posing as Neal or forcing him to make the demand.

She almost wished the third possibility the lawyer had suggested were true—Neal was trying to extort money from her. Only that choice meant her son was safe. But he'd never do that.

Rosenbaum might be wrong. What if Neal was tied up with a hood over his head in some filthy hovel, guns pointed at him? Just because the Rear Detachment number hadn't worked for Rosenbaum didn't mean it was bogus. From Dwight's and Neal's stories, she knew the army was capable of screwing up a perfectly foolproof system.

Flipping through the log, she noticed the calls she'd made to Tillman Rosenbaum's office and remembered his accusation that she blocked his calls. Could Lucifer be pulling another stunt to confound her? Kahlil had showed her various icons to push when she got stuck. The only problem was she never remembered how she'd backed herself into a corner in the first place. She tried tapping on various prompts. An unfamiliar screen popped up with Rosenbaum's numbers displayed. Below it, a box was checked: *Disconnect incoming.*

Did that mean her phone rejected his calls?

Kahlil had explained sometimes settings changed accidentally from jostling around in her pocket. "You've heard of *butt dialing*?" he'd asked with a mischievous smile. She'd laughed, but that only gave her another reason to hate the smartphone. If it disabled functions without you knowing it, that sounded like a big fat inconvenience—anything but smart.

She unchecked the box. At lunch, she'd ask Rosenbaum to make a test call and see if unchecking fixed the problem. That is, if she ever got a word in edgewise.

People clustered at the entrance to the ballroom. Tawny drifted over to join them. Under her dressy suit, nervous perspiration made the silk camisole stick to her back. Around her, lawyers chatted. From listening, she figured out *CLE* meant *Continuing Legal Education.* Other snippets of conversation touched on Rosenbaum's upcoming presentation.

"The legislature needs to address policing for profit. Cops make a fat commission when they turn over assets to the feds. Too damn tempting."

"It's armed robbery. If dopers do it, it's illegal; if the feds do it, it's legal. The net effect is identical."

"Tillman's a showboat, but he gets the job done."

"I'll endure anything to get a day out of the office, even listening to this prick. At least he's entertaining."

At the door to the ballroom, a woman checking off names directed Tawny to Table Three, near the podium. She wove among round linen-covered tables set with sparkling glasses, candles, and fresh flowers. Despite the elegant surroundings, even the women attorneys wore jeans or casual gear, as if on their way to yoga. Maybe lawyers only dressed up to appear in court. Several offered polite, curious smiles and leaned their heads together to speak softly. She thought, *They're probably wondering who this overdressed woman is.*

Rosenbaum engaged in intense noisy debate with a group near table three. Tawny slid into a seat, wishing herself invisible, regretting that she'd accepted his invitation. She sipped water and pretended to read the program notes. When he lowered his lanky body into the chair beside her, she almost jumped out of the way.

His long arm waved at a server. When she approached, he demanded a bowl of hummus instead of butter, not even saying *please*. Then he turned to Tawny. "I called Max. After my presentation, we're going to his office."

"Where?"

"Here in Helena. Might as well get this taken care of today, save us both another trip." He must have noticed her look of surprise because he added, "You not leaving right away, are you?"

"I—I guess not." Nothing required her to rush home. It didn't really matter where she was when Neal contacted her. If Rosenbaum got the feds off her back, the trip was worth it.

"Good." He reached into a basket of pita chips and dipped one in hummus, crunching while he continued to talk. "When we meet him, keep your mouth shut. Even if he asks you a direct question, don't answer. Let me handle it."

Fine with her. Rosenbaum seemed intimidating enough to handle a federal cop. "OK."

In her tote, the phone rang. She pulled it out to silence it. Kahlil. She'd talk to him later. But it reminded her of the blocked calls. "Uh, you said you couldn't reach me. I checked my phone. It's new and I'm not very familiar with it, but it seems I must have accidentally hit something that rejected your calls. I think I fixed it."

"Let me see that." He reached out, practically snapping his fingers. "I just bought my son the same model."

She gave it to him. He swiped through several screens, then frowned at her. "You can't *accidentally* reject calls. It requires a specific app and takes about eight steps to activate. See?"

He thrust the phone under her nose. She fumbled for her glasses, peering at the screen. "I've never done anything like that. I don't even know how."

"Well, there it is, right in front of you."

Tawny shook her head. "I haven't had the phone very long. My son sent it to me as a gift, and I'm totally lost trying to use it. A friend has been helping me . . ." Unspoken worry niggled at the edge of her mind.

"What is it?" The lawyer squinted suspiciously at her.

The image of Kahlil, resetting mysterious screens, floated through her memory. "I wonder if my friend did it." But why would Kahlil set the phone to block calls from the lawyer?

"Who's this friend?"

"Someone I recently met. He taught a class on how to use this instrument of the devil."

An angry-looking stout woman pushed between Tawny and Rosenbaum, facing the lawyer. "We need to talk. Now!"

He jumped up and moved away from the table with the woman. Their noses practically touched, like feuding cats spitting at each other, while they muttered in low, emphatic tones.

Tawny studied the strange screen, perplexed.

A chime sounded for a new message. She played it back. Kahlil's gentle voice said, "Tawny, you do not have to worry anymore about your son. The money is available whenever you need it." A pause. "I miss you."

Her heart clenched. This man she'd only known for a few weeks was handing over a quarter million dollars, without hesitation, to rescue Neal. Again, she marveled at his touching generosity. But she couldn't in good conscience take the money without paying him back. She'd ask Rosenbaum how to sign over her house to Kahlil, *if* the feds didn't seize it first, and *if* the abrasive lawyer ever gave her an opportunity to speak.

But . . . had Kahlil made a mistake setting up a call-blocking app on her phone? All his work seemed so precise, calculated. He was anything but sloppy, and he knew how badly she needed legal counsel. Surely he wouldn't have done anything intentionally to block the lawyer's calls.

Would he?

She glanced around to see if she had time to sneak outside long enough to call Kahlil back. But servers crowded among tables to deliver steaming lunch plates.

Rosenbaum returned to his seat and immediately joined an ongoing discussion with others at the table. Tawny understood only one in every three words bandied back and forth. She ate in silence, glad to escape the line of fire. The lawyer picked at his food, apparently more interested in talking.

After most people had finished eating, he gestured to an emcee, who introduced him, the ham actor eager to take center stage. He strode to the podium, told a few jokes to warm up the audience, then began in earnest.

"Ladies and gentlemen, you already know me and my passion to protect the civil rights and liberties of American citizens who are being victimized every single day by draconian measures law enforcement is wielding under the questionable auspices of the Patriot Act. Today, I wish to tell you the story of my latest client. She is a widow and the mother of a young man serving in the army. While her son is overseas risking his life to fight terrorists to protect the constitutional rights of every person in this county, his own mother has been deprived of her property without due process by the very same government that sent her young man into peril.

"This lovely woman sitting at my table . . ." He motioned for Tawny to stand. "Mrs. Tawny Lindholm, ladies and gentlemen."

Blood rose to her cheeks. She wanted to crawl under the table, but she bobbed up briefly before quickly dropping back to her seat. *Jerk.*

"This poor widow," he continued, "has not been *convicted* of any crime. She has not been *charged* with any crime. This woman has not even been *accused* of any crime. Yet the Department of Homeland Security seized her bank accounts, without notice, without due process, without a shred of evidence against her, rendering her penniless and unable to even pay for her own lunch."

That son of a bitch! He invites me to this damn lunch, then turns it around to make me look like a charity case.

"This very morning, she asked me, 'Mr. Rosenbaum, will I lose my home to the government?' Ladies and gentleman, can you imagine an innocent widow with a son in the armed forces having to ask such a question? Look at her! Is she a terrorist? A drug smuggler? A money launderer? A threat to national security? I ask you, ladies and gentlemen, if our government can commit such egregious abuse to a woman as innocent as Mrs. Lindholm, what chance does any citizen have against government entities seizing their life's work, businesses, homes, and possessions? Are we returning to the era of jackbooted thugs busting down doors and confiscating property in the name of der Führer?"

I'm going to kill him. Tawny hunched low in her chair, burning with shame. She wanted to flee the packed room. The arrogant prick had a lot of nerve, using her, without even asking, as his excuse to make a splash to an audience.

Rosenbaum went on. "Am I being melodramatic, ladies and gentlemen? Over the top? Exaggerating? You may think *yes*, but you do not know my family's history. My grandmother, my *bubbe*, was a little girl in Poland in 1939. An innocent child. She was no threat to the government, no criminal, no danger to anyone. Nor were her parents, who had their business and home confiscated by a government they had trusted to protect them. My *bubbe* was yanked from her mother's arms"—he gestured as if grabbing a child from the air—"and taken to a concentration camp. She survived, the only member of her family to live through the Holocaust."

He leaned forward over the dais, embracing the audience. "I still remember, as a little boy of ten, *Bubbe* told me her story. She did not cry or beat her breast, just matter-of-factly told me what life had been like for her when she was the same age as I was."

His voice dropped low, almost whispering into the microphone. "She showed me something she had never shown a living soul before, not even my grandfather. She pulled her lip down, and there was a tattoo, her number from the concentration camp." He paused and wiped his eyes.

Silence reverberated in the room.

"So, ladies and gentlemen," the booming baritone recovered, "that is why I am passionately devoting my life to defending the citizens of this county from the insidious, creeping abuses I see taking place in the name of national security, victimizing innocents like Tawny Lindholm, as they did my *bubbe*."

Next, Rosenbaum reeled off cases that he displayed on PowerPoint, talked about decisions, case law, and appeals, while Tawny huddled in her chair, feeling eyes on her from surrounding tables. Finally, he wrapped up his speech to enthusiastic applause. Lawyers waved their hands or pushed forward to ask questions. In the shifting movement of the crowd, she took the chance to slip out of the ballroom, head down, past people staring at her.

She hurried through the lobby and out the doors to the parking lot. Pausing to lean against a pillar, she sucked in gulps of cold air and let the chill breeze cool her seared face.

That son of a bitch. Paraded her problems in front of a hundred strangers like she was a trashy lowlife on reality TV.

After five minutes of deep breathing, she made a decision and hurried to the Jeep. Screw him. Screw the meeting with his buddy Max. She'd had enough of this lawyer feasting on her misery like a buzzard. She was going home.

Then she realized she'd left the tote bag with the money and her laptop under the table.

Damn!

She pounded the steering wheel but knew she had to return.

Gritting her teeth, she hurried back to the ballroom, where a few lawyers still lingered, chatting. She pulled the tote bag from under the table and started to leave when Rosenbaum caught her.

"Where have you been? The appointment is in twenty minutes. We barely have time to get there." He loomed above her, glowering.

She spread her feet in a boxer's stance. "Forget it. It's off. I'm sorry your grandmother suffered what she did, but you had no business blabbing my private problems to a ballroom full of strangers without my permission. Isn't what I tell you supposed to be confidential? You humiliated me just to give yourself an opportunity to show off to a captive audience. I don't care what a big hotshot you are, I don't want anything to do with you."

Rosenbaum glared at her for several seconds. She didn't break eye contact, even though her heart pounded in her ears and she was shaking.

Abruptly, he dissolved into laughter, guffawing so hard he grabbed a chair for balance.

She watched in amazement. Was this jerk laughing at her? He was beyond a jerk. She stalked away.

"Wait! Mrs. Lindholm! Tawny, please." His long legs quickly caught up to her, and he planted himself in the doorway, blocking her exit. Laugh lines still creased his face, but he held out his hands in supplication. "I'm sorry. I truly am. You're dead right. I had no business sharing your story. I get carried away sometimes."

"Oh, really?" She started to push past him.

"Look, I know I'm an asshole. But I'm an asshole on a mission. I really believe I can help you. You've gotten screwed big time. That's what I'm fighting against: the little guy versus a bullying government. The Patriot Act was the worst piece of legislation ever passed in this county. If I can overturn even part of it, my life's work will mean something. I'll have made a difference. I'll have saved other people's *bubbes* from tyranny. Will you give me another chance?"

Did she believe him? Was he sincere?

His dark eyes bored into hers. She saw something there—the light of a crusader.

A sincere asshole, she decided. "All right."

He linked arms. "All right, then! Let's go kick some federal ass."

As they walked to the parking lot, Tawny asked, "This morning, how did you recognize me among all those people?"

He grinned. "That's easy. You were the only one in the hotel without gleaming, sharp teeth."

Chapter 12: Dumbfounded

While Rosenbaum's Mercedes purred through traffic across town, he said, "You have the video of the woman posing as you?"

"Yes," Tawny answered. "On a thumb drive in my bag."

"Where'd you get it?"

No way would she mention Lupe Garza's name to this big mouth. "I won't say. It would break a confidence." She stared hard at him.

He got the message, all right, but quickly moved on. "Your house has been broken into and your car tampered with."

She nodded.

"It's clear enough you're being set up. When did you first hear from your son about this supposed kidnapping?"

"About a week ago."

"What else strange has happened in your life in the last few weeks?" He ticked off items finger by finger on the steering wheel. "You got a new phone, supposedly from your son. You met this guy who's helping you with the phone. Was this before or after the bank transactions happened?"

She lifted her chin and closed her eyes, trying to remember. Recent weeks had been such a whirlwind of turmoil and confusion. "I guess about the same time."

"You just meet this guy. He fiddles around with your phone. And all hell breaks loose at your bank. Is that what you're telling me?"

An uncomfortable itch started creeping up her neck. "Do you think they're related?"

"And then your son is supposedly kidnapped? All at the same time? Well, duh."

Tawny pressed back against the leather seat, as if pushed by an invisible hand, stunned as the sequence of strange events popped into sudden, nauseating focus.

Until this moment, she had not realized that every crazy episode in the past few weeks had occurred since she met Kahlil. Starting with the first flick of his finger across Lucifer's screen, a line of dominoes began to crash down, knocking every aspect of her life into chaos.

But how could that be? The man had been so tender and empathetic. He knew her mind better than she did herself. He understood her loneliness and fears. She had fallen for him and he for her.

Hadn't he?

What if it was all an act?

Was he somehow involved with the mysterious money appearing and disappearing in her account? Was he setting her up to the feds?

Was he in league with the woman who looked like her?

"Earth to Tawny."

She jerked back to the present with Tillman Rosenbaum. She tried to concentrate, but a black shadow kept drifting in front of her eyes.

"We don't have much time. Let's keep moving here," Rosenbaum said. "You contact Albritton. He reaches out to me. I try to call you, and your phone rejects my calls. This call-blocking app finds its way onto your phone without your knowledge. Obviously someone is trying to keep you from obtaining counsel." He turned to face her. "What the hell is wrong with you? You look sick."

Sick? Beyond sick. Inside her, something shriveled and contorted into death throes. Her heart. Trust. Beliefs. Faith in her own judgment.

Lunch threatened to come up. She pressed an arm across her stomach while her hand clamped her mouth shut.

Dammit to hell.

"What is it?" Rosenbaum pulled into a parking place and shut down the engine. A light dawned in his eyes. "That phone guy. You're involved with him."

Ashamed, Tawny nodded.

"Really involved." Not a question, a statement of fact.

"Yes."

He unfastened his seatbelt. "Come on, we're late."

Did she have to go? She wanted to stay in the car, hoping for the waves of nausea to subside, for the shock grinding against her heart to wear down its sharp edges.

With leaden feet, she plodded beside Rosenbaum into the federal building, up the elevator, down the hall to an office. Dizziness made her sway.

Pull yourself together. Don't pass out. Focus.

In a conference room, Maximillion Grosvenor and Tillman Rosenbaum greeted each other like two cobras, shaking hands but never taking their eyes off each other. Grosvenor was much shorter, on the heavy side, with glasses and a bald head fringed with reddish hair. He probably had freckles as a kid. Now he looked hard, cynical, suspicious.

They sat at a long table; Grosvenor on one side, Tawny and Rosenbaum opposite.

"First, let's get one thing clear," her lawyer said. "Is my client under arrest?"

"Not at this time."

"Has she been made aware of charges against her?"

Grosvenor folded his hands across his stomach. "Formal charges have not been filed."

"How about *informal* charges?"

"Your client is under investigation because of suspicious banking transactions."

"Did you give her proper notice her accounts were being seized?"

Grosvenor shifted in his chair. "I'd have to check my files."

Rosenbaum slapped the official letter on the table. "I'll save you the trouble. You did not! You left this with the bank manager, who held off giving it to my client until she physically showed up at the bank to find out why her money was unavailable." He yanked the paper back. "Cut the crap, Max. She has no criminal record, no ties to organized crime, not even a traffic ticket. Why are you targeting her?"

"I can't comment on an ongoing investigation."

Rosenbaum jumped to his feet. "Fine, you play Billy Badass. Tomorrow morning, I'll file a complaint stating that you executed the seizure without proper notice and without due process of law, in violation of the Fifth and Fourteenth Amendments to the United States Constitution. Come on, Tawny."

She stood and followed, scampering to keep up with his long strides, her mind trying to tread water in a dark, bottomless sea.

When they were alone in the elevator, she asked, "You're going to file a lawsuit for me?"

"Damn straight. If they haven't charged you, I'll petition the court to release your money."

The elevator jerked, and she grabbed the handrail for support. "Will they?"

"Depends on the judge. I'll argue your clean record, not a flight risk, no ties to terrorism, blah, blah, blah. But meanwhile, we have to get to the bottom of who's setting you up and why."

"Shouldn't Grosvenor or the FBI be investigating that?"

"*Should* and *will* are two different species. Max is a government bounty hunter. His job is to fatten the coffers. He doesn't much care who he takes the gold from, as long as he gets the gold. But I wanted him to see you, see what he'll be up against if he insists on pushing it. He'll have to sell a jury on the idea you're a ruthless criminal, and I don't think he wants to do that. And when the media gets a look at you, well, 'Katy, bar the door.' He's sunk."

"Media?" This freight train was picking up speed, dragging her life along with it. She wanted to jump off.

He sighed with exasperation. "Cases are tried in the media. You're a drop-dead gorgeous widow whose rights are being trampled by the oppressive feds. You're mediagenic. They'll eat you up. You won't be able to change channels without seeing your face. You'll be tweeted all over the planet."

Tawny clung to the rail as her knees threatened to buckle. "I don't want to be famous. I just want my money back."

"Doesn't matter what you want."

The truth of his words smacked her. She had lost control of her life, her emotions, her . . . destiny and fate.

How phony those last words rang now.

The elevator door opened. They stepped out and left the building. Tawny's head swelled with pain, while Rosenbaum's step had a jaunty spring to it. He was even smiling. What the hell? How could he be so cheerful when her life lay in shambles?

At the Mercedes, he opened the passenger door for her. She looked up at him. "You love this, don't you?"

"Absolutely. If I didn't, I'd be nuts to keep doing it."

She shook her head. "How does your wife stand you?"

"She doesn't. We're getting divorced."

Tawny instantly felt crummy for sniping at him. "I didn't mean—"

He shrugged. "I already told you I'm an asshole. It's no secret, especially not to my wife."

Tawny slid into the leather seat, and he closed the door. When he climbed in the driver's side, she touched his arm. "I really am sorry."

Again, the flicking hand. "Forget it. My only regret is the kids."

"How many do you have?"

"Two girls and a boy, fifteen, fourteen, and eleven."

"Tough age for their parents to split up."

"Any age is a tough age for parents to split up." That sounded like the voice of experience. She wondered if he still wore his wedding ring in hopes of reconciling.

They drove in unaccustomed, though welcome, silence, but the momentary distraction of the lawyer's personal problems didn't last. The sick feeling returned to Tawny's stomach.

She couldn't turn away from facts that pointed to Kahlil as the cause of this horrible mess. He'd betrayed her, used her, played her as a *patsy, pigeon, mark*, all those names Rosenbaum had called her. She'd welcomed Kahlil into her body and soul. She had been blind. Naïve. Pitiful.

Long ago, her father had pronounced her "beautiful, but dumb." For years, she tried to overcome that haunting label. Kahlil's sweet, seductive words almost convinced her that she was smart. But her father had been right all along.

Rosenbaum parked in the hotel lot. "Let's go in for a drink. I want to see that video."

The last thing Tawny wanted was a drink.

In the bar, they sat in a corner booth. It was quiet and empty, too early for happy hour. The server brought ginger ale to settle her stomach and a single malt scotch for him. She opened her laptop and played the video for Rosenbaum. While he watched, he asked, "You can prove you weren't in Helena on these dates, right?"

"I guess so." She never thought she'd need an alibi for not being someplace.

When the video ended, the lawyer mused, "OK, she never spoke more than a whisper, so there's no way to get a voice print. Smart." He reached over and replayed the part where the teller handed the check to the imposter. "But not that smart. She just received a worthless piece of paper. The bank undoubtedly put a hold on the funds until the feds seized them." He pulled on his chin. "Did you see any physical characteristic that proves it's not you? A mole, a scar, some telltale flaw?"

Tawny shook her head. "She'd fool my own mother. Except . . ." A detail chafed in her memory. She ran the video back again. After the woman signed the receipt for the cashier's check, she slid it toward the teller with her left hand. Tawny hit "Pause," then zoomed in. The picture enlarged, growing grainier. Yes! "Look, no wedding ring."

The lawyer's lower jaw jutted to one side. "So?"

She held up her left hand. "I broke this finger, and the knuckle stayed swollen. Even if I wanted to, I couldn't take my wedding ring off."

Rosenbaum's face split into a grin and he high-fived her. "Bingo! OK, email this to me." He gave her a business card.

She carefully typed his address and sent the video while he chattered happily about subpoenaing the signed receipt and contacting handwriting experts to compare signatures. "Whoever it was at the bank that gave this to you, they did you a helluva favor."

Tawny remembered how cowed and fearful poor Lupe Garza looked. "I'm not going to tell you the name."

He stared down his nose at her. "Newsflash, Tawny, any IT geek can figure out whose computer this video came from, surer than a fingerprint."

Her mouth fell open. "You can't let anyone . . . Please. I promised. The person could lose their job."

Rosenbaum snorted. "He or she could lose more than a job. Could be charged with a federal rap for interfering in an investigation."

Her fists clenched. Lupe had risked even more than Tawny realized. Had she ruined the woman's future by trying to save her own?

Rosenbaum rattled on. "You wouldn't believe how the regulators can strangle banks. The feds treat them like revenue agents, raking in money for them. But if a bank cmployee tipped a customer off about the investigation, the feds would stomp the bank into regulatory hell. Now, I don't have any particular affection for financial institutions, but they're getting shafted just like the rest of us citizens. We're all guilty till proven innocent under that goddamn Patriot Act."

Tawny rubbed her temples. She'd heard enough sermons today from this lawyer.

Rosenbaum must have noticed her eyes glazing over because he changed focus. "Now, about this phone guy."

She cringed at Kahlil being called a *phone guy* despite the sharp sting of betrayal. "His name is Kahlil Shahrivar. He's helped me a lot, not just with the phone. He offered to pay the two-hundred-fifty-thousand-dollar ransom for my son."

Rosenbaum's snapping, dark eyes narrowed. "Have you seen this money?"

"He's got it available . . . from his accounts, I guess."

"If you haven't seen the long green, he's full of shit. I can tell you I have three billion bucks in my left sock, but if I can't put it in your hand, it's smoke. Same as your son's alleged kidnapping. Don't you see? Your son is pretend-kidnapped, ransomed with pretend money."

Tawny pondered his words. "But why?"

"Ask your phone guy." He took a swallow of scotch. "On second thought, don't ask him. Stay the hell away from him."

The pain of betrayal corrupted the sweet memories of their time together. But she had to ask Kahlil why. "I can't."

Rosenbaum rolled his eyes in exasperation. "Of course you can! And don't start defending him to me. He's poison."

Tawny's back stiffened. She sat as straight as she could, staring up at the lawyer. "Wait a damn minute, here. I'm being punished like I'm already guilty without ever having a chance to face my accuser or defend myself. You want me to do the same thing to Kahlil? Pronounce him guilty without giving him a chance to explain?"

Another eye roll. "Don't get all righteous and noble on me. I can smell this dude across the state without ever laying eyes on him. Your problem is that you're nice and honest and good-hearted, so you think everyone else is, too. Well, lady, it's bubble-busting time. The world is full of assholes preying on the weak, the naïve, the nice. Do unto others before they do it unto you."

His insults stung, but she was starting to get used to them. "No matter what you say, I owe Kahlil a chance to explain. Otherwise I'm no different than the bank or Maximillion Grosvenor treating me like I'm guilty until proven innocent. I can't be like that."

"'I can't be like that,'" the lawyer mimicked in singsong. "As Bambi said to the hunter who's pointing a .458 magnum at his head."

"If the world is full of assholes, and you admit you're one of them, why should I put stock in what you say?"

He grinned, lower jaw jutting. "Because I'm *your* asshole." He downed the last of his drink. "I'll get my investigator on this tomorrow. In the meantime, don't be calling this guy. Got it?"

Tawny didn't answer and pressed the chilly tumbler of ginger ale against her forehead. Ice didn't stop the dizzy throbbing.

Rosenbaum seized her arm, slamming it and the glass on the table with a dull thud. Ginger ale slopped over her hand. "Listen, Tawny, forget about debating me over who's more righteous and fair minded. I'll kick your butt around the block, and I've got case law precedents to prove it." He bent his head and leaned in so close, the scotch vapors assaulted her nose. "You need to avoid this guy like Ebola. He means danger to you."

Chapter 13: Death of Illusion

Tillman Rosenbaum left at three p.m. to drive back to his Billings office. Tawny decided to spend the night in Helena, not daring to return to Kalispell where Kahlil waited for her. She found a cheap old motel orphaned by the interstate. After checking in, she changed into jeans, a long-sleeved T-shirt, and sneakers, desperate for exercise to release the tension thrumming inside.

As she walked the historic streets of Last Chance Gulch, she struggled to suppress her emotions over her muddled confusion. Kahlil had targeted her from the start. He wooed and romanced her with his empathy, his almost-psychic ability to read her thoughts. Played to her vulnerability, uncertainty, and loneliness after Dwight's death. Flattered her while exploiting her weakness.

How desperately she'd craved what he offered. He shared her burden of loss, relieved the crippling emptiness, and offered the nourishment of hope.

How foolish she'd been. How gullible. Rosenbaum had pegged her in under five minutes—a *patsy*, *dupe*, *mark*. No matter how insulting, his judgment of her was spot on. He'd immediately recognized the truth; so obvious to him, so invisible to her.

Rosenbaum seemed convinced Neal's kidnapping was phony. The texts Neal supposedly sent didn't sound like her son. But he could still have been abducted. How badly she needed to hear his voice.

She sat on a park bench and tried Neal's number again. This time, it rang eight times, then went to automated generic voice mail. Finally. "Neal, it's Mom, please call me. As soon as you can. I love you, son."

Well, that didn't solve the mystery. The number could belong to anyone. If only there was a way to pinpoint the phone's location. Kahlil had said no.

But . . . if Kahlil had lied . . .

She retraced her steps on the uneven pathways, clambering down the hillside, trying to remember where she'd passed a cell phone store. Maybe someone there would help. Then she spotted the Lewis and Clark County Library.

Old fear settled in the pit of her stomach—the fear of words she couldn't read, books she couldn't finish, knowledge that smart people took for granted but, like clouds in the big sky, floated beyond her grasp. She desperately needed to grab that cloud now. Knowledge, facts, and truth were the only way to sort out what was real and what was illusion. Or delusion.

Sucking in a deep breath, Tawny entered the building, comparatively new in contrast with surrounding historic sites. The librarian directed her to their technology guru, a pale, unsmiling girl named Sierra with stringy hair, black glasses, and tattoos climbing up her neck. Tawny asked about tracking Neal's texts.

Sierra ran through various screens on the smartphone. Tawny noticed her fingernails, with chipped black polish, were bitten down to the quick, but her familiarity and deftness rivaled Kahlil's. After several minutes, she said, "There's, like, some unusual apps on here."

"Unusual? What kind?" Tawny asked.

"I'm not sure. I haven't seen anything like them before. Where did you say you got this phone?"

"I thought my son in Afghanistan sent it to me."

"You're not sure?"

How could Tawny explain? "Now I'm wondering if it came from someone else, someone who's maybe playing a trick on me."

Sierra blinked hard several times while peering at Tawny. "It's totally weird. There's, y'know, functions on here that aren't regular consumer-type apps. Maybe military or something. They're, like, password protected, so I can't get into them." She offered the phone to Tawny. "If you want to enter your password, I can try to see what they do."

Tawny took the phone, stared at the unfamiliar screen. The only password she'd ever used was the one to access the bank. She laboriously tapped in the complicated sequence of letters and numbers.

Password error. She repeated the entry. Same message. "This is the only password I know, and it's not working." She gave the phone back.

Another strange look from Sierra. These days, it felt like a lot of people gave Tawny strange looks. "I can't get any further."

Tawny brought up Neal's messages. "Can you just tell me if these texts came from Afghanistan?"

Sierra worked the phone for several seconds. "Not really. There's apps you can install, y'know, for parents who want to know where their kids are, or like if you wanna find out if your husband's cheating on you."

Tawny shook her head. "No, no, he's dead. And he never cheated . . ." She caught another strange look from Sierra. *Stop babbling. Shut up about your life story and focus on the problem.* She squinted through her glasses at the display. "You can't trace where the texts came from?"

Sierra's face scrunched. "That's, like, a whole ginormous controversy, y'know, with the NSA and cops and everybody. Yeah, the location can be traced, but the carrier won't release it without a subpoena. Privacy and all that crap."

"What if it's an emergency, like a kidnapping? Can't the cops find out a location to save someone?"

Sierra shrugged. "Probably. But you'd have to ask *them*. Me, this is all I can do."

Tawny leaned against a work station, weak with disappointment. No way to find Neal. No way to verify if the kidnapping was real. Unless she went to the feds, who were busy trying to build a criminal case against her. She felt as if gravity pulled her down through the floor.

"Hey, you OK?" Sierra asked, peering close.

"Yes. Yes, thank you very much for your help." She took back the phone and started to leave but stopped. "Sierra, could you do one more thing for me?"

The girl did her hard blinking, but she appeared willing.

Tawny asked, "Can you make sure the location tracking is disabled?"

"Sure," as if that was the easiest task anyone had asked Sierra to do all day. She held the device so Tawny could watch her actions. "Go to settings, then to this screen, see? Just slide the switch from *on* to *off*. Done."

"Is that all?" Tawny remembered Kahlil had taken several minutes to disable it, making the steps appear complicated and difficult. "Wait a second. Was the tracking on or off?"

Sierra gave her another strange look. "On."

Kahlil had not disabled the tracking after all. Not only could the feds trace her, Kahlil could also, a thought that frightened Tawny.

Sierra added, "Another thing. This location tracking is just, totally, lame. Y'know, it's used to report the weather where you are, what restaurants and malls you drive past, all that data Google and Apple and those guys collect for advertising. Even if you turn this tracking off, 9-1-1 and cell towers still know where the phone is. If you want to make absolutely, positively sure nobody can find it, just pop the battery out. Then you disappear, like totally, invisible."

"Invisible?" Tawny repeated, as if in a dream. "Would you show me how to do that?"

"Sure." Sierra thumbed the back off and used a ragged black fingernail to pry a flat battery out. She held it up for Tawny to see. "If you want it to work again . . ." She clicked the battery into its slot and replaced the cover. "That's all there is to it."

When Sierra handed her the phone, Tawny felt as if she'd accepted a poisonous snake. The feds—and Kahlil—had known her location all along, no matter his reassurances.

The girl cocked her head to one side. "Y'know, if you need to figure out more functions, there's plenty of tutorials on YouTube. Just type in the model and your question, and you'll find all kinds of answers." A few more blinks, then, "Good luck."

Stunned by Sierra's revelations, Tawny left the library and walked briskly down the street, as if being pursued. She forced oxygen through her lungs, trying to counteract the feeling of strangulation that constricted her throat.

Kahlil knowingly left her wide open to be found, by the authorities or himself.

She'd allowed her fear of technology to intimidate her into helplessness. She put herself completely in Kahlil's hands because he performed magic. Yet Sierra just showed her how simply she might have found solutions by herself instead of being mystified and controlled by Kahlil's expertise. He'd taught her only basic tasks, keeping her ignorant of what went on behind the curtain, from where he manipulated her.

While Tawny pondered, she turned a corner and ran smack into the bank branch where her evil twin had deposited the cash into her account. She stopped at the entrance, thought about walking inside to see if employees recognized her. No, with the revolver in her waistband, she didn't dare. No sense getting herself arrested now. That was all too likely to happen in the near future.

Instead she crossed the street and bought a bottle of water from a store. She sat on a wall, sipping, and watched cars move through the drive-up, imagining the lookalike Jeep pulling in and the imposter stacking cash in the drawer. The money hidden in her coat felt heavier than ever.

How she longed to talk to Dwight. He'd know how to figure out the crazy mess.

The desire to hear his voice again welled up inside her. She called her home number to listen once more to his last cherished message saved on the answering machine. The familiar words repeated, weak and raspy: "Hey, love, I'm done with the infusion. If you come pick me up, I *might* be persuaded to take you out for an ice-cream cone."

Listening gave her comfort and anguish at the same time. She closed her eyes and imagined Dwight's face.

Then the machine announced, *"New message."*

Damn. Probably another bounced check.

"Mom, sorry I missed your birthday," Neal said. "Been on a mission and couldn't call. Just got back. I owe you a birthday dinner next time I'm home. Don't forget to ask for the *senior* discount. Love you, Mom."

Tawny gripped the phone tightly, pain stabbing her swollen ring finger. Could it be? She repeated the message.

Yes!

Neal's voice. Neal's blessed, beautiful, teasing voice, time stamped at 11:15 this morning.

Like flash cards, realizations cascaded in her mind.

Neal. Alive. Safe. Not kidnapped.

Neal had missed her birthday.

He hadn't sent her Lucifer after all.

Tawny stared at the smartphone.

The events of the past few weeks replayed. Connections jarred into place like cinder blocks dropped from the sky. The *chance* meeting with Kahlil. *Fate* and *destiny* whirling her into a romance with him. The mysterious deposits and withdrawals at the bank.

The seizure of her money. The text messages supposedly from Neal that didn't sound like him. The phony ransom demand. The disconnected number for Rear Detachment. The calls from Rosenbaum that didn't come through.

Kahlil *had* set her up.

She'd welcomed him into her heart and body . . . memories that now made her flinch. If she ever saw him again, she didn't trust herself not to cry. How could he treat her with such tenderness yet cause her unimaginable misery? Why did he choose her? And for what?

As the afternoon sun extended shadows, she stared at the instrument of the devil in her trembling hand. She wanted to fling it into traffic, let the tires of cars and semitrucks crush it into dust. Destroy every trace of connection to the handsome, charming, treacherous Kahlil.

No. She had to be smart. As much as she longed to get rid of it, the phone might be evidence to prove her innocence. Instead, she opened the back as Sierra had demonstrated and removed the battery. Relief flooded her veins, as if she had dismantled a bomb.

* * *

Kahlil pressed the accelerator harder. The rumbling police interceptor engine of the dark-blue Ford Crown Victoria easily passed slower vehicles on the uphill grade.

If Tawny's conversation with the Jew attorney had ended after the first few minutes, as it should have, the original plan could still have worked. By employing a combination of endearments and technical jargon she did not comprehend, her suspicions could be mitigated. But when she did not answer Kahlil's call, and the lawyer proved to her that his number had been blocked, the damage turned irreversible.

While he listened to the attorney's relentless barrage, months of methodical planning eroded away. The precise but delicate framework on which he'd built the myth to ensnare Tawny had shifted, folding in on itself like the slow-motion collapse of a building, floor by floor. The attorney was smart and cynical. Formidable.

The plan needed to adapt to new circumstances. Instead of Tawny unwittingly triggering the climax, now she needed to be forced.

Azarmina was en route to their rendezvous. They would leave the Ford, no longer needed to simulate federal surveillance, and drive the rest of the way together in the lookalike Jeep.

For one last time, Kahlil allowed himself to open the compartment in his mind where he kept the secret treasure of moments with Tawny. He did not believe in useless dreams for what might have been if they'd met under different circumstances. Yet during the brief weeks he had spent with her, the strange prickling deep between his belly and groin had grown stronger, more insistent, unable to be ignored or repressed.

He now knew last night had been the final time he would make love to her. Never again would he chuckle when she teased him, savor the joy of watching her delight in the pleasure he gave her, or feel her gentle touch to his body and soul . . .

He forced himself to close the compartment for the last time.

Once, he had hoped to spare her life. Impossible now.

He sped over the summit of MacDonald Pass, bearing down on Helena.

Chapter 14: Caught

"Tawny."

She jerked upright in bed. Murky darkness surrounded her. Had she dreamed Kahlil's voice? She grabbed for the revolver under the pillow.

Gone.

Then she felt his presence on the bed beside her. "I am right here, Tawny."

Oh my God.

How did he get in the motel room? She'd double-locked the door. Heart in her mouth, she reached for the bedside light, clicked it on. Squinting in the brightness, she saw him, lying on his side, atop the spread, elbow canted to prop his head up. Unshaven, dressed all in black—turtleneck, windbreaker, and jeans.

Smiling.

"How did you get in here? How did you find me?"

He shrugged one shoulder slightly, indicating *no big deal.* "Lock picks. The tracking device I put on your car."

"Why?"

"Because I must." He rolled upright and sat cross-legged, reaching one hand to touch her cheek.

She jerked away.

"You are so lovely. So dear to my heart."

Bile rose in her throat. How could he lie like that, looking deep into her eyes, a faint smile under the brushy mustache? She jumped up from the bed and stood tall, facing him, wearing only the panties she'd slept in. Damned if she'd let nakedness embarrass her in front of this man turned monster.

"What do you want?" she hissed.

"To be with you. We will be together for quite a while, now." He rolled across the bed and picked up the smartphone she'd left on the bedside table. With a quick, efficient movement, he replaced the battery and pocketed the phone.

A weapon. Tawny needed something to attack him. She glanced quickly around the grubby little motel room. A lamp hung from the ceiling on a chain, only a shade and bulb. A flimsy aluminum luggage rack leaned against the wall beneath a rod with permanently attached metal hangers, where her clothes hung. The

TV was bolted to a table that was bolted to the wall. Anything heavy enough to do damage was secured against theft.

"I have your gun," he said. "Please do not resist me. I do not want to harm you."

She clenched her jaw. Could she run outside, scream for help?

As he had done so often before, Kahlil appeared to read her mind. "I have secured the lock so you will not be able to open it. Please get dressed now. We have work to do." He rose, pulled her T-shirt from a hanger, and handed it to her. She took the shirt and tugged it over her head, although his touch on the fabric made her skin crawl. She hungered to defy him. "I know my son was never kidnapped."

Kahlil reached for her jeans hanging on a hook. "It guaranteed your cooperation when I needed it. Now"—he shrugged—"the ruse no longer matters."

She pushed past him, yanked the jeans away, and slid her legs in, zipping up. While putting on socks and sneakers, she wondered how she could've ever feared breaking down in tears when she saw him. Instead, cold rage gripped her heart and turned it to a chunk of ice. She tasted hate. She did not know how he intended to use her, but if she was destined to die, she was taking him with her.

The jacket filled with cash hung before her. Below it was the folded-up luggage rack, a rickety frame with mesh strapping, about as strong as a flimsy lawn chair. Pitiful, but the only possible weapon at hand.

She snatched the rack, spun, and thrust it at his torso, its legs hitting him in the chest and crotch. He doubled over with pain and surprise. Again she thrust it at him, pounding with all her might. Its legs bent and collapsed. She threw the tangle of broken aluminum at him and ran for the door.

She wrestled with the dead bolt, trying to unlock it, but it was jammed, as he'd warned. Kicking and pounding, she tried to break through the metal door. Nothing. No give, no yield.

Drapes hung across the window. She wound up for a sideways kick through the glass, but Kahlil grabbed her from behind in a bear hug, pulling her away from the window. He flung her onto the bed, then straddled her, pinning her arms. He panted from pain and exertion. Sweat dripped from his face onto hers. Fire flared in his green eyes.

The power of his grip on her wrists felt as if he could crush her bones. Strong legs clamped hers tight together in a wrestling hold, preventing her from kneeing him in the groin. She felt tingling as his weight and pressure cut off her circulation. In a few moments, numbness would prevent her from standing, let alone fighting him.

She stopped resisting, went limp. *Wait for another opportunity.*

They stared at each other. Dark circles under his eyes had deepened since she last saw him. Lines of strain cut vertically in his cheeks. His mouth looked pinched. When his breathing slowed, he smiled. "Well, that was invigorating." His head tilted. "Please do not make me hurt you. Will you cooperate?"

She broke eye contact and nodded.

He released one hand and stroked her cheek with the backs of his fingers, a caress that had thrilled her only the night before . . . a lifetime ago. Then he pulled a nylon zip tie from his pocket, like cops used for makeshift handcuffs. Gripping both hands in front of her, he bound her wrists together. "I fear I cannot trust you to remain passive. I am sorry." As he cinched the locking tab, he gauged her reaction. Tight enough that she couldn't wiggle a hand free, but not too tight to cut off blood flow. "Are you all right?" His tone sounded genuinely concerned.

How could he pretend to worry while he terrorized her?

As he had so often done, he read her thoughts. "I am not a sadist, Tawny."

"What are you going to do to me?"

He lifted her up to a sitting position, then to her feet. "You are going to help me."

"How?"

"By being with me. Come, now." He led her to the door, then inserted a small curved tool into the jammed lock. It opened. "Your coat." He reached for the jacket and put it around her shoulders, smoothing the denim. That touch—sensuous, even while he abducted her. He apparently didn't feel the hidden cash pockets. For all the good the money could do her now.

Kahlil guided her from the room to the parking lot, where Tawny had left her Jeep. Now an identical green-and-tan model sat beside hers, no doubt the one the imposter had driven. In the dimness, Tawny made out a figure sitting in her driver's seat. When Kahlil opened the passenger door, the dome light shone down on her evil twin.

I'm staring at myself.

The woman's face was eerily like her own, with only small differences: the nose a bit wider, the angle of her forehead a little steeper, deeper brackets around her mouth. Heavy makeup coated her skin, skillfully shaded to match the contours of Tawny's face. Her brown eyes met Tawny's with steadiness, but they were empty of expression, almost dead.

Tawny blurted, "Who are you?"

One side of the woman's mouth turned down. She glanced a question at Kahlil.

He didn't respond and pulled the passenger seat forward, gesturing for Tawny to climb into the rear. Awkwardly, she stepped up on the pipe running board, turned sideways, and braced herself with hobbled wrists. Getting into the back of the Jeep had always been a challenge, even with both hands free. She twisted and sat down hard, sideways on the narrow bench on the folded emergency blankets. He slid the passenger seat in place and climbed in.

The woman started the engine. Tawny caught a faint whiff of perfume, the same scent the intruder had left behind after the burglary at her house.

Before reversing, the woman glanced over her shoulder at Tawny. For a second, their eyes locked.

You look like me. You violated my home and belongings. You destroyed my reputation.

Dead brown eyes answered, *So what?* The woman broke the stare, pulled out of the parking place, and headed for the street.

A primal urge pulsed through Tawny. She hungered to loop her tethered hands over the front seat and choke this villainous couple who had destroyed her life. But she couldn't disable both of them. In the middle of the night, the streets were deserted. Her only hope lay in attracting someone's attention. She suppressed a raw impulse to attack, biding her time.

They drove to the interstate without speaking. The woman headed toward Great Falls. Tractor-trailers made up most of the light traffic. The dash clock read 2:36.

Tawny broke the silence. "My son didn't send me the phone. It was you."

Kahlil turned in his seat. "I needed to monitor you."

The library tech, Sierra, had commented on the unusual apps. Tawny said, "You tampered with it. It's not just a phone."

"You made me smile when you named it Lucifer. Out of the mouths of babes . . ." He jostled her phone in his palm. "I have heard your every conversation. I knew when you cried for your husband, when you fought with bankers, when you met with the Jew attorney. I have never been as close to another person as I was to you." He removed the hearing aid from his ear. "You were with me always."

Son of a bitch made eavesdropping sound like intimate foreplay.

He polished the screen with his sleeve. "And soon Lucifer will perform its most important task."

"What are you setting me up for?"

"I won't go into too much technical detail, but in a short while, you will make several calls that authorities will eventually trace to your phone. Meanwhile, those calls will trigger chain reactions at various power-generating stations, setting loose a worm to infect computers that control the electrical grid in the northwest quadrant of the United States."

Tawny blurted, "You're a motherfucking terrorist!"

The woman let out a whoop of laughter. She spoke to Kahlil, "I thought you said she was a timid little mouse."

Instantly, Tawny recognized the voice—hoarse and husky, with the indefinable accent. The voice of Sergeant Stuart at Rear Detachment.

The phony Sergeant Stuart.

Kahlil's dark brows crinkled, and he spat a sharp foreign word at the woman. The only harsh tone Tawny had ever heard from him.

She watched the imposter, who didn't shrink at Kahlil's rebuke but turned attention to her driving again, a defiant set to her shoulders and chin. *She has contempt for him. They work together, but they don't like each other.*

Kahlil faced forward. Tawny studied the back of his head, the dark hair curling over his turtleneck. He had rigged the smartphone to redirect her calls to this woman, this terrorist, instead of Rear D, just as he'd blocked Rosenbaum's calls.

No wonder he anticipated her questions and was always prepared with quick, glib answers. He knew her doubts and how to deflect her concerns with convincing—but false—reassurances. She had believed he spoke easily, without hesitation, because he spoke the truth. But it was lies, all lies.

Again, the idea of strangling him with her manacled hands clouded her mind. She had to push the hatred down.

When someone angered Dwight, he always went silent, the quiet emanating from him louder than most people's shouts. He also grew calmer, as if his emotions froze. He never spoke in anger. But the recipient of his rage always regretted it. Tawny needed to follow Dwight's example. Stay cold, unemotional, until the right moment.

When the woman turned off the interstate toward Choteau, Tawny's hopes caved in. Highway 287 wandered through mile after empty mile of desolate country. Only an occasional pinprick of light hinted at a remote ranch house. If the terrorists were heading back to Kalispell, they'd chosen an extralong, out-of-the-way route. In the next twenty miles, they met only one oncoming vehicle.

No point trying to escape until they reached a town. But few settlements dotted this route, and their sidewalks rolled up at dusk. At this late hour, even bars were shuttered.

Dwight's plastic toolbox sat below her under the rear seat. Tawny tucked her foot around the corner of the box, trying to coax it out without making noise. She nudged it with her toes, moving the heavy container only a half inch at a time. Soon one foot cramped, so she used the other.

When they bounced over a pothole, the box lurched forward on the floorboards, striking the backs of her legs, jamming her knee into the front seat. Pain shot through her, but she swallowed the groan in her throat.

The nylon tie bit harder into her wrists, now swelling with bruises from the earlier crush of Kahlil's iron grip. Her fingers felt fat, like sausages, difficult to bend, prickling with numbness.

She leaned down, awkward fingertips touching the toolbox latch. She waited until they were passing a semi, then flicked the latch open, hoping the noise from the big rig covered the sound.

Kahlil turned to look at her. For a horrifying instant, she feared he was reading her thoughts again and tried to force her mind into blankness. But he couldn't, not without eavesdropping with the smartphone. He did not have that power over her anymore.

His gaze rested on her, her curse ignored, pleasure now evident in his green eyes. Always before, that look had preceded a kiss, a caress, or the warm press of his body. Now she shuddered.

"Are you cold?" he asked.

She shook her head and stared out the side window. A sign read Junction 89, leading to a wide spot in the road called Dupuyer. Not likely to find help there.

Tawny waited until Kahlil faced ahead again, then leaned forward, stretching her fingertips to reach under the toolbox lid. She lifted it, but the low seat blocked the lid from opening more than six inches. She felt inside, identifying tools by touch, until she found the wire cutters she'd hoped were there. Carefully, she slid them out, letting the lid down quietly. They'd clip through the nylon tie securing her wrists.

For the time being, she slipped them into her jacket pocket and reached down to feel for other tools, something heavy enough to bash in a skull. Thoughts of violence that disgusted her in the past now became justified, necessary. She wished she had listened more to Dwight and Neal's conversations about hand-to-hand combat instead of retreating to another room, sickened when the two men she loved most calmly discussed how to kill people quietly and effectively. How badly she needed their advice now.

But at least she had the basic knowledge from the self-defense class. Targets of vulnerability: eyes, nose, Adam's apple, and groin. Stomp on the instep, kick the knee.

Better if she found a weapon. When they'd owned the shop, Dwight had an impressive tool collection for working on big trucks: twenty-inch crescent wrenches, four-foot-long breaker bars, sledge hammers . . . any of which she could swing with devastating effect. But this toolbox held only smaller wrenches, sockets, pliers.

Then the blade of a screwdriver scraped her thumb. She pinched it and straightened up in the seat. Holding it between her palms, she wondered if she had the strength to drive it into a chest, a back, a neck. No—she remembered something Neal had said: Aim for the eyeball or ear, vulnerable places where the skull didn't protect the brain. She added the screwdriver to her pocket.

The back seat of the Wrangler was a cramped little prison without any easy way to get out. The rear window and tailgate opened from the outside only. The spare tire mounted on the tailgate further blocked that escape. The front seats wedged her long legs in an awkward sideways position. The tight quarters didn't allow her room to use her pitiful arsenal of hand tools. Even if her attack succeeded, she'd remain trapped without the means to get away.

She longed to clip the tie around her burning wrists, but Kahlil and the woman would know immediately when they let her out, eliminating the element of surprise. Better to leave the nylon shackle in place until she saw a chance to run.

The woman gestured to Kahlil, pointing at the gas gauge. Tawny's trip to Helena had used up most of the tank. She'd planned to fill it before starting home in the morning. At this hour, on this stretch of road, an open gas station would be hard to find and her only chance.

"I need to use the bathroom," she said. A public place, with people around. *Please.*

Kahlil looked over his shoulder. "I believe there is a rest stop in about ten miles."

No! Not a deserted rest stop in the middle of the night. She wished she'd kept her mouth shut. *Think, think.*

"No one is going to believe," she said, "that I masterminded a plot to take down the grid."

He smiled at her. "We would not expect them to. You are one of several who are triggers. I have prepared ample evidence against you and the other decoys to occupy federal investigators."

"That's what the money was about." The strange deposits in her bank account. "You set me up to make it look like I was getting paid to do this."

"And to bring attention to you. Law enforcement is well aware of you. Your suspicious activities gave them reason to watch, but not enough to arrest you . . . until after the attack happens. Then you will be arrested quite quickly."

A small measure of justice occurred to her. Between the frozen accounts and the cash Tawny had secreted, he'd lost more than $140,000. "Your money's gone."

He shrugged one shoulder. "The cost of doing business. An investment in a greater return."

Tawny grasped at desperate straws. "I've already told my lawyer about you. He'll know I was forced. My best friend knows, too."

"The only information your friend Dr. Belmonte can contribute is that you have a new boyfriend who looks like Omar Sharif." His green eyes crinkled. "You flatter me."

Tawny burned but no longer from embarrassment.

He cocked his head to the side. "I am disappointed. I cannot cause you to blush anymore." He shrugged. "As for your lawyer, he has a reputation for flamboyance and exaggeration. He will say anything, no matter how outrageous, to defend his client. Judges frequently find him in contempt of court. He might wind up in jail beside you."

Kahlil reached between the seats and laid his palm on her leg.

She jerked away. Only yesterday she'd hungered for his touch. Now it disgusted her.

"Poor Tawny," he continued. "The bereaved widow cracking under the pressure. You were desperate for money to ransom your son. Driven to the edge of madness, doing something you would never do ordinarily."

"The kidnapping is a hoax."

"It does not matter. By the time investigators confirm that, my colleagues and I will be gone. Your function is to be the distraction meanwhile."

The distraction.

Tawny did not allow herself the luxury of rage over being reduced to a distraction. To him, she was of so little consequence that he'd ruined her life, tortured her with fear for her son, and would soon cast her away as a scapegoat, with no more thought than ending the life of an ant he stepped on.

If she survived, then would be time for cursing him, for damning him to hell. Now she must focus, concentrate.

"You said there are others. Other patsies like me?"

He gazed at her with a look she had once mistaken as love. "Not like you. No one was like you." He sighed, then went on. "But yes, there are other decoys. People deep in debt, alcoholics, compulsive gamblers, all willing to do anything for another stake. For two years, I have deposited cash in their accounts, which are also at your bank. Amounts under ten thousand, so as not to raise scrutiny. When money magically appears, they do not question their good fortune. They wish to believe they have won the lottery of life. Greed is a powerful tool. Coupled with desperation, it becomes irresistible. You were the only one who tried to give the money back. Everyone else succumbed. Except you. Quite extraordinary."

Tawny frowned, puzzled. "But you put bigger amounts in my account. Why the difference?"

"Ah." Kahlil smiled warmly. "A sign of high intellect is the ability to recognize subtleties. Did I not tell you that you are extraordinarily intelligent? You have perceived an essential aspect of my plan. Not everyone does." He cast an accusatory look at the imposter.

The woman's shoulders flinched, but she didn't speak. Tawny wondered about her expression. Anger? Defiance?

Kahlil shifted to face Tawny. "You see, employees of electrical generation companies are carefully monitored by their employers. If I had put too much money in, that would have raised the alert to a possible security compromise. One does not warn a target before one attacks. But you"—his smile broadened—"not being a current employee and only seasonal, did not fall under such stringent monitoring. Large deposits drew the attention of bank authorities, but they will not connect you to the dam . . . until after the attack occurs. In retrospect, they will realize you, plus many others, have been receiving money to facilitate the breach. They will focus on employees, the distractions, until we are gone."

The distractions. Again, that cold insult. Tawny asked, "How many others?"

Before Kahlil could answer, the woman made a sharp guttural sound. Was she warning him about saying too much? Tawny needed to keep pumping him for information. If she escaped, she needed all the evidence she could muster to defend herself.

Kahlil looked sideways at the imposter but said nothing.

"What about *her*?" Tawny nodded toward the woman.

"She will disappear as soon as she takes off the wig and makeup and removes the contact lenses that change her eye color." He flicked his hand, tossing aside an imaginary disguise. "Without them, she does not look much like you at all, except for height and figure. She is a skilled and convincing actress, is she not?"

The imposter pointed at a sign for the Dupuyer rest area. Kahlil nodded and the woman pulled off the road.

As Tawny feared, the parking area was deserted, with not even a big rig driver stopped for a nap. Quickly she moved the wire clippers and screwdriver from her jacket pocket to the waistband of her jeans.

Kahlil pulled the passenger seat forward to release her from the prison of the rear seat. In the awkward twisting movement of getting out, the jacket around her shoulders started to slip off. No! He'd spot her weapons. She threw herself against the front seat. The screwdriver blade dug into her hip. She clamped her mouth tight to stifle a cry of pain. But she kept the screwdriver and wire cutters out of his line of sight.

He caught the slipping jacket and draped it back in place over her shoulders. His palms rested there for an extra few seconds, the heat of his hands penetrating the fabric.

Warm hands, cold heart, she thought.

He helped her to the ground, then leaned in the Jeep to speak to the woman. She made an annoyed noise but got out of the car. "She will accompany you," he said to Tawny. He handed the woman a small revolver, which Tawny thought might be hers, the one he must have eased from under her pillow at the motel while she slept. The woman pointed the gun at Tawny and followed as she walked to the restroom.

Strategies whirled in Tawny's mind. The area was too desolate to make a run for it, but maybe she could disable the woman and even the odds. She pushed through the swinging door and saw two sinks and two stalls. Inside one stall, a mop sat propped in the back corner. She headed for it and started to close the door. Her evil twin banged the door open with an outstretched palm, gun in the other hand. "No!" she ordered.

Tawny gave her an imploring look. "Please? Some privacy?"

Her twin squinted a warning, then stepped back, allowing her to close and latch the door. Immediately, Tawny pulled the clippers out of her waistband. She faked a cough to cover the faint noise of her snipping of the nylon tie. Her hands sprang free. She flexed feeling into her fingers, then touched the rag mop in the corner. A metal handle, good. She threaded her arms through the jacket sleeves and placed the screwdriver and clippers in her front pocket, accessible. She peeked through the crack in the stall partition. The woman leaned against the sink counter, arms folded with the gun resting in the crook of one elbow, looking bored.

Tawny flushed the toilet and grasped the mop handle.

Was she ready?

As ready as she'd ever be.

She inhaled deeply, then whipped the door open and charged, jabbing the end of the handle into the woman's stomach. Her twin *woofed* as she doubled over. Immediately Tawny changed her grip to that of a baseball bat and swung hard, coming down on the back of her skull with a sharp crack. The woman dropped to her knees, hands outstretched, struggling to aim the gun at Tawny.

Again and again, Tawny hit her, on the skull, on the back, and the arm holding the gun. Another being inside her body took control and guided her attack, generating strength far beyond her capacity, raining blows with cold, accurate aim. One hit knocked the braided wig from the woman's head, exposing short, matted, platinum hair, turning red with blood. Her body jackknifed on the cement floor under the attack. The revolver fell with a clatter, landing near Tawny's feet.

She dropped the mop and scooped the gun up, relieved to recognize her own weapon.

She backed away from the woman, whose blood spread in a pool under her head. Had she killed her twin? Half of her mind felt cold pride at her handiwork. The other half wondered what depths this unexpected blood lust had come from.

"Tawny."

Kahlil stood at the door, pointing a semiautomatic pistol at her.

She aimed for his heart and pulled the trigger.

Click.

Click.

Only hollow clicks, all the way through the five shots that should have been in the cylinder.

Chapter 15: Don't Waste Your Death

Tawny's legs started to buckle. She fought to stand.

Kahlil shook his head slowly, regretfully. "I removed the bullets." He glanced at the crumpled unconscious figure. "You are not to be trusted, my treasure."

She lunged for the mop lying on the floor but stopped when she heard the snap of his pistol cocking. Part of her urged, *Take the chance, go after him.* But the icy part of her mind cautioned, *Wait, don't die unless you take him with you. Don't waste your death.*

She straightened and stared into his eyes.

He took the useless revolver from her hand, pocketed it, and tipped his head toward the door. "Now you have made more work for yourself. You must get her back to the car."

Tawny's mouth gaped. But of course he wouldn't leave his accomplice behind. If she lived, she'd be questioned.

"Do it." He aimed the pistol at her. "Please."

She bent down and grasped the woman under the armpits. When Tawny lifted, the twin let out a ragged breath. While Kahlil held the restroom door open, Tawny dragged dead weight, equal to her own, outside. She struggled backward across sparse grass, tugging the unconscious burden, trying not to look at the bleeding head that lolled back and forth on her thighs. The woman's heels left snaky lines in the dirt. By the time Tawny reached the Jeep, sweat poured from her despite the cold night.

At the rear of the vehicle, Kahlil opened the hatch and tailgate. "Move away," he ordered, aiming the pistol.

Panting, Tawny lowered the woman to the ground and stepped aside.

Kahlil squatted next to his comrade, never taking his eyes from Tawny.

Opportunity! She waited until he gathered the woman in his arms, then sprinted as fast as she could. *Look for someplace dark, where he can't see.* She spotted a line of trees and headed for them, zigzagging away from the lights of the parking lot.

A shot rang out. Kahlil shouted, "Stop!"

Ahead, a broad cottonwood offered cover. She ran toward it, but another bullet zinged past her ear. She heard a thud as it imbedded itself in the tree, still twenty yards away.

"I will not miss again."

She couldn't outrun another bullet.

Heart pounding, lungs burning, muscles rigid, she skidded to a halt.

"Stay where you are. Do not move."

Facing away from him, she couldn't see what he planned next. She imagined him taking careful aim and waited for the next bullet, perhaps this time in her spine. Seconds passed. Then she heard the slam of the Jeep's rear hatch.

Kahlil called, "Now, turn around and come back quickly."

Tawny pivoted and realized the woman no longer lay on the ground. He'd loaded her into the rear seat while Tawny's back was turned, as she waited for a bullet that didn't come. She should have tried another sprint . . . maybe. Too late now. She trudged back to the Jeep.

He moved to the driver's side and motioned to her. She felt herself obey, as if a puppet master manipulated her limbs with long strings.

Holding the pistol with one hand, he ran the other over her body and quickly found the wire clippers and screwdriver, which he dropped on the ground. His palm paused on the hidden pouches where she'd sewn the cash. He pulled the jacket off her and ripped the lining open. When he saw the cash, he nodded.

She had nothing left. He'd stripped her of her puny weapons and the only security she'd been able to protect.

He opened the driver's door and threw the jacket in the back seat, where the crumpled woman lay covered with the emergency blankets. "Now you will drive," he said.

They climbed into the Jeep. Tawny started the engine, put it in gear, and entered the highway. Her breathing slowed, and she felt weak from the letdown following the adrenaline rush. Lingering echoes of the shots rang in her ears.

Beside her, Kahlil reloaded his pistol and replaced the bullets in her revolver. She caught a possible tremor in his hands in her peripheral vision but couldn't be sure.

Would she have done anything differently in the restroom if she'd known the gun her twin held was useless? No point in going there. Every gun was loaded, even when it wasn't.

But why had Kahlil given an empty weapon to his accomplice?

Tawny gripped the wheel and noticed stickiness. Spots of the woman's blood speckled her hands. She tried to wipe them on the legs of her jeans but found more blood there. Guilty sorrow welled in her throat, but she fought it down. She had to stay strong, not let regret cloud her mind.

If she couldn't escape, she again vowed to take Kahlil with her when she died.

They drove in silence through rolling, dark prairie for the next half hour. Tawny tried to block the image of the bloody platinum hair from her mind, but she felt compelled to keep checking the woman in the rearview mirror. She groaned from time to time but never moved from her crooked slump on the cramped back seat.

"My sweet Tawny," Kahlil's velvet voice interrupted her thoughts, "you are not a timid little mouse after all."

She glanced sideways at him, stunned to notice his admiring gaze. Was he pleased that she had beaten his cohort to a bloody pulp? Or that she'd tried to escape?

He had put on such a convincing act of empathy, gentleness, and compassion. Thinking back on the weeks she'd known him, she didn't recognize any occasion when he'd slipped and allowed his true self to show. His gentlemanly facade had been unerring and perfect. His appearance of grieving, the sorrow they shared for losing their mates, his kindness, his immediate generosity in offering to pay Neal's ransom.

But of course he'd set up the phony kidnapping. He could have offered her a billion dollars with equal ease, knowing the hollow promise never needed to be kept.

She damned herself for falling for him, welcoming his tender touch. His warmth had filled the vacuum her life had become since Dwight's death. Loneliness was a powerful force that propelled her into his arms.

The gas gauge needle hovered near *Empty*. She guessed the Jeep might last another thirty or forty miles before it sputtered to a halt. How much farther to a station with people and help? What if they ran out before they reached a gas pump? Would Kahlil kill her then? She fought down panic.

No. He needed her alive for some purpose. Otherwise, he would have shot her at the rest stop.

As they crested a long, rolling hill, a glow shone below in the desolate black night. Tawny's heart leaped. Browning.

Kahlil noticed it, too. "We will stop there," he said.

Ten miles farther, she veered into the merger between 89 and Highway 2. The truck stop was small, not crowded. A couple of tractor-trailers sat parked in a side lot, engines still running but dark, the drivers curled in their sleepers. The convenience store was brightly lit, but the only person inside appeared to be a drowsy clerk, nodding off behind a glass partition.

Two islands jutted from the c-store. On the right, a lone man fueled a diesel pickup. The left island was empty.

Kahlil pointed to the left. "Go there."

She drove next to the pumps and shut off the engine, wondering if she dared honk the horn and scream to the man at the other island. But the pistol lay in Kahlil's lap, a half second away.

He took two more zip ties and secured her wrists at the ten and two o'clock position on the steering wheel. This time, he pulled them tight, cutting deep into her skin. "If you defy me again, I will shoot between your eyes. Do you understand?"

His words chilled her. Now his tone sounded flat, without emotion, without mercy. She nodded.

He got out of the Jeep and inserted a credit card. While he pumped gas, she peered through the windshield, hoping to spot a security camera, but she couldn't find one. If only another vehicle would drive in. But none did.

After a few minutes, Kahlil had filled the tank and returned to the passenger seat. He opened a pocket knife and cut her shackles. Raw grooves remained in her flesh. She rubbed her wrists for a few seconds until he said, "We must go."

She drove out of Browning on Highway 2, watching the rearview mirror as the bright little oasis, an empty promise of help, faded from view.

"I am glad you cooperated this time." He took her right hand in his and gently rubbed the indentations on her wrist. "I truly dread hurting you."

She wanted to pull away, but something told her to let him keep holding her hand.

How strange he sounded. One minute threatening a bullet between her eyes, the next full of regret and sorrow.

"Where are we going?"

"To my work."

"At the dam?"

"Near there. That is where your phone will activate the worm."

"Worm?"

"That's what the malware is called. Perhaps you heard on the news last year about Stuxnet? Your NSA and the Israelis disrupted the Iranian nuclear program with cyber-sabotage. My work is similar, boring into unsecured areas to access PLCs, Programmable Logic Controllers. Once the machinery fails, the overload will cause a switch to the next generation station down the line, which will then overload, causing another switch, another overload, leading to an unstoppable chain reaction. Each failure builds momentum until the entire northwest grid goes dark."

Oh God. Tawny bit down hard on her lip and tried to visualize life without electricity—no heat, light, refrigeration, TV. The oxygen generator Dwight had depended on would fail. Traffic lights, air travel, gas pumps, computers, smartphones, supermarkets, banks, all these and more, paralyzed. She couldn't think of any aspect of life that didn't depend on electricity.

Millions of people helpless. The destruction staggered her. History would change because of this monster sitting beside her, caressing her hand.

She tasted blood from her lip. Somehow, she had to suppress her rage and keep him talking. "How long have you been working on this . . . plan?"

"More than three years. My jobs take me to electric generation plants in different locations. No one pays attention to a psychologist, unlike an engineer or programmer. But that gives me unlimited access to personnel files, where I discover security weaknesses. While I am in each location for a few months, I cultivate what you called a 'patsy,' a scapegoat who will be blamed for the sabotage. After the attack, these scapegoats will become the first suspects because they cannot explain cash payments to their bank accounts nor the apps on their smartphones giving them unauthorized access. This plan required years of painstaking work to prepare."

Tawny spoke slowly, choosing her words carefully. "Are you doing this alone?"

"No. I have colleagues who do the mechanical engineering, advanced programming, and so on. I oversee what you might term the *human* engineering."

"Have you set off a plan before?"

"On a smaller scale. You have probably heard in the news of widespread power outages for the past decade. Many of those have been the work of my colleagues and me. When obsolete infrastructure is already teetering, it is quite simple to push it over the brink. Many of our projects have even been classified as 'accidents' rather than deliberate destruction. People accept 'accidents' readily."

"Do you want recognition for . . ." She wanted to say *for your vicious terrorism*, but chose different words. ". . . for bringing down the grid?"

"Oh, I do not want credit. Only people with petty egos need name recognition. In fact, I much prefer anonymity. One accomplishes far more when one remains invisible."

Kahlil continued to stroke her arm and massage her hand as it rested in his lap. She forced herself to allow it, not jerk away from him. Touching her seemed to reassure him . . . about what, she didn't know.

He sighed deeply. "I do regret my wife is not here to see the plan come to fruition." He shifted in his seat. "She did not understand, and she preferred direct overt action. I tried to explain to her that, yes, bombs make a dramatic emotional statement, but the damage doesn't last. My plan more accurately parallels the effect of an earthquake that wreaks widespread, long-term damage."

A thudding sound drew Tawny's attention. Kahlil's knee jittered back and forth, bumping the center console.

He went on. "Maryam died believing I would never be more than a dull plodder in front of a computer, while she courageously faced death each time she detonated a bomb. But cyber-sabotage is far reaching, difficult to detect, and so elegant. Keystrokes on your phone will send commands to the other phones around the northwest. Simultaneously, all will begin the upload to infect computers that control electrical plants. The generators and turbines will run faster and faster until motors overheat and they thrash themselves to bits. The malfunction will not be recognized until the machines explode from the inside."

His knee jittered even faster. Never before had he shown such agitation. His kneading of her hand now bordered on painful.

"Maryam never appreciated the subtlety." He gave Tawny a strange smile. "But *you* recognized it." The rubbing stopped, and he pressed her hand hard to his mouth.

For an instant, the warm pressure of his lips, the tickle of his mustache, reminded her of the electricity she'd felt when she first met him—the false hope of a new relationship, now turned so bitter. Then he lowered her hand again to his lap.

"What really happened to your wife?" she asked.

His chest swelled with a deep inhalation before speaking. "We were to be at a meeting with an affiliated group. As I do so often, I became lost in my work and was late. Maryam had gone ahead. I arrived three minutes after your government's drone hit the building." He swiped the back of his gun hand across his eyes. "Three minutes, a mere blink."

Amid so many lies, Tawny sensed his genuine grief, perhaps the one true thing he'd shared with her. Now, though, she wondered how much stemmed from his wife's death. Or was the greater anguish that he could never prove his worth to her?

His shaking knee gradually slowed to stillness. Tawny's hand rested loose in his grip, as if he'd forgotten he was holding it. She slid free and held the steering wheel with both hands.

Miles droned on in silence, headlights piercing black emptiness as they made the long mountain climb outside East Glacier. She had to blink hard to ward off the hypnotic effect of the yellow-striped center lane and the white fogline on the right shoulder. The lines seemed to point toward the relentless route to disaster.

"This is only the pilot project."

After the extended quiet, Kahlil's voice startled her. She looked sideways at him. He, too, appeared mesmerized by the yellow lines striping the road.

"Once the northwest quadrant has been disabled, bigger missions must follow," he continued. "Within a year, I estimate my plan will result in catastrophic failure of the grid across the entire country. It will affect more people, cripple more industry, and promote more anarchy than the mightiest bomb Maryam could have ever conceived. The economy will never recover from the trillions it will cost to rebuild infrastructure. Your country will fall to its knees."

Tawny wanted to scream, *No!*

Kahlil was brilliant and monstrous. Was there any way to disrupt his horrifying plot?

"You want revenge on three hundred million people because a drone killed your wife?"

Kahlil chuckled, a reaction that shocked her.

"What's funny?" she demanded.

"You are, my dearest one. Everything is so simple and straightforward to you. Right, wrong; black, white."

Did he mean to insult her or compliment her? She couldn't tell.

"No," he said. "To answer your question, my plan long predated Maryam's death."

The woman moaned for the first time in an hour. Kahlil reached between the seats and adjusted the blankets over her.

"If she doesn't get to a hospital," Tawny said, "she's going to die."

"She understood the risks." His jaw clenched. "As did my wife."

The question Tawny had held back moved forward in her mind. If she was ever to find out, now would be the time. "Why did you choose *me*?"

He smiled, resting his heavy-lidded gaze on her. "Why would I not choose you? You are beautiful, intelligent, charming, lovely in every way. I have been a fortunate man these past few weeks."

"You speak as if you care about me, but from the very beginning, you planned to destroy me. I don't understand. If I cared for someone, I could never intentionally hurt them, cause them to suffer."

"That, my treasure, is your most charming quality. Your innocence. You will never know how much being with you has lightened my heart. But I have a mission that I am driven to accomplish. You are a part of that mission."

"A cog in the wheel."

"Exactly."

She glared at him. "When the wheel turns and crushes me under it—"

"Then I will remember the precious time we had together as I go forward to my next mission." He reached over and brushed her hair. "Sometimes death is a reward."

She wanted to yank her head away but resisted. *Keep him talking. Keep listening.* "What a strange thing to say."

"I did not understand that for many years." His voice took on a faraway quality, as if he spoke from another time. "My father tried to teach me that lesson when I was a little boy, but I did not realize his wisdom then. I only cared for the selfishness of living."

Tawny wondered at the meaning of his odd words. "To live isn't selfish."

"Oh, but it is. Death is the ultimate sacrifice of one's love. To give the gift of death to save someone you love from suffering."

A haunting image of Dwight floated in her memory, ravaged, emaciated, in agony despite massive doses of morphine. She remembered thinking at the time, *Why doesn't he ask me to end his suffering?* She would have done anything to relieve his pain, even if it meant arrest.

She stared directly at Kahlil. "You mean, mercy killing?"

"The way you put the injured deer out of its misery?" He shook his head. "No, my treasure. Not quite the same."

"Then what?"

He caressed her shoulder. "So innocent."

Why did he keep touching her? She forced herself to remain still, fight the repulsion.

"Your country has not been kind to my family," he said. "My father was an esteemed scientist. Many years ago, he offered your government a great gift that would have improved the lives of millions. But they scorned him. And scorn was not insult enough. They discredited, disgraced, and destroyed him."

While his left hand massaged her shoulder, the pistol in his right pointed at her. She could no longer stand to look at him, hear his voice, or listen to his rationalizations. She fixed her gaze on the road ahead.

He released her shoulder. "You would have liked my father. You are both trusting innocents, too gentle for this world."

"What happened to him?"

Kahlil did not answer. Seconds ticked by. Then minutes. Finally, as they reached the summit of Marias Pass, Tawny sneaked a sideways glimpse.

His jaw worked, grinding his teeth. His Adam's apple moved up and down. At last, he whispered, "I killed him."

She jerked in shock. New fear coiled inside her. A plan to destroy millions of lives was almost too abstract and unreal to comprehend. But to murder his own father, a man he seemed to revere? That horror struck too close. Afraid to keep driving, she pulled to the shoulder, stopped the Jeep, and faced him. Unable to breathe.

In the dimness of the dash lights, his expression startled her, almost as if his eyes wandered independently of each other. "I was eleven years old. I came home from school and found my mother lying on her bed, cradling my three little sisters in her arms. They were all dead. My father sat in a chair beside the bed, weeping. He said, 'I waited for you, Kahlil. I want all of us to leave together.' I screamed at him, 'What have you done, Father?' He reached out to me, to kill me also. I ran from the room, but he caught me in the kitchen. He was sobbing, trembling. I grabbed a knife from the sink and stabbed him in the heart."

Tawny's insides lurched.

Kahlil's face had visibly aged during the telling. Again, she noticed his eyes wandering, unconnected to each other.

Before she could stop herself, she touched his rough, lined cheek. "You don't have to go through with this. Please."

He took her hand from his face, held it for a long second, then placed it on the steering wheel. "Yes, I must. We still have far to go." He nodded for her to pull onto the highway, descending the mountain.

Chapter 16: Final Sunrise

The blacktop ribbon stretched before them. Tawny estimated at least another hour to reach the dam. Her tongue stuck to the roof of her mouth; her throat ached with dryness. Now she really did need to go to the bathroom, but Kahlil would never allow her another chance. Her discomfort increased mile after mile, through the peaceful, sleeping settlements of Essex and Nyack. Muscles in her back seized from being in one position too long. Her hands went numb on the steering wheel.

Minutes before dawn, Kahlil directed her to the dam turnoff. They drove across the curving monolith, wind whipping whitecaps in the angry gray water of the reservoir. The sheer concrete face dropped more than fifty stories. Water passed through turbines to generate electricity for hundreds of thousands of people down the line—electricity Kahlil intended to destroy here and in many other locations.

In a gravel cutout a short distance from the dam, a silver Subaru sat near a trailhead where people often left their vehicles while hiking. It appeared empty.

"Park next to that car, please," he said.

Tawny pulled beside it and shut off the engine. She tried to peer inside, looking for an indication of campers who might return soon. Kahlil dashed that hope immediately when he pulled out a fob, thumbed it, and the Subaru's lights flashed.

His getaway vehicle.

"We will move now." He leveled the pistol at her as they exited the Jeep.

The temperature felt below freezing, and a blustering wind buffeted the canyon walls. Despite the wind chill, Tawny stretched for a few seconds, trying to release the knots in her back and hips from the long drive. He watched her but said nothing. When her teeth began to chatter, he opened the Subaru passenger door for her. She huddled inside, away from the gusting wind, shivering without her jacket. He closed the door, went around to the driver's side, and got in.

Exhaustion weighed her down. Her arms felt leaden from gripping the steering wheel without a break. Thirst parched her throat.

Kahlil slipped the pistol into his windbreaker pocket, pulled out her smartphone, and began to swipe and tap the screen. He must be doing the final programming.

Tawny could not prevent him from destroying the power grid. She'd tried—and failed—to talk him out of it. The plan surged forward, no matter what. He'd made that clear.

Shame again overcame her. How foolish and gullible she'd been. She'd been betrayed and used like an empty-headed puppet to commit evil that would affect millions of people. Was there any point in going on?

Her children no longer needed her. Her husband was gone.

Dwight once told her the most dangerous human being was one who had nothing to lose.

She had nothing to lose.

Kahlil finished programming the phone, then wiped it clean with a cloth. Still holding it with the cloth, he offered it to her. "Please take this."

Fingerprints, she thought. *He wants my fingerprints on the triggering device.* She folded her arms and stared at him.

Green eyes gazed deep into hers. Surprisingly, she didn't see anger in them but rather sadness. "As you wish." His voice sounded strangely resigned. He laid the phone, wrapped in the cloth, on the dash. "Would you like some water?"

Although she wanted to resist him, her mouth begged for moisture. Her head throbbed from dehydration. She gave in and nodded.

He reached in the back seat and brought forward two bottles of water. She unscrewed the lid and swigged down the best part of the pint. Her grateful throat ached from swallowing.

In her peripheral vision, she saw him sipping from his bottle, watching her.

When she paused for a breath, she noticed a bitter aftertaste. Kahlil regarded her even more intently, a laser focus. Flecks of residue settled at the bottom of the bottle. The water had already hit her stomach, making it gurgle.

Poison!

Kahlil gently took the bottle from her and put it in the back. "I am sorry. I had hoped to spare your life. If things had worked out as I originally planned, you would have been arrested and almost inevitably been convicted because of ample evidence against you that I provided. Your attorney would have worked diligently to save you, but he would fail. You would be sent to prison. But you would have lived."

Poison coursed through her body. How long did she have left? Minutes? Seconds?

A sliver of sun edged over the mountains. Rays sliced through dark clouds and sparkled on the whitecaps of the reservoir. How beautiful. Her last sunrise.

Kahlil reached to cup her cheek. Frozen in shock, she did not move. His warm palm rested against her face, caressing it slowly as if savoring the last opportunity.

"It will be painless, my treasure. I truly never wanted to cause you hurt. You will drift off, and it will be over. I will return you to your Jeep with a suicide note and press your fingerprints on the phone. My colleague and I will be gone in the Subaru before anyone finds you."

Buzzing grew loud in her ears. Dusky blurs floated across her vision. She tried to keep her eyes open, to focus, to stare at his face. *Stay awake.* Her surroundings drifted away, as if she were in a boat passing a vague, foggy shore. Heaviness deadened her limbs. Her neck wobbled, weakening under the weight of her head. She allowed her face to rest in his hand because that took less effort than to hold her head up.

He gathered her in his arms. No strength to resist.

His lips brushed hers tenderly, sweetly. "I will go now because I cannot bear to watch the life flow out of you, just as I could not bear to shoot you at the rest stop." He laid her back against the seat. "I will be close."

Her head lolled sideways. She felt herself sinking, melting into the seat.

He murmured, "Everyone I have ever loved dies." Then he got out of the car and closed the door.

Tawny forced her eyes open. She watched him walk away from the car, then break into a run, arms and legs pumping hard, the back of his black jacket ballooning in the wind, dark hair whipping.

Coward!

Anger galvanized into a solid, unyielding pillar inside her. *Stay awake!*

Kahlil ran across the road toward the parapet overlooking the dam. About a hundred yards away, he slowed. Stepped up on the sidewalk. Stopped. Leaned on the parapet, looked down to the river below.

Anger cleared Tawny's mind. *Don't claim you love me, you monster.*

The wind howled. Or was it the roaring inside her head?

Images drifted in her brain. Emma. Neal. She'd never see them again, never tell them how much she loved them.

Dwight. Would he be waiting for her?

A brief sparkle of memory flashed. Teenage Emma stumbling home after drinking too much at a party. Neal, the experienced older brother, pulled her by the arm into the bathroom, bent her over the toilet, and shoved his finger down her throat to make her vomit. "You'll thank me in the morning," he'd said. "The less alcohol absorbed, the easier the hangover."

Would that work with the drug Kahlil had put in her water bottle? Another memory flickered of her first-aid training when the children were little: *In case of poison, induce vomiting.*

She leaned over the driver's seat, rammed her finger down her throat. Water and bile came up quickly. She retched sour bile until her stomach was empty. Cramps gripped her, but maybe she'd gotten rid of at least part of the poison before it entered her system.

Her mind felt a little clearer. If nothing else, she thought with grim humor, she'd ruined the place where Kahlil had to sit. Small revenge.

She straightened and stared through the windshield. He seemed miles away, like looking backward through a telescope. He leaned across the top of the waist-high wall, forearms resting on the ledge, staring down.

Could she stumble that far? Keep him from destroying millions of lives?

Lucifer lay wrapped in a cloth on the dashboard where Kahlil had left it.

The battery.

If she removed it, would that stop the action he'd triggered? She had to try.

With fumbling fingers, she pried the back off the phone and snapped out the battery. The parts slipped from her feeble grip to the floor. Already she felt loss of control in her hands. But she wasn't done. He could simply replace the battery. She had to stop *him*. Permanently.

With difficulty, she grasped the door handle and opened it.

The wind caught it, yanking her sideways. Bitter, bitter cold. Maybe fresh air would revive her. Swinging her feet out, she tested them on the ground. She pulled herself up, holding onto the door. Rubbery legs flexed under her weight but held. *Dammit, I can do this. I will do this.* Anger supported her as she took a few tentative steps. She gulped air. It felt invigorating, but she immediately began to shiver.

How far away was Kahlil? Miles . . . hundreds of miles. Wind pinched her cheeks and penetrated her T-shirt, piercing deep to chill her core. She staggered toward him, one slow step after another. Her paces gradually quickened. But it was so cold.

Her feet wove back and forth in a drunken grapevine. Just like Zumba. *Stand up, don't fall, keep going.* A pulse throbbed in her ears—a drumbeat, the rhythm section to her relentless march. *I must reach him.*

I. Must. Reach. Him.

Closer. Getting closer. Now what?

I'm dying, but I'll take him with me.

The howling gusts echoed off the canyon faces. *Don't let him hear me coming. Only let him hear the wind. Don't let him sense me coming.*

His shoulders shook. The wind blowing his jacket? No, a different movement. He was crying, leaning on the wall, sobbing.

You motherfucker. You murder me, and then cry over it.

Anger inside her was solid ice, even colder than the outside temperature.

She rushed him, right hand balling in a fist.

The second before she reached him, he turned, saw her. Wet, red-rimmed eyes widened. Mouth opened.

With all her strength, she rammed her fist into his Adam's apple. A strangled gag erupted from his mouth. He clutched his throat.

She drove both thumbs into his eyes, feeling the wet softness yield under the force. Her fingers twisted tight in his long hair, gripping his head while her thumbs wedged deeper into his eye sockets. He howled in agony. Blood ran down his cheeks.

His arms shot up between hers, knocking her hold loose. But he was staggering, pawing at his bleeding eyes.

She plowed her shoulder into his chest, knocking him backward on the parapet. Legs flailing, he writhed on his back on the narrow ledge, fighting for balance. His desperate fingers scrabbled for a handhold on the concrete.

She grabbed his ankles, trying to roll him over the edge.

His hips bucked. Powerful legs kicked, breaking her grip. One foot grazed her shoulder. The other connected with the side of her head, tearing her ear.

The head blow made her legs wobble. She fell forward, the parapet catching her. Dodging his kicks, she seized one ankle, this time clinging to it with both hands.

Keep him on his back, off balance, like an insect. Don't let him get his legs under him.

Hold tight.

The gun in his pocket. If she could reach it . . .

He twisted. She let go of his ankle and went for the pocket of his windbreaker, felt the hard shape of the pistol, but it was tangled in fabric. He thrashed, blind yet still so strong, powerful. One arm snaked around her head while the other braced himself on the parapet. Her torn ear screamed from the friction of his hold. He pulled her on top of him, then rolled her over till she teetered on the edge.

She yanked her head free from his grip. For an instant, the vertical drop of the dam wall flashed into view, beckoning her. Nausea lurched in her stomach.

She made another desperate grab for his pocket to seize the gun. Still twisted in the jacket. He sat up, blind and disoriented. That gave her the chance to throw herself toward safety on the side of the wall toward the road. Again his arm pinned her head, pressing it hard against his chest, pulling her toward the precipice. But the poison was sapping her strength. She couldn't hold out much longer.

She went for his eyes, a finger poking deep into one bloody socket. He screamed and released her, both arms thrown across his face. She jammed her hand into his pocket, at last touching metal. *Where's the trigger?* Her thumb went through the loop of the trigger guard. She pulled with her last bit of strength.

The shot deafened her. She didn't know if he'd been hit or the bullet went into the parapet. But his back arched and he twisted, rolling to his side, closer to the edge of the wall.

Push!

She threw all her weight against him, driving her shoulder into his floundering body, shoving with both hands.

And then he was gone.

She collapsed across the ledge and watched him plummet down the curving wall of the dam, slamming into the concrete over and over. Down, down, down, hundreds of feet, his limp body bounced.

She couldn't see him at the bottom. He'd disappeared from sight. Or her vision had failed.

The poison overcame her. She went limp, sliding down the parapet to the sidewalk, consciousness flowing away like spilled water.

I'm dead, but I took you with me.

Chapter 17: Interrogation

Dr. Virgie Belmonte closed and double-locked the front door of her condo against protesting voices. A mother tiger could not protect her young more ferociously than Virgie had protected Tawny from sheriff's deputies, federal cops, and the media. Drapes darkened the living room against morning sun and prying eyes. Gradually, the clamor outside faded away.

Tawny huddled on Virgie's velvet couch, covered with a fleece blanket, trying to hold a mug of tea. One sip and her trembling hand threatened to spill it. She set the mug on the end table.

Earlier that morning, Virgie had brought her up to date on the past two lost days of her life. An employee arriving for work at the dam had found Tawny, shivering violently, near death, at the side of the road. She'd stopped breathing in the ALERT helicopter as it rushed her to the hospital. ER personnel revived her, but she remembered nothing of the next forty-eight hours in ICU. Law enforcement showed up, demanding to question her, but Virgie had spirited her out a back exit, bringing her home, claiming, "My patient requires monitoring twenty-four seven."

In the kitchen, Virgie talked on her phone in a low voice. When she hung up, she returned to the living room and ran her hand softly over Tawny's forehead, brushing away limp hair. "That was Tillman Rosenbaum," she said. "He's flying in from Billings. Be here by four this afternoon. Strict orders that you don't talk to anyone or answer any questions until he's with you."

"As if I had the strength." Tawny's head fell back against pillows Virgie had propped behind her.

"Between hypothermia and respiratory arrest, my dear, you'll be feeling puny for some time to come." Virgie curled one leg under her in the chair next to the couch. "When I heard you'd stopped breathing, I thought we'd lost you. Your core temp was ninety-three degrees. Thank goodness the ER doc recognized a benzodiazepine overdose on top of hypothermia. If he hadn't ordered that tox screen, they might not have found the Valium. Once the doc gave you Romazicon, you came around. I suggest you put him on your Christmas list."

Tawny nodded weakly against the pillow. She thought about asking Virgie the doctor's name, but talking required too much energy.

Virgie leaned forward, elbows on her knees. "In addition to lawyer–client confidentiality, there is also doctor–patient confidentiality. Anything you tell me, I can't talk about."

"Nosy, aren't you?"

Virgie grinned. "Curiosity is eating me alive. A pal at the sheriff's office told me a game warden found Kahlil's body at the bottom of the dam. They're reviewing the surveillance video to determine if he fell or jumped."

Or was pushed. They'll know exactly what I did.

Virgie went on. "Inside his rental car, there was a weird typed suicide note, except it's supposed to have been written by you. *Typed.*" She cupped her chin in one hand and tapped her cheek. "If my memory is correct, you type about sixty-five mistakes a minute."

"I didn't write it."

"Didn't think so. Lots of rumors flying around. Love triangle. Murder–suicide pact. A woman with a fractured skull slumped in the back of your Jeep. Cash found sewed into your coat. And something about a terrorist plot. Your smartphone is being processed for evidence." She tucked the blanket closer around Tawny's chin. With a wry smile, she added, "Can't imagine why I'd be curious."

Tawny closed her eyes and tried to summon courage. "Virg, Kahlil was a terrorist. He set me up to take the fall." Speaking that many words sapped her strength.

"Those strange deposits to your account? That was to make it look like you were getting paid by terrorists?"

Tawny barely moved her head, nodding.

"What about Neal? The kidnapping?"

"Phony. Kahlil did it to force me into helping him." Tawny jerked up, sending a shock wave through her brain. "Neal! Can you get a hold of him?"

"Already in the works. When you tried to die on us, I contacted the army and tracked down his unit. They're flying him back on emergency leave."

"Emma?"

"Found her on Facebook. Sent her a prepay card because her cell is shut off again. She'll call later."

Tawny sighed with gratitude. "You're the best."

"Why don't you nap now? That lawyer's going to be here pretty soon, and he sounds like the kind of guy who'll run a girl ragged."

"You got that right." Tawny snuggled under the blanket.

Virgie turned off the table lamp, darkening the room. "Oh, hey, I almost forgot. That bank that's given you so much trouble? Heard on the news last night the FDIC locked them down. Chained the doors shut, wouldn't let any of the employees out."

* * *

"I killed two people." The words tasted bitter, and Tawny's stomach twisted.

Tillman Rosenbaum sat in Virgie's dining area, knees high, looking like an NBA player in a kindergartener's chair. "OK, the first lesson you must learn is never, never, never say you killed anyone." He glanced over his shoulder to make sure Virgie remained in her bedroom, door closed, to preserve attorney–client privilege. "Now, take me step-by-step through everything that happened after I left you in Helena."

Tawny leaned her elbows on the table, resting her aching head in her hands. She reviewed what she'd done after becoming suspicious of Kahlil, talking with the tech guru at the library, scoping out the bank, hearing Neal's phone message. Then waking in the motel in the middle of the night, with Kahlil lying next to her. She shuddered at the memory. "He knew everything because the smartphone was rigged. He'd listened to every conversation, everything I've said or done since he sent the damn thing to me. He knew I couldn't be fooled any longer, so he abducted me to force me to carry out his attack on the power grid."

Rosenbaum scribbled rapid notes on a yellow legal pad. "You were kidnapped, under duress."

She nodded.

"Good."

"It was *not* good!"

He kept writing. "It was terrible, but from a legal standpoint, it's good, really good. Just keep talking, and let me worry about the details."

Tawny told him about finally meeting the woman who'd impersonated her and the stop at the deserted rest area. Then she began to cry. "I beat the woman to death with a mop handle."

"Oh, *shut up*," Rosenbaum muttered. "She held you at gunpoint. You were being abducted by armed terrorists." He reached across the table to pull back the sleeve of Tawny's robe. "Look at you!"

The zip ties had carved dark magenta lines around Tawny's swollen wrists. Kahlil's powerful hands had left purple-and-red bruises all over her arms. Her neck screamed whenever she turned her throbbing head. Spasms knotted her back and legs, despite the pain pills Virgie had given her.

Rosenbaum whipped out his cell and snapped a picture. "Dr. Belmonte said your whole body is one big mess of contusions. She's going to take photos later today while they're fresh." His fist dropped, thumping the table. "You were in fear for your life. That's self-defense, Tawny. And don't you dare forget that."

Sobs choked her words. "I didn't have to kill her. Kahlil gave her a gun without any bullets in it. But I didn't know that till later."

"Doesn't matter," he growled. "You were in fear for your life. How many times do I have to tell you?"

Tawny's question from that night came back. Why had Kahlil given an unloaded gun to his accomplice? Then the answer snapped into place. "He didn't want to take the chance she might shoot me because he needed me alive. He knew I'd fight her." She stared down at her mottled hands, remembering the sticky feel of blood contaminating her fingers. "She looked like my twin, and I never even knew her name."

"Azarmina Hodja."

"What?"

"That's the name of the woman found unconscious in the back of your Jeep. She's in the ICU at the hospital here. Been on an FBI watch list, although it doesn't sound like they were watching her very closely. Reportedly an actress, touring in road companies around the United States."

"She's alive?"

"So far."

"Thank goodness."

Rosenbaum rolled his eyes. "You are beyond comprehension." He flicked on his tablet. "My sources in Homeland Security tell me *Kahlil Shahrivar* is an alias, no surprise there, but what's really interesting, he's related to Azarmina Hodja. She's his wife's sister."

Tawny recalled the tension between Kahlil and the woman in the car. Did she blame him for her sister's death? "At first, he told me his wife died in childbirth. Then later he said a drone killed her."

"From her dossier, the wife sounds more like someone who'd *eat* her children. Suspected in several bombings, including a sidewalk café in Jerusalem two years ago."

"Oh God." She covered her eyes with both hands, pressing hard against the headache. Was it possible? Had Kahlil's wife killed the Roths? Then *he'd* moved into their home? How sick, how depraved.

What kind of strange marriage did Kahlil and his wife have? Tawny had believed his grief was as genuine as her own. But now, she wondered.

Rosenbaum continued jabbering while she drifted back in the memory.

She revisited Kahlil's last expression. Eyes red rimmed and tearing. Agonized. Suffering. He'd believed she was dying in the car.

And he finally let down the mask, the act he had maintained since the first moment they met.

Was it possible he really did regret murdering her? That he did love her, in a perverted way she would never understand?

Rosenbaum flipped a pen between his long fingers, tapping it annoyingly on the table to retrieve her attention.

She forced herself back into the present.

"Anyway," the lawyer continued, "the feds knew she was working with someone."

"Excuse me. Who?"

"Azarmina," he said with exaggerated impatience. "Kahlil was harder to pin down. He evidently had flawless credentials to give him access to installations he'd targeted."

"He was a psychologist."

"Figures."

She didn't know what Rosenbaum meant, but asking required too much energy.

"So go on with what happened."

Tawny described the plot to bring down the grid Kahlil had revealed to her on the long drive, his peculiar tale of the death of his family, and killing his father. When she got to the part about drinking the poisoned water, she started to shake. Cold again, deep into her bones.

"Let's take a break," Rosenbaum said. He helped her to her feet and led her back to the couch, where she flopped down, exhausted. He pulled the blanket over her.

Gradually the shivering subsided. But memories tumbled in her mind, crashing into each other. Their lovemaking mixed up with Kahlil's betrayal, the trust and safety she had felt with him collided with his duplicity. Yet how could she feel such agonizing regret for causing his death? She buried her face in the back of the couch.

Rosenbaum's hand on her shoulder squeezed with more comfort than she would have imagined the usually rude lawyer was capable of. He handed her a tissue. She blew her nose, pulled herself to a sitting position, and continued with the part of the story she dreaded the most.

"He gave me the drugged water. I was terribly thirsty and guzzled it. He kept looking at me strangely." She wiped her still-sniffling nose with the tissue. "Now I know why. He wanted to make sure I drank enough to kill me. But there was something else in his eyes, too. He said he didn't want to watch me die, so he left me in the car, alone.

"I hated him. I was so angry. That's all that kept me from passing out." Tawny wadded a handful of blanket into a ball, knuckles whitening. "Anger, hatred, revenge. If I was going to die, I'd make him pay for it. I made myself throw up, trying to get rid of some of the poison."

Rosenbaum raised his eyebrows. "The cops noticed the vomit in the Subaru at the scene. Pretty smart move. That probably saved your life."

Yeah, I'm a regular genius. That's how I got myself into this mess. "I pulled the battery out of the phone, hoping to stop the destruction." She glanced at the fixture in the dining area, the lamp on the end table. Bulbs burned brightly. Electricity still flowed through the wires.

Rosenbaum nodded. "Yeah, you interrupted the upload. Another smart move. Big bonus point for your defense."

Defense against a likely murder charge. She plucked at the blanket, pulling it tight to her chin. "I knew I was going to die, but I wouldn't let myself go until I stopped him. I forced myself to stay awake, to go after him. When I reached him, he was crying."

Pain pierced her heart at the remembrance. "But I was fixated. We struggled."

The ear Kahlil had torn throbbed. She touched behind it, feeling the stiff thread of stitches.

Her next breath almost strangled in her throat. "I grabbed the gun in his pocket and shot. I don't even know if it hit him. Then I pushed him over the dam. He bounced and twisted . . ." She imagined the sickening crack and splinter of Kahlil's bones, sounds she knew she couldn't have heard above the wind. Yet her imagination made them real. She began to tremble again.

Rosenbaum moved to sit on the couch beside her. He gripped her upper arms as if he meant to shake her. She recoiled against the pain of her bruises, but he didn't let go. "Listen to me, Tawny. He damn near succeeded in committing deliberate homicide. The only reason you're not lying in the morgue next to him right this minute is because you kept your head, and luck was with you when that guy showed up early for work. You have as strong a case for self-defense and justifiable homicide as any client I've ever had. But do not ever repeat to anyone what you just told me. Do you understand?" His dark eyes bored into hers. "You have been through hell, but you don't want to put yourself in an even worse mess out of some misguided sense of morality."

Tawny pulled away from him, hugging the blanket around herself. "I hated him, but now I hate myself for killing him."

Rosenbaum shot to his feet, fists whipping through the air in frustration. "Goddammit, Tawny! You are the most aggravating client I've ever had." He stalked around the living room, hammering his thighs. "This motherfucker uses you, pins a federal rap on you, almost destroys the country's infrastructure, practically kills you, and you feel guilty about stopping him? I don't believe you."

The door to Virgie's bedroom crashed open, and she rushed out, looking from Tawny to the lawyer and back again. "Baby, are you all right?"

"It's OK, Virgie," Tawny answered. "I have a talent for annoying him."

Her friend studied the situation for a moment longer, then backed into her bedroom. Just before closing the door, she lasered a warning glare at Rosenbaum.

The lawyer paced across the living room, which only required three steps because of his long legs. Finally he flopped in the chair before Tawny.

"OK," he started, "let's hit rewind. Let's say you didn't push him over the dam. What the hell do you think he would have done with that magnanimous opportunity?" Rosenbaum's long arm swept through the air so fast that she felt the breeze. "Is he going to whip out an antidote and save your life? Is he going to call off the attack he's been working on for years? Is he going to turn himself in, name names, and bring down whatever network of terrorists he's affiliated with?" He stared at her, hands spread, demanding her answer.

Tawny closed her eyes. Of course, Rosenbaum was right. When Kahlil had handed her the bottle of tainted water, he fully expected her to die. Maybe he felt remorseful, but he did it nevertheless.

"There's surveillance video," she said. "They've seen exactly what I did. They know I killed him."

"Sacrificing yourself on a pyre of misplaced guilt doesn't undo anything, Tawny." Rosenbaum leaned forward. "You believed you were dying. With your last ounce of strength, you did what you had to do to prevent a diabolical plot that would affect millions of people. You stopped a vicious terrorist. And that's what you will say to every single person who questions you, from the FBI and Homeland Security, on down to the dog catcher and the meter maid."

Tawny pondered his words. She *did* stop a catastrophe. If Kahlil had lived, he meant to spread his destruction across the country. She *did* save the lives of thousands, maybe millions.

Rosenbaum cocked his head to the side. "You've got to ditch this Pollyanna conscience of yours. I can't properly defend you if you won't defend yourself. Are you with me on this?"

She looked into the depths of his harsh dark eyes. She had saved her own life only to live with the pain of killing.

Rosenbaum's expression changed. A flicker of . . . what? Understanding? Wisdom? "Do you believe in the Ten Commandments?" he asked.

"Yes." What was he driving at?

"Did you know that both Hebrew and Greek translations say, 'You shall not murder'? Murder is different than kill, Tawny. You killed, but you did not murder."

Tawny leaned her head against the couch and closed her eyes. Was Rosenbaum right? Could she learn to live with her acts? Maybe . . . in time.

She had to trust in a greater understanding than she had.

The chair squeaked as Rosenbaum stood. She opened her eyes and looked up at him. "OK. I'm with you."

"Good. Let's get back to work." He offered his hand.

She grasped it and let him pull her to her feet, head woozy from the movement. "I don't know how I'm going to pay you. Do you think you can get my money back?"

He snorted. "After this? Piece of cake." He gestured air quotes. "'*Widow foils terrorist plot, saves the grid.*' By the time I get done, you'll be a cross between Joan of Arc and Wonder Woman."

Tawny held onto furniture for support. "Hardly. I'm just a small-town widow with dyslexia who can barely operate a smartphone."

Another eye roll from Rosenbaum. "Your humility is charming, but stuff it."

She sank into the chair at the dining table. "I'm a pretty troublesome client."

He gripped his pen. "No client who worries about paying me is troublesome. However, I must admit, only one other woman has irritated me as much as you do, and I married her."

Tawny smiled weakly. As he'd said before, he might be an asshole, but he was *her* asshole. "I hope that's not a proposal, because I'll have to turn you down."

Rosenbaum grinned. "Proving beyond any reasonable doubt that you are a very smart woman."

* * *

For the next two days, Tawny met with a rotating kaleidoscope from multiple alphabet agencies: FBI, JTTF, DHS, FDIC, Bureau of Reclamation, county detectives—too many to keep track of. Rosenbaum sat close beside her, one hand always on her arm. Sometimes he squeezed to stop her from answering certain questions; other times, he patted gently, letting her speak. She didn't always understand why he objected, but she went along, trusting he knew how to keep her out of prison.

Tawny's children arrived home. Emma hugged her as she wept through extralong false eyelashes that looked as if she'd borrowed them from a carousel pony. Fresh colorful tattoos ran down her arms like long sleeves, although she'd ditched the boyfriend. New lines creased Neal's handsome face, aging him, making him look more like Dwight. Tawny's heart swelled every time she rested her gaze on them, savoring the sweetness of reunion.

Neal spent most of the time either on his laptop or cell, talking to comrades in the intelligence community. One afternoon, he left for several unexplained hours. When he returned, he'd somehow teased out new information on Kahlil and his plot.

At the breakfast bar, over the dinner of macaroni and cheese Emma had microwaved, Neal filled them in. "Shahrivar had worked at Grand Coulee, Bonneville, and other installations, from Seattle to Minneapolis, as far south as San Francisco." Neal tipped back a bottle of Moose Drool, then continued, "In his house, they found hard drives indicating he'd hacked into computers at electrical utilities all over the country."

"Who was he working for?" Tawny asked.

Neal shrugged one broad shoulder. "Don't know yet. Have to follow the money, see who financed him. We may never know for sure. One of the counter-terrorism guys thinks he and his wife might have been lone wolves who started their own cell with family members. His sister-in-law is being interrogated." He grinned at Tawny. "You sure did a number on her. Fractured skull. Never would have figured you were so feisty."

Tawny tried to swallow a bite of macaroni. It stuck like a lump of steel wool, scouring her insides. "I—I'm glad she lived."

Neal gave her a playful punch on the arm. She tried not to flinch from the pain of her bruises. "I'm proud of you, Mom. For an old lady, you swing a mean mop."

So like the way Dwight used to make her laugh away sadness. She couldn't help but smile and half rose from the bar stool, as if to lunge toward her son. "Not too old to whup your butt."

Neal raised both hands in surrender. "Abuse! Emma, call Child Protective Services. Ma's beatin' on me again."

Emma rolled her eyes and spooned more macaroni onto his plate. "Eat up and shut up, bro."

He shoveled in a big bite. "Hey, this is almost as good as Kraft's."

Emma grunted. "It *is* Kraft's, stupid. My crowning achievement in the kitchen."

Tawny squeezed her eyes tight so tears couldn't flow from the fullness in her heart.

Neal finished the beer and reached behind him to the refrigerator for another. "Bizarre how Shahrivar wound up renting Mr. and Mrs. Roth's place."

Tawny crumpled her napkin. "It was intentional. I think his wife set off the bomb that killed the Roths in Jerusalem. He moved into the neighborhood to get close to me." She bit her knuckle at the remembrance.

Neal studied her, frowning. "You told the investigators that, right?"

She nodded.

"Good." He planted an elbow on the counter, rolling the beer bottle in circles. "While the evidence techs were processing his house, they turned up an old newspaper clipping from 1982. The article was about this brilliant scientist–engineer who'd fled Iran with his family in '79 when the Shah was deposed. He took his research to DC and testified in front of Congress, claiming he'd developed a method to harvest unlimited hydroelectricity from ocean waves. He was discredited and started railing against the government, saying they deliberately destroyed his invention to keep the power status quo."

"So?" Emma put on her bored face.

"So," Neal went on, "the guy went home and overdosed his wife and three little girls with Valium, then killed himself with a knife in the heart."

Emma grimaced. "How awful."

Kahlil's image tried to drift up from Tawny's memory, but she pushed it back down.

"There was another kid," Neal added. "A boy, eleven, they never found. Figured dad must have done away with him someplace else and disposed of the body. Why would the Roths hang onto a morbid old newspaper story?"

"It didn't belong to the Roths," Tawny murmured, remembering the clipping she'd found the day she first discovered Kahlil living in her old friends' home. He'd thrown it in the wastebasket but must have retrieved it later.

Emma's butterfly attention span skipped ahead. "Hey, did anyone bring in today's mail? There's gonna be coupons for sixty percent off at the Buckle."

Tawny stared down at the bright-orange cheese staining her plate. She couldn't suppress the memory of Kahlil's haggard face and faraway eyes as he'd related the story of his father. She barely noticed Emma leaving the breakfast bar and returning a moment later, shuffling through the mail.

"Look at this, Mom." She held out an envelope hand addressed to *Neal Lindholm and Emma Lindholm*, with a return address from Mailboxes, Etc. "That's weird. Who'd be writing to both of us?"

Weariness pressed Tawny's shoulders. "You better open it and find out." She closed heavy eyes and listened to the ripping of the envelope, the rustle of paper unfolding, then Emma's sharp gasp.

Her daughter stood holding the letter, hands trembling, gray with fear. "Jesus, Mom, it's from the guy who tried to kill you."

Neal grabbed for the letter, knocking over his beer. Dark foam fanned across the counter.

Wooziness swept through Tawny. "Read it, please."

Her son recited:

Dear Neal and Emma,

I am the man who took your mother's life. If you receive this letter, I am also dead. If my plan succeeded, this letter may be delayed for months or years. Perhaps you will never receive it. I pray your anguish will lessen with time.

Please be reassured your mother did not suffer. She drifted off to sleep and felt no pain. She was a remarkable woman who brought great joy into my heart.

Everyone I ever loved in my life has died, including your mother. Death is a friend who brings peace and an end to suffering. Your beautiful mother is at peace, as am I, at last.

Kahlil Shahrivar

* * *

On a balmy October evening, with the cinnamon tang of fall leaves in the air, Tawny and Virgie sat in the patio behind Tawny's house, drinking wine.

Virgie dipped a cracker into a plate of melted Brie. "So what do you hear from your crazy lawyer?"

Tawny stretched her legs and wiggled her toes in her sandals. "My case is still working its way through all the different jurisdictions—federal, state, county. He thinks he's finalized a deal to get the charges ruled as justifiable homicide without going to trial. Knowing what a showboat he is, he'd much rather have his day in court, but I want it over and behind me. Besides, he got plenty of attention with the media coverage of my arraignment and preliminary hearing."

"That was brutal. All those bloodsuckers." Virgie shook her head. "One good thing about the media is that they've got the attention span of a three-year-old. Now they've moved on to the United Bankcorp scandal."

Tawny tugged on her braid. "Rosenbaum told me the latest on that. Seems the bank was complicit in terrorist money laundering." She spooned Brie onto a cracker. "And get this: after that asshole manager skipped town, he tried to flee to Belize with other bank officers in their Learjet but got left standing on the tarmac. Seems they took off without him."

Virgie laughed. "Sometimes a little justice prevails."

Tawny watched the sky turn pink and orange as the sun dropped. She wondered if memories of Kahlil would ever recede far enough for her to review them like an old movie, events that happened to someone else while she watched.

Virgie poured them both more wine and lifted her glass. "From here on, only good times."

Tawny clinked glasses. "OK by me." She sipped, then remembered her other news. "Hey, I might finally have a job."

"Yeah? What?"

"Rosenbaum's starting a class-action suit by people who had their assets wrongly seized by the government. He wants to hire me to interview them and do research."

"Oh, really." Virgie's lips puckered, trying to suppress a grin. "You know, if he ever stops with the motormouth, he's kind of cute. So tell me—is his divorce final yet?"

Tawny glowered at her friend. "Don't even start."

"How do you know I'm not asking about him for my own interest?"

"Because, Virgie, he's too tall for you."

"But the perfect height for you."

"Not in this lifetime. Or the next. Or the next . . ."

THE END

About the Author:

Debbie Burke likes to take perfectly nice fictional folks and thrust them into nightmarish circumstances. Her nonfiction is less dangerous than her fiction and appears in international magazines and blogs. She loves to mentor young writers and plumb their vivid imaginations.

A Message from Debbie:

Thanks so much for reading *Instrument of the Devil*. I hope you had as much fun reading the book as I did writing it. If so, I'd greatly appreciate a brief review of it on Amazon.
Further adventures for Tawny are coming in *Death by Proxy*. Visit www.debbieburkewriter.com for updates on new releases.